THE TRADING OF KEN

The Trading of Ken

A Novel by

Rebecca Guevara

OXIDE BOOKS

First Edition

ISBN 0-9770424-0-5

Text copyright © 2005 by Rebecca Guevara

Covert art copyright © Jamie Chipman

This is an Oxide Books book, published by
Juniper Press.

Edited by Mark A. Taylor
Design by Jamie Chipman
Photos: Getty Images

Printed and bound in the United States

Library of Congress Cataloging-in-Publication Data

Guevara, Rebecca.,

To Sam and the Hovering Voice

ACKNOWLEDGEMENTS

Thanks to First Thursday Book Club, Lori Giovannoni, Troy Roper, Gloria Spiking, Mark A. Taylor, Karen Wilson, my son Zachary and his family for simply being.

CHAPTER ONE

Cotton garden gloves protected her hands as she lifted a single marigold with dry coiled roots from the last spot in the plastic six-pack. The gloves were irritating and distancing from dirt and young flower, like a blanket separating a mother from her baby. She shook them off and held the bare-rooted plant with her fingers. Red nails clipped the dry dirt as she moved the plant to her palm. The small effort at life was perky and thriving without water in the dry nursery loam. How long could it last without sustenance? An hour, maybe overnight, but not through another day. The small hole for the plant had been dug. She placed it tenderly and pushed hard on the dirt around it.

Catalina Margaret Daniels Overton was planting petunias and marigolds in her backyard and waiting for the children to be home. Ten-year-old Justin would return from baseball practice and eight-year-old Margaret, her MoMo, would return from visiting a friend after school. The house loomed behind, a realtor's dream of fetching phrases aimed at the almost affluent who believed buying ahead of secure income and inflation would save money and assure family happiness.

Three years ago their curly headed, too energetic female agent had waved at Cat in the front seat of the BMW and Ken in the back, "You must see the houses being built in Sunshadow Estates. You won't believe how beautiful they are. They make Utah look like a little bit of France." She winked at the local joke as they passed the faux river rock fence sign bordering the development. "Sunshadow Estates – *a return to elegance with the casual pleasures of today.*"

"Return to what elegance?" Cat wondered. She had never lived in elegance and neither had Ken. What Utah native had, really?

Sunshadow Estates was a nook in the southeast corner of the Salt Lake Valley where the Rockies crumble into the Wasatch

1

Mountains. The name did make sense. Early sun brightened the western part of the valley, keeping the moneyed, fancier neighborhoods of the city in morning mountain darkness.

The house was the current acquisitive beautiful. Two stories high, it was stacked like children's play blocks in a new style plan imitating a French village castle; a recent trend copied from Utah's envied stepsister, California. Cat liked the family room surveying the backyard through French doors with brass handles. Ken liked the large garage and the feeling of grandeur; space he needed to put his body strength in perspective. They both liked the downstairs bedroom for visiting grandparents and private master bedroom with bath a few steps away from the children.

It had been easy to leave their thirty-year-old, one-thousand square foot brick 'beginner house' - as the newspaper ad read. They soon settled into the spaciousness and convenience of Sunshadow Estates where successful growing families live in the ample belly of the American West. It was a larger, more beautiful home than Cat ever imagined for herself. The 4,500 square foot house did fulfill the developer's promise. Their lives became Western elegant and casual; at once larger, more beautiful and filled with pleasure. Cat was a gardener at heart and surrounded the house with flowers, shrubs and trees. She only worried about cost when she remembered her childhood.

Today, with the warm May sun on her back, the earth was finally ready for summer's flowers to marry root to earth. She started with white petunias in the pots on the patio. "Plant me. Don't plant me," Cat imagined the flowers taunted. "I'll grow leggy, tall and without blooms by August anyway." The red ones had more verve to survive but they would go the same way as the white. Planting petunias was love duty. Love duty to effort and making a house, a home, a place for family to be comfortable and feel loved.

When the petunias were planted in the pots surrounding the patio, she took the two six-packs of marigolds and walked further out, to the back of the yard. The marigolds just "did," she thought. They never complained. They just survived. A little water, not too many snails and they were fine. Their hearty beauty quietly gained momentum through October, becoming more alive in ever shortening days. Their smell was brash, near sweat. When she looked from the family room she would see them as perky, as vibrant, as uncomplaining in the teasing warmth of May as they would be wrapped in the first snow of winter to meet their death. Petunias, with their cloying perfume, reached too far with ever weakening and grasping arms. They succumbed to autumn's touch, folding like a lacy parasol.

The phone rang and Cat stood quickly. She dashed was over grass, patio, through French doors to the kitchen counter where she found the phone behind an iron interpretation of a sunflower.

"Hello."

"Lina." The sound of printing presses methodically drummed a beat behind her husband as he called her by the name only he and her parents had ever used.

"Hi, Ken. How are you?" Her voice lifted, hearing him.

"I'm going to be late."

"Oh. Ok. What's going on?"

"Late work. Can't be helped."

"Oh."

"I'll be home as soon as possible."

"Oh."

"Bye, love."

"Bye, Ken."

She put the phone down and returned to gardening. Slightly irritated she gathered her thick curly red brown hair that touched her shoulders and coiled it in a twist under the band of her visor. As she walked back to the flowers she saw her white winter legs. April sun had begun to tan her arms, but she knew it would take diligence for her legs to ever brown. She was quite sure no one had ever gotten cancer on dough colored legs that refused to color. Meanwhile, she was avoiding every ray of sun on her face with the visor in the hopes of kicking in preservation genes. By June she was going to look like a human checkerboard but at age 38 there was just enough wear on her face to cause regret for high school sun seeking summers. Still, Cat was a 'lovely woman,' as she had been referred to, with twilight blue eyes that reflected light from the inside out and an inviting curving softness of body that presumed a softness of soul. All she saw in the mirror was twenty pounds too much but others recognized a home of acceptance and security for the people she loved.

It would be a pleasant dinner with her children and she knew she should enjoy their company more than she would. The three of them would have a nice dinner conversation and then watch TV to laugh at characters and plot, but she would be lonely without Ken. They were a family and whenever one of them was missing from dinner it was as though an extra plate should be put out for a ghost who was missed and dear. Kenneth. She thought of her husband who worked so hard at his business. Nine years he had put into the printing company that three years ago finally began to reward all of them. The house had been the biggest reward.

As an always fidgeting, too busy for his own good eighteen-year-old, Ken was hired by the University of Utah printing department for his work-study assignment. He ran a one color 11x17" press that was used for official campus flyers, odd teacher demands for class materials and by hopeful writing students who paid to have their ravings reproduced so others could suffer with them. Paper and ink smells are intoxicating to three groups of people: writers, readers and printers. Ken began to breathe the rhythm of printing and found it more suitable to his body need to be busy and absorbed in deadlines with the demands of a real today rather than the elusive hopes of what a degree in something he hadn't decided might ever offer. In the middle of his second semester, to his parents' great distress, he left college and got a job at Presson's Printing - *We Press On*. John Presson taught him the trade and when he was settled in a marriage, with two young children, Ken announced he was leaving the company to start his own. Presson was not surprised.

Presson had been surprised the young energetic Ken had married a feather of a girl with too much education. She was a second grade teacher which was certainly a good fallback to the economic whims of printing, but the girl herself was too fragile for the daily grind of hard sell, hard thinking, hard living of printing. A scrappy woman with an edge would have been better for him. Presson didn't realize Ken needed the borrowed benediction of education.

The company began as Overton Overnight Printing, "a double O for double value," was Ken's business slogan. With two 11x17" presses, a pre-press person, one full-time and one part-time pressman, and a counter person, he began to build a list of customers and a reasonably steady return. Cat helped where and when needed and did the book work. That time of young children and a new company had been a busy, "focused life," as some business consultants bullet point in

4

lifestyle choice presentations. It revolved around a business with more promise than profit but it was enough and Ken's enthusiasm and dedication always made Cat believe in a greater approaching comfort.

Ken's day began at 5:30 with kissing Cat's flattened hair angled like a sloppy triangle around her head. By six, he left the house, worked nonstop and often did not come home until eight Cat rubbed his shoulders while he ate re-warmed lasagna or chicken and rice and talked of careless employees, picky customers and unreliable equipment. Before going to bed he and Cat visited the children's rooms where they leaned and kissed them goodnight. Life was a cocoon of children, work and more work.

They also lived in a city where 'the buck stops here' had a unique meaning. "I can work 24 hours a day and keep my prices the lowest in town, but if someone comes along with a sweeter face than mine, I'll lose the job," Ken would say over dinner. "How this city feeds its children I don't know. I lost a job today I know was below cost. It went for paper alone." Earnestness wore on his face in a vertical line of concentration above his brow increasing the intensity of his clear, uncompromising assessments of people and situations. Silver hairs half-mooned his ears. The man she married when she was 26, and he was 30 had the strong muscles of constant movement, but not those exercised with regular time or care from sports or the outdoors. His intent face evolved from a carelessly arranged good-looking young guy into an experienced man's intrepid stare at the bald, uncompromising face of business.

Five-years-ago he surprised her with an invitation to dinner. It would be the two of them in a dark quiet restaurant where they could talk. For no reason, he told her. She dressed carefully and sensually, preparing herself for unacknowledged fantasy. Too bad there had been a reason. Past the pre-dinner drink, the opening of a wine bottle, the salad and into the entrée he began a gentle, persistent presentation. His full dark eyebrows lifted and furrowed with expression. If she would just be patient, just be understanding, just believe, he was sure the company would succeed beyond anything she had imagined. It was time to expand. Time to move the company to a new level. Where he was would only become a dying dead-end. New printers and copiers were making it possible for any decent size company to do the same work themselves. Who would need Overton Overnight when they thought they were doing it better, cheaper and with more control in their unused room down the hall. If she would just believe. Overton Overnight would become Overton Printing. A full printing house. All they had to do was take out a second mortgage on their thousand-square-foot brick rambler and use it as collateral to a bank loan that he had already been approved for and they would make the transition. A transition. That's all it would be. Their success with Overton Overnight had been evident. He knew how to run a company from the ground up.

Bankers recognized his success. She was a banker's daughter, she knew what that meant. He had an established business name in printing. It would just be a broader, brighter focus. Cat would still help with bookkeeping. He would hire one sales person and there was enough in the loan for a trained pressman on a good used four-color press he had found, and he would keep the pressman he already had for a better two-color press and it would work. There would be a few more people, of course, but he knew he could do it. When it succeeded the first thing they would do was buy a new and bigger house. As an officer of the company he needed her opinion. What did she think?

Finished with the vodka Collins, a spinach salad, starting on chicken pasta something, a half glass of wine and the delicious attention of her husband, she agreed. Yes, of course it would work, and she believed it would. Play for the evening was quashed but business was accomplished.

Cat imagined Ken and the children treated her life as a backboard in games of growing up and running a business. Their days were out in the world learning and living, but when they came home they bounced their lives, disappointments, victories around and on her. She felt their wins and losses as her own. Where they needed help she jumped to be there. When they needed applause and support, she believed she provided it in the stable, reliable routine of the home they returned to and the presence of her love.

Her life was melody of movement with time as comforting background music. Tasks and responsibilities were carried on and fulfilled without notice while more important action, more important music, was played by other people. She enjoyed the simpler, repetitive routine of her days that supported. It justified the very pleasant circumstances of her life.

Monday, Tuesday and Friday were house care days dotted by occasional charity work. To enhance business standing and contacts Ken urged her to be "involved."

"People with money support cancer," Ken said, underscoring her need to smile, be gracious and mention Overton Printing. Or arthritis, if she preferred, he offered, knowing rich older people wrote checks for their own diseases. Cancer was her choice; the disease that had taken her life worn, gentle, ever patient father. She was active in the fundraising dinner dance for Cancer Care House, a Home with a Heart. Her widowed mother was her example with weekly volunteer work at a similar care house.

"You'll enjoy it, dear. It's been therapeutic." Twice a week they talked on the phone. Several times a year the children spent weekends with her. She still lived in Cat's childhood town of Logan, 80 miles northeast from Salt Lake City. Ken's mother, Kathleen, had groaned at Cancer Care House, "Oh god, Cat, is that still the funnest way to spend time in Salt Lake?" His parents had taken leave of Salt Lake to follow the sun and warmth while still keeping the glow of Salt Lake's sanctity in St. George, a growing town of Utah retirees at the southwestern end of the state. Life with cocktail hours, tee-off times and designated pre-planned grandchild visits suited Kathleen and Robert Overton well.

It was love of books and the fatherly Bill Shiner's deliberate power walk that kept her spending Wednesdays where she had worked since college. Cat knew her time at Shiner's Bookstore was a true interest but she wondered if it was also a reluctance to leave an indefinable cocoon.

Cat spent Thursdays at Overton Printing, where her involvement had changed through the years. When it began she was 'on call' for any duty. If paper needed picking up for a rush job she drove to the paper distributor. When Ken needed to be away to pitch a new customer or attend a lunch for the litho club she would run the counter while the employee was at lunch and answer phones. There were miscellaneous tasks of wiping up the break room or bringing a birthday cake for an employee. For years she was in charge of keeping all finances straight. Ken would make deposits and she would figure who needed money now and if they could take a little extra out for themselves. Years ago she sat on the couch and hand wrote checks on her lap with Good Housekeeping on her knee and a young child on either side, propping her as their best-loved book while they watched Sesame Street.

The only part she didn't like was her 15th of the month over 45 days call for payment. Ken said she was to use her lilting feminine voice as a gentle reminder. One morning every two weeks she was also expected to make telephone calls to potential customers and arrange appointments for Ken. He bought a sales lead list and insisted, "These are only strangers waiting to be friends." Now, with a larger company, more employees and the children in school, it had settled to a gentler routine. She still brought in birthday cakes, but she flatly refused to clean the break room and toilet. A cleaning service came in once a week. If she wasn't an employee it was only that she didn't draw a paycheck or have regular time or claim social security hours.

Her main duty was to fulfill Ken's trust. He trusted her and wanted to guarantee the bills and invoices given to the accountant were accurate. A desk was kept for her in the corner and she felt important and needed each time she went to work. Papers were piled high, waiting for her organization. Working at Overton was a decision of convenience and family effort for success. She had worked part-time since its opening days to please and appease Ken. Searching just a little bit deeper there was pleasure and conceit that Ken enjoyed having her about the office, even on an irregular schedule. The work gave her a sense of his life and pressures and gave her the freedom to spend time with the children and create a comfortable home for all of them. Cat wasn't a business partner.

"You're the best pinch hitter since Manny Mota," Ken cooed as he kissed the top of her head. "Overton thanks you. I thank you for all you do." The freedom of schedule, Ken's appreciation, the change of scenery in the days of a full warm life with Ken and two beautiful children was enough.

Today was Tuesday and the children came home from school and read in chairs by the TV while Cat prepared dinner and set it on the dinner table in the open family area.

"MoMo, are you thinking the horse camp would be better or the writing camp?" she asked over dinner. The forms needed to be completed and mailed.

"Horse camp. Annie said they do writing there sometimes,

too, and there's more to do than at writing camp. Just write all day? No fun."

"What about you, Justin? I guess it's decided with the Outdoor Adventure camp?"

He leaned his elbow on the table over his food, "Ya, that sounds fine." Good. Both children were settled and she could now rest that she was giving her children interesting summer experiences in the first week of August.

After dinner Justin went to his room to entertain himself on the computer and MoMo and Cat watched TV. The documentary on the condition of zoos in urban areas was interesting but her real focus was replaying the conversation with Ken. She didn't remember hearing when he might be home. Or exactly why he needed to be late. In the beginning of Overton Overnight he would explain reasons to be late in detail, as though he needed to let the air of worry and fear leave him before he could organize his thoughts and get tasks accomplished. She was told about the details of jobs, the frustrations of his days. But now, as they grew in the face of greater financial responsibility he had slowed the telling of daily stories. Perhaps not to worry her, she thought. Perhaps they were more complicated. Of that she was sure.

At 8:39 as MoMo was brushing her teeth the three of them heard the city jungle roar of the Ford Expedition before the garage door opened. Kenneth, Daddy, had returned. The door and echoing engine noise across the garage cement walls was comforting in its large man father call as it settled to stay for the night. MoMo and Cat ran to meet him at the door. "Daddy, Daddy," He stooped to kiss her. "Ken, you look exhausted," Cat said as he hugged her.

"Hello, Justin," he yelled up the stairs and winked at both of them.

"Hi, Dad."

Cat put the covered food she had kept for him in the microwave and pulled the salad from the refrigerator. The three of them sat at the kitchen table.

"Come down, Justin, I want to see you," yelled Ken before putting the fork in the salad. The kitchen was close enough in the make believe French castle that Justin heard.

This is the part of the day I like best, thought Cat. We're

reunited at the end of the day. A family of four that loves and needs one another.

"Lina, I went through hell on that job for the museum," he began to tell the story with his gestures of salad or chicken on a fork also directed at the children. Catalina had lent itself to many names through her life. Cat, Catty, "C", but she liked the privacy and warmth of when Ken called her Lina best.

The children were put to bed. Justin's hair ruffled, MoMo's cheeks kissed and Ken and Cat went to their bedroom to watch TV until one of them would turn to sleep. Cat lay in bed and listened to Ken remove his clothes in the room sized closet and she was happy. So lovely, all of this was so lovely.

New employees of Shiner's Bookstore - A Community Gathering Place, quickly learned the ritual of saluting Mr. Shiner. "Hello, Mr. Shiner," said clearly and with a slight nod of the head was expected by every employee the first time he was seen on any shift. Usually he was whisking between the old wooden shelves where he had walked for almost forty years in a jumbled pattern between aisles, displays and chair arrangements making sure patrons were in the store and book displays looked fresh and book wormy luscious. After a first hearty hello he did not require or want recognition. Employees should be paying attention to their duties.

Seldom were there new employees. Of the five fulltime and five part-time employees, only one was expected to turnover in two years. Book people implode where they stand. They can't help themselves. Being surrounded by books is an addiction as sure as liquor or heroin and once caught they simply don't often have the inner strength to leave the fold. There is a smell to books as seductive as skin and there is a look to bookstores as endearing as a lover's hair blowing by a wind. Cat felt a familial comfort in Shiner's Bookstore. It was a soothing place for customers and employees who entered the store and were willing to consider Mr. Shiner a surrogate father. And so many people did. Fathers can be so hard to find.

"Hello, Mr. Shiner," Cat said the next Wednesday afternoon.

"Hello, dear girl." Mr. Shiner growled as he walked deliberately and quickly. The wind of his 6'2" lean and running old body circled her. In peace. Reliability. Since college days Cat had been a part-time employee who took from six months to a year off to get married or have a child, but the unspoken understanding between Catalina and Mr. Shiner was they would grow old together thirty-years apart and in separate lives. As he would with several of his employees who he held in his heart as children and in his bank as employees.

If Cat wondered when she was with Ken whether Shiner's was important to her because of a simple interest in books or it was a secret place to hide from life, she never wondered when she was at Shiner's. It was recognition of self, demonstrated through something of value - the disseminating of books. And there was personal greed for books, just to touch them. Just to breathe in something that was beyond what she understood or may ever understand. Happy as she was, she knew a simple wife, mother and part-time worker in Salt Lake City was unlikely to absorb the deeper answers and probing insights of the books she touched at Shiner's. Perhaps being around was enough.

Today she was shelving. A one shift a week person didn't get the best jobs but that was all right. Shelving new and reordered books allowed her to become familiar with everything in the store. The preferred job, one she occasionally got, was to be buzzed on the intercom when someone needed help to find what they needed. "What mystery would you recommend?" "Where is British history?" "Has Mayle written anything new recently?" Then she could talk to people about what they liked.

A book she was squeezing in was one of the store's second string sellers; not a top ten, but consistent in leaving the shelf over the last two years. The business and pop psychology title, *Married to Business* was about the advantages of being married to your business partner. Several times she had skimmed through the pages, reading headlines and a few paragraphs, but she was careful. A book with a bend spine or smudged page was unsellable. People wanted the promise of perfection handed to them for $23.95. Perhaps, she now thought, not so different than a perfect prom dress or shoes or a lipstick that had been opened though never used. We want fealty. Something already used and touched by others must surely have split loyalties, affectionate attachments and dirty secrets without us. Americans are virgin worshippers of uncharted lands, she thought and they want to own, not share; not appreciate temporary, mutually ben-

11

eficial, liaisons.

Scrunching her back and turning sideways she read, *"Lines of responsibility need to be clear."* She bristled and shook her head. "Like a marriage, like a business. Someone in charge of the garden; the children's schedule, payroll, dinner, quality control. So what's so damn different? Whether you work around Tide or toner? How much you're paid? The money you can charge on a credit card without being questioned? Probably an author who had never been married and certainly never cared about home.

There was more, *"If one heads marketing the other should not tread on the claimed territory."* How would that work at home? If one accepts cleaning the toilet should the other not use it? She knew the flaws of the comparison but didn't care.

There were subtle differences in working at Shiner's and Overton. Employees at Overton always treated her with a smidgen of respect in their voices that her coworkers at the bookstore only had when they talked to Mr. Shiner's son, Elliott - or El as he was called. At age thirty with seven full time years and a previous childhood of part-time experience, it was assumed El would one day be their boss. It was a smidgen for him, too. By hearing each one of them say hello to El she recognized the voice Ken's employees used with her. Not quite deferential, but a near enough relation that El, or she could never complain to Mr. Shiner or Kenneth about the attitude of so-and-so.

"I knew I'd find you here," the rustling ethnic skirt of Eme Collins was unmistakable. How a woman's soft skirts could sway with come hither love for mankind and total irritation at the idiocy of one man, Cat had yet to understand. Eme's forty pounds extra weight always danced. It wasn't heavy, it was an orchestra of life and energy that carried her to places that conservative Cat would never visit. Her brown deer eyes were forest floor earth, impenetrable depths that made Cat look away to her thick wavy hair, full lips, high large cheeks for answers because the eyes were too embracing; too seeing.

"Are you disturbing my work time for Mr. Shiner?" Cat looked at her friend from college. Emeraude was named for the citrus playful Coty cologne popular in the 1960's because her mother thought it an exotic and melodic word she hoped would imprint her daughter. She was a woman riddled with hopeless imagination and few practical life skills from a lonely childhood in Utah where dreams are large, but seldom connected to originality. She had instilled soulfulness in her daughter but her dream of scooting her into a life of adventure, where she would be quoted in biographies died in teen-age fear. When the girl with dark hair so thick it held brushes at angles and skin so clear it always looked newborn came home from school with the nickname Eme, she was crushed. Eme was protecting herself. She knew in a 1970s classroom of Salt Lake girls the name Emeraude among the Stacys, Amys and Leslies would brand her exotic and worldly, which was a cousin to slut. Instead of her mother's hopes of an adventurous life in Paris bistros, Eme had pioneered upsetting Utah men. Perhaps not a difficult, but still a laudable thing to do.

"I've got a man problem."

"Sheldon?" Sheldon was the most permanent fixture of the last eighteen months. Both Cat and Ken liked him. He and Eme were the same height at five-foot-seven and it wasn't hard to imagine Eme puffing out her chest during a disagreement while the more fragile Sheldon enclosed himself in upstanding dignity. Still, he was a man of quiet forceful inner strength and a steady humor that appreciated people's foibles. Especially Eme's.

"No."

"I'm still interested."

"He isn't."

"Sheldon?"

"No."

Cat looked at Eme quietly waiting.

"I met this guy. I know I should have called you," Cat stirred and Eme stopped her, "but I couldn't. He was just too special and I wanted to bring him over to meet you. Not just talk without proof of existence."

Over the last twenty-years there had been a long path of proof that Eme attracted men. She was equal parts overweight sweet-faced woman who kept fresh cookies flavored according to the season in a cookie jar laced with porcelain grips, and seductive earth woman with ample cleavage and arms that held hard. When she left a man she wrote his name on a seashell and crushed it with a meat tenderizer before adding it to a four-foot high apothecary jar she kept in the living room by the fireplace. When a man left her she wrote his name on a rock, hit it with the meat tenderizer and had a ceremonial burial at

13

the new moon. A time to rid oneself of difficulty. Not included in the seashells and rocks were memories of men she had only passed and spoken short sentences with - auto repairmen, shoe salesmen, passers-by in movie lines. Eme could talk of them for months. Replayed scenes became momentous interludes of attraction and coyness and even if reservations were clear and wedding rings glistened from obvious display, they had provided Eme with a collected memory to be dusted and remembered when a man she was sleeping with emptied the cookie jar on his way out the door.

"Remember Ryan the produce manager?" Cat nodded and she continued, "Well, we talked for a good five minutes yesterday over the Macintosh and Granny apples and I found out he isn't married."

"Oh." Best to be quiet.

"He said his daughter lives with her mother," she paused and there was a catch in her throat. "Well, he acted embarrassed he'd let that information out so I was casual about it, but a few minutes later I asked him if he would like to meet for coffee and he looked down hedging before making his way to the tomatoes."

Cat was quiet to make sure this was the end of the story. "Well, you never know."

"Know what?"

"Maybe he was being shy or it's too soon after a divorce. You've moved from apples to tomatoes before and still been interested. Just afraid."

"Yes, but not from me. Men like to touch me."

"Maybe his wife was a carrot stick and you're scary new territory."

"What should I do?"

Cat hated being asked what to do in Eme's relationships. Cat's experience with men was zilch next to hers, next to anybody's.

"I don't know, Eme. Be with safe, adoring Sheldon. Men are a mystery to me."

Acknowledging the truth of the statement, Eme moved to a new subject, "What are you reading now?"

"I'm putting this book away." She fingered the spine, "it's about working with your husband. It's getting to be a popular thing to do."

"You do it."

"Not really. I go in one day a week. That's all."

"Well, you have a stake holder position with inside information."

"You make me sound so astute."

"I just want you to realize your value. And you're an officer of a corporation."

"Thank you."

"I know you're busy and Mr. Shiner saw me come in, so I'll leave now. Lunch next week?" They touched hands good-bye and Cat moved her cart to biographies and began shelving.

Her shift ended before the children were due home from school so she stopped at a discount store and looked around for bargains to decorate the house. There were none. She went to the grocery store for a 'few staples' as her mother would have said. Ryan was in the produce department when she turned the corner. He was down by the apples, across from an ever-growing display of exotic mushrooms, surrounded by fresh herbs, dressings and packaged salads. Though his arms were folded he seemed to be enjoying the words of a woman who only reached his armpit. There was a smile and a slight hip shift forward. Ryan didn't know Cat; wouldn't have known her by name or sight. He was only known to her by Eme's description and current desire. It wouldn't do to tell Eme about this. If she mentioned the visit at all she would say only that 'I saw him and he was talking to a customer.' End of story.

The total was just over $40. There was cereal for the children's breakfast, lettuce and tomatoes that she never bought more than a few days ahead and a substantial pile of 'Daddy Food'. The children thought it comical Ken had special food that he monitored for inventory. He would always share and never really seemed to mind if it disappeared with someone else's hand, as long as it also quickly reappeared. It would be dark and quiet as the four of them watched a TV show when Ken would jump up, get a Daddy Food and bring it back for everyone. Pretzels, potato chips, various ice-cream bars, sometimes frozen buffalo wings and refrigerator chocolate chip cookies that he would bake before presentation on a tray with paper napkins. Everyone happily munched together and it was assured the family store would soon be replenished. Cat brought home 'experiments' such as frozen won tons, gourmet chips or popcorn and everyone voted on whether each should join the ranks, even if occasionally, as Daddy Food.

Ken walked in the door at seven. Beat looking. Cat didn't say anything though her voice modulated and tried to extend caring through deference that he may or may not have evinced as a fleeting gift of silent care or weakness, inability or inattention. Giving spousal care without observed declaring of "I'm giving," hearing a "Thanks," and saying "You're welcome," is an ephemeral gift of self that carries great unspoken weight toward future. Emotional gift-giving that is not recognized is enough to cause divorces but it feels so self-serving to draw attention at the moment. And so deserved to receive without appreciation.

"Dinner's almost ready," she kissed his cheek and returned to the kitchen. A few weeks ago some of the women at Shiner's were talking about husbands. How romance had dimmed. How the nearness of him was, well, near. Innocently, Cat reported she kissed Ken every time he came in the door from his workday. There was laughter and congratulations to her for 'carrying on so long.' She liked it.

Dinner with the children was restorative. Ken and Cat always felt good in the company of their children. They liked their small daily tiptoes toward adulthood. The longer their childhood took the better because at each stage both parents were happy, pleased to be with these lovely young people and see them through.

Before going to bed they walked into each room to kiss them goodnight in their sleep. MoMo slept with a frog night light on. Her honey red hair glistened like spring pond water under sunset. Long curling strands covered clear pale skin on fat young cheeks. Her whispered sleeping breaths were through practical, near straight and lovely lips, not too lush, not too afraid of life and love. The small curled body underneath a bedspread of opened butterflies was small, slight, a bit wasting or perhaps waiting until it was awakened. She was a John Warehouse painting, Cat thought. Where her ethereal brushstrokes body came from she did not know. She was without precedence in their families, a small sprite child. Singly, they leaned and kissed her before going to her brother's room.

Justin was a direct pip-squeak of his father. Dark haired, wide cheeks, dark brows, at once purposeful and alert. His ten-year-old body had not blossomed to the breadth and power of Ken, but he had energy and sinew that declared him male. Cat would sometimes find herself overtaken by the hazel blue-green mystery of her son's eyes, now hidden by long lashes. Cat leaned, to kiss the matted hair of her boy child, smelling of day, sun, growth coming from within. Ken did the same.

They each performed their bedtime rituals and then sat on the bed, side-by-side and watched the news on TV. There was conversation about local events, assurance their lives were in order compared to others, and finally a call to love and sleep to the next day.

On Memorial Day weekend Cat brought a dozen geraniums to Overton and placed them in pots on either side of the front door. A week later as she walked by them she was pleased they had taken well. She passed under the metal sign of Overton Printing and through the double doors with a feeling of accomplishment and recognition of being part of building something grand and successful through her efforts. Overton gave Ken a work in life he enjoyed; a way to make a living that wasn't the endless repetition of days she imagined her father felt during his morning drives to the bank. The company lived from Ken's purposeful breaths and provided a good life, a very good life, but Cat could not justify existence on her need and satisfaction alone. So she reasoned and was pleased the company also provided a quality business service to the community where they lived peacefully and it meant salaries and shelter to the families of twelve employees. The effects rippled out from them creating a tree of life. Families and lives she would never meet were part of something she had helped start.

Mary Ellen was the office manager, she controlled phones, everyone's schedule, did the simpler vendor ordering and was good at barking sufficiently at the back shop workers who were not keeping up with client phone demands and Ken's posted schedule. Rhonda was her assistant, working relief phones, paper cutter, shrinkwrapper, errand runner and go-fer at Ken's demand to deliver, will calls and lunch orders. Dan was a young sales guy with only a year's experience at a smaller shop, but he was inspired to succeed by the needs of a pregnant wife and a child. An easy going guy, he smiled through disappointments and knew how to make people comfortable. Todd ran the 11x17" two-color press and did odd jobs with Rhonda. James ran the small art department. He declared himself a designer, but he also

17

hustled through prepress production and did what he was told to do. Darrell ran the four-color during the day and Miguel came in after five when it was needed to run either press. The last employees floated and changed, not quite secure in printing or aligned with Overton's style. Ken did the rest. Bidding, scheduling, bartering for better pricing, big customers, soothing of employee personality conflicts, hiring, firing.

Everyone nodded Cat's way as she walked to her desk in the corner. When Ken asked which desk she wanted Cat reasoned since she benefited the most from the profits of the company and yet spent little time there, she would take the oldest desk that was bought used when they had started Overton Overnight. She felt comfortable with it and people who spent the most time there could have new desks. The front desk was broad oversized oak, designed to put room between visitors and Mary Ellen. To the far side and ahead of Cat was Rhonda of the helter-skelter duties.

Incoming bills, delivery receipts, copies of bank deposits and samples of jobs with their tickets were in individual stacks ready for Cat's well-spent hours at Overton Printing - Your Complete Printing Source. An hour passed before Ken came in through swinging doors that separated office from press area. He had returned from visiting a client with a bid and waved at Cat as though she were a long-loved sister. He dodged to his office and stayed there until he needed to leave his desk. His head bobbed between the computer, the phone and the direction of the door as people stopped by with questions and scheduling problems. When needed, or just to stretch, he went to the back and helped Rhonda and James cut, shrinkwrap or box a job. Ken often carefully adhered Overton Printing stickers to the boxes ready for delivery. His private signature of quality.

Rhonda ordered two pizzas for lunch and placed them on the table in the break room. Once a week pizza was ordered as a ritual thank you to staff. They could eat it or not and it was only there until it was not. Sometimes a last curling wedge would be room temperature after five when someone picked it up to eat on the way home. Cat gathered three pieces on a paper plate, two napkins and two sodas from the vending machine before going to Ken's office.

"There were some good deposits this week."

He looked up with satisfaction, "Great, huh?"

"Yes. It's amazing to me how that press that costs so much

can make so much."

"I know. I'm looking at a new folder to keep up with it. The one we have only does 5,000 an hour. We need something that will do at least twice that." The unspoken price sat between them like a priest's confessional.

They were chewing pizza so she just nodded but wouldn't have said anything anyway. It frightened her to think of going more, more, more into debt. Shouldn't there be a natural point where good income meets with expenses instead of always upping the ante? Maybe she was being a banker's daughter. Conservative. Afraid. She quit talking. It was dangerous to upset Ken's fragile optimism.

"How was MoMo this morning?" She had a stomachache last night and Ken left before she woke.

"She's fine. I think it was the popcorn followed by the ice cream bar." Again he nodded. Their lunch conversations were congenial, mostly about nothing and often interrupted by phone calls or someone popping a head in the door with a question. The door never closed and everyone respected their lunches together as well as possible but they knew work was first and no one waited until lunch was over if it needed asking.

Cat was finished mid-afternoon with her duty of rearranging the stacks of paperwork into meaningful accounting piles. Arranged carefully in a leftover paper box she clipped and banded the piles with respective disks for the company's accountant.

"I'm leaving now, Ken," she popped her head in the office door but did not go inside. Affection when an employee might suddenly appear bothered her more than him. He nodded from his computer then lifted his head to look at her. "Ok. See you at home."

The twenty minute drive to The Lewis & Smith Group - *Your Financial Advisors*, was her time to think about dinner, garden tasks, the children's schedule, whether she needed to call Joel for a hair appointment. It was mid-day reorganization time and Cat felt wrapped in her car with the radio. Ken bought her the silver Audi when it came off a lease two years ago. She was reluctant to spend so much for a car when a used Toyota would do, but he'd insisted she have the most expensive car of her life. Now she enjoyed its austere European luxury. The next year Ken took out a lease through the company for the huge never driven off the lot dark green Expedition. It was the benefit of owning a company, he said and they used it for work. Ken, Rhonda and Cat traded-off driving it for errands. When she first climbed up to the wide leather seat that had sight above three-quarters of all traffic, she was intimidated by the feeling of bullying and remoteness from other drivers in its padded American luxury. Now she enjoyed it and recognized a disquieting sense of power in being big enough to expect traffic space. When she heard Ken leave or return home she thought of a rumbling bear coming down the road unaware and uncaring of the rights of small critters in the forest.

This afternoon she spent a few minutes talking to Don Smith of Lewis & Smith about how the quarter's business was looking. He was a colorless man in his forties with thinning hair, a growing jowl and he was always pleasant but never friendly. His mouth curved for a smile but it seemed more an animal's warning of intruded space. Cat couldn't tell if he was an afraid man living an unfulfilling life or a straightforward single goaled man who lived easily in the terms of his talents and desires.

"Thank you for bringing this by, Cat. Your business is doing well. Always a good thing to see," he tipped his head in deference to numbers.

"Thanks, Don. Both Ken and I appreciate how you explain what those numbers really mean." Further conversation was stilted so she gracefully took her leave from the Utah divide. They understood the business of one another but could not penetrate the humanity, so there was little talk.

Cat heard the carpool van stop in front of the house to let MoMo out. Now that school was out parents traded trips to the recreation center and baseball practice. Next week it would be her turn to run the children about. Every sixth week was hers; it was one advantage of this neighborhood. More parents were able to share in the delivery duties of children. Her week was shared with two other moms with cars the size of her efficient Audi.

"How are you feeling, MoMo?" She looked into her daughter's eyes. They were shaped like Ken's, straight, deep and heavy-lidded with high eyebrows.

"Fine. I'm going to my room."

It must have been the ice cream. Her stomach was much more tender than Justin's. Justin soon followed home with his friend, Walt, to play games on the computer in his room. The children weren't even teenagers and already they were making separate lives with interests that didn't always include her. She folded towels and headed up the stairs to hear their noises through the walls and know they were okay, peacefully and happily doing what children do to grow up.

At five-thirty the phone rang. "I won't be home until at least eight, Cat. Go ahead and eat without me."

"What happened? Everything was fine."

"Well, it's not fine now. The catalog for the pewter company isn't coming off the press right and the customer is here for a press check. It may take longer than eight." Pewter had nothing to do with Salt Lake. Overton got the 32 page four-color 100,000 run from an advertising agency with a long eastward arm. It was important to succeed.

"We'll miss you." If they did a good job it would be back next quarter or next year. However often they print. It was important to secure this higher-up the rung clientele. "Run with the next pack of big dogs," Ken said.

"Where's Dad?" asked Justin when she called them down to eat. Cat heard Walt use the phone to let this mother know he was leaving for the walk two blocks home. What was wrong with the world that every move of children needed to be planned and recorded in this secluded middle-class neighborhood of sufficient incomes and supposed security? Where nothing had ever really happened to any child that she knew about. Fear cloaked over childhood today in a way she never had to experience.

"He's working late. Problem with a job. So we're having it easy. Macaroni and cheese with your favorite, fried hot dogs." She smiled at him.

"Great. Can't understand why Dad doesn't like it." MoMo wasn't as enthusiastic but she ate and they talked. Cat told them about her talk with Don Smith. Justin told of a history lesson on China, "Who cares?" MoMo was upset she had been assigned to write about frogs.

"Think of it as your friendly room froglight," Cat suggested. They were sitting at the table by the kitchen and family room where they had most their meals. The formal dining room gathered more dust than family memories.

At eight, she was reading while the children were in their rooms. She was on the beginning pages of The Stone Diaries by Carol Shields, *"The minutes tick by, become an hour, sometimes two. These segments of time are untied to any other time she recognizes. It happens more and more frequently, these collapsed hours, almost every day since the summer weather came on."*

She looked across the room through the glass French doors and windows to the petunias in the back yard. They were holding their own in June's warming light.

CHAPTER TWO

"If that cat scratches the screen one more time, I'll kill it," Suzanne said out loud. She considered herself capable of such an act but perhaps unwilling to carry through; at least in her brother's estimation. But then what did he know? He knew plenty and was the only one who judged her by standards up to Suzanne's ideas of what was worth any time at all. No one else ever mattered, didn't matter now, and would never matter. Even Michael's opinion was only important as an anecdote. It was to be enjoyed like an after dinner mint; neither adding nor subtracting from the meal, though it was a sweet favor to enjoy. Oh, all right, she would admit she valued his opinion and expected his approval.

Where was Michael anyway? He promised to be here an hour ago to help paint the bathroom and he wasn't close enough for her to hear his three-year-old oversized blonde-siren red show-off truck. When he turned from Ninth East into her block long row of thirty-year-old apartment buildings she would hear. She thought of this anonymous overlong driveway as her street. It was lined on either side with three straight-cut boring two-story brick buildings of nine apartments on each level. One-hundred-eight white front doors with grey wire screens faced the middle driveway with a living room window beside each one. It was her street. Nobody else wanted it. But right now she was only interested in painting the bathroom coral. Coral like the necklace she brought from St. Thomas last month when she had gone with John. Old John. A waste of time. Not that he was that old. And not that she didn't have a good time on white beaches, under a kindergarten blue sky. The time he had spent on her with rum soaked drinks, late dancing, early diving and hot cool afternoon naps of sex and sleep were a good memory. A memory. Best to be rid of someone who couldn't carry on a conversation that didn't end in trailing fumes of, "Yes, I am magnificent with enough money to trap you and your body is all I want and what you're worth."

The days had color as bright as a school play's backdrop. The morning call was an invitation of sex splashed in the bottom of a tequila sunrise with grenadine. Days of deep fabric color touching the blues, yellows and greens of native dress . . . so alive and pulsating her ears and eyes itched with life to take it in. Sweeping oversized orange sunsets in strokes so broad they painted half the world and left one breathless before the moon appeared. Well, at least Old John had shown her the world of coral. Skeletons of marine life growing in geometric convoluted arms of spiky nodules protecting themselves. Coral. She brought it home.

Now she lightly tapped the window to stop the cat from scratching the screen. She heard Michael's truck turn the corner and come down the private street.

"Where have you been?" she stood holding the wrought iron balcony railing outside her door and looked down, tensed and ready as a race horse to curse chance and lay blame. Michael looked at her through years of being a younger brother who once idolized and now knew. He had shared tee-shirts, bath water, peeled oranges and parents with this female who was eighteen-months older and no other woman would ever surprise him like she did.

"Screwing your bosses daughter."

"Good, I hope I get something out of it."

"Only what you put into it."

"I want more than that."

"So how long am I sentenced to this painting?" He passed her into the apartment only two inches taller than her at five-foot-nine.

"Maybe two hours if you don't take time to pee."

"So where's the beer? We'll time it."

"Oh for godsakes, Michael. You know." She turned saluting with the same upturned butt he remembered when she was fourteen. It talked to men and he knew it because he watched every fourteen through eighteen-year-old in the high school watch it. Though it never talked to him, he understood the language. She had taught him the language of her butt and dark eyelashes, flashing eyes and soft-cropped yellow hair jutting to say, "touch me and don't touch me" at the same time. She had been a good teacher and now that he was twenty-six he was grateful. Understanding the call of a woman is at best a dangerous jungle and he at least had learned from an older sister who was willing to teach, if not with chalk and outlined notes, by expressive example.

"You're painting the bathroom that color?" his male sensibilities of a bland and comforting home to return to after competitive posturing over pool tables and forced encounters with antiseptic urine smelling bathrooms was upset. Home should be welcoming and soft. "Are you trying to haunt the place?"

"You don't like Jamaica Kiss? She sharpened her life piercing glance of a falcon on him.

"Is that a color or something you did last night?" he looked away. "It's just bright."

"It's from Old John."

To still his voice he picked up a paintbrush. It was his hope Old John would be Suzanne's answer. The guy was close to geezer at 48 but he had money, fading looks that were a handsome sunset, a kind way of making people comfortable and a sincere affection for Suzanne. He was sure of that. Michael hoped Suzanne would find him agreeable enough. Maybe for years. Or a lifetime. Now he was careful to say anything.

"He liked this color," Michael was noncommittal.

"I like this color and its coral."

"So how is it from Old John?"

"I found coral in St. Thomas. There isn't a natural color here like it."

Michael nodded. His dark hair and square face were in direct opposition to the creamy fairness and round invitation of his lithe sister. If her defined shade of coral was not available in all of Utah, it must be true. She knew color as well as she knew how to use drama. "I'll show you the necklace Old John bought me after we paint."

Two hours and two beers later he rubbed the coral necklace with his thumb while Suzanne filled glasses with ice and poured water from a bottle. She might call it a coral necklace but Michael thought it was as much a gold necklace. The cabochon in the center was over two inches wide and at least half that high. The marine life peacefully unmolested in clear Caribbean waters since Europe had touched it in the 1500s laid as stolen innocence in his hand. It was framed in heavy gold, a quarter inch around, 18 carat he guessed and it tapered ever narrower to a clasp with a dangling hook.

"I don't know about coral but the gold on this necklace will add pounds to your walk."

"Then I won't wear it when I weigh in," she appreciated his jokes even at her expense. "Michael, you're the only person who can criticize or tease Suzanne roughly and not die in the process. Be Suzanne's conscience. She hasn't developed one of her own." Their mother spoke with clear eyes looking directly into his the month before she died of cancer. The words to Suzanne had been, "Take care of Michael. I don't want him alone." Suzanne thought this funny. As if Michael would ever be lonely with the packs of women waiting ahead and behind him. She laughed to herself, but when she told Michael last Christmas it sputtered out with seriousness and a heart-felt vow to always be with him. Michael laughed softly; happily accepting her holiday hug. He never did tell her what their Mother had said to him.

"Where is Old John now?" If he had doubted the man's bank account he wouldn't again. Any man who bought a woman a souvenir of this heft had money.

"I don't know. Still looking for the right one I suppose."

"Why aren't you the right one?"

"I am. But not for him. He had money but it was caged money he would keep to himself in the end. Oh, I could have money to spend, but not anything to build."

"Why was it caged?"

"It was all 'earned' as he said and now it had 'earned' a right to be caged for him. It was tucked in places I would never know about. He liked showing it, bringing it out to make my eyes shine, but he didn't need me. He wanted a breathing, pretty blonde-haired bank account with no active interest, no accrued investment and few questions. All to make him look powerful."

Michael nodded. Suzanne was always objective about people's motivations, including her own, "I want access to a man's gut level. I'm not an earring." She turned. "There's that cat again," and headed to the front door of the small apartment. A large grey and black male cat strutted inside, it's tail lifted like a candy cane. "All right, Mr. Crichton, you can come in, but don't go in the bathroom. It's still wet." Suzanne was sure the author Michael Crichton would be a perfect husband. His mind was alive with intrigue and the ability to write it so people enjoyed the products of his mind. He was paid well and respected. He was busy all day writing which meant his wife could be free to build her own life's portfolio. With a little good luck he also had an author's insecurities and was finished with youthful games. Suzanne imagined herself as seducer nurse, describing the insecurities first until he felt ill and then supplying the answers to solve, soothe and entertain.

"Hello Mr. Crichton." The cat jumped on Michael's lap, lifted his head for ear stroking and purred.

"He likes you," she stated.

"We understand each other."

Suzanne's head lifted for an explanation.

"We've both lived with you."

Again she laughed at his joke on her.

"Are you up to clubbing tonight?"

"Yes, let's start at Jumper's. You know," she rolled her shoulder and fluttered her eyelashes, "where it itches." They laughed at Jumper's motto. Without meaning - just like the place. Sometimes they met friends when they went out, but they were a good team for the club scene without anyone else.

Stunning is what an aunt had called them at their mother's funeral six years ago. Good bait for the rest of us is what Aaron said over a first drink a few months ago. Suzanne Flint was reed slim and bone dainty feminine with enough breast to draw a gently sloping artist's profile. The body was young fresh healthy cream but it was the face people noticed. Life glowed from surreal eyes the colors of tree brown green through a prism of morning rain. The depth and awareness made them look bigger than they were. Only when she closed them would a person realize the small slits that had sent light to observe from windows as secure as a tank protecting what she thought and now knew about them. Proportionate is how her mother described her face at age twelve, not wanting to unleash the power of her beauty before she was ready. The slightly bowed mouth, and straight nose with the slightest ball at the end were as simple as the eyes, but they sparked an energy that glowed across a dark barroom. Blonde hair with purposeful dark roots was an inch too long to be spiky and an inch shy of requiring more care than slight waves genetically blessed.

Michael was compressed dense power. He held it in shoulders, arms, legs, hips, only sharing when he wanted. Rhythmic daily work as a carpenter ever bending, fitting, piecing one angle to another gave him grace, litheness, patience. Power bubbled, rippling waves holding strength in check, seeming to slow graceful movements with energy held back. Dark bordering on black of twilight before night sky hair was short, trimmed and in control as was his lean jaw, straight nose and level, straight shooting eyes. The blue eyes were direct, open and easier to approach than Suzanne's He looked with the clarity of a ship's captain, surveying subtle changes below surfaces, seeing action in wind others overlooked, knowing the approach of calm in chaos.

There was a routine to walking in a bar. Michael opened the door at Jumper's as though they were a date and Suzanne stepped lightly aside, within six feet of the door where they were most visible. She would stand alone with her limbs loose and pleased as though she had just had sex. As she surveyed the room with a slight smile in approval, Michael would slowly come to her side without touching. Without posing overlong, they walked toward a table of friends. He took her direction for seating, and as most of the bar watched, Suzanne would seat herself, while Michael sat next to her. Interesting strangers they had already observed could not tell if they were lovers or friends. Brother and sister never occurred to them. Michael and Suzanne planned it that way.

Everyone shifted and moved closer together to make room as the siblings arrived. Raylene and Aaron were on one side and Sierra and Eddie were on the other. There were no couples so seats and conversations changed constantly through an evening or as strangers came to venture a meeting. Raylene was Suzanne's friend since high school and Sierra had been Raylene's co-worker at her last job in the office at a car dealership's car repair and servicing department. Aaron they picked up as a regular from O'Riley's where they often went for beer, hamburgers and pool. Eddie was Michael's roommate. They had been friends since apprenticing together as carpenters.

It was a loose "association" as they called themselves, no dues or gossip. Last year when Raylene temporarily went with a former loser boyfriend and the others talked about her, Suzanne stood up from the table of two empty pitchers and six glasses, swayed once from the beer and announced, "We are here for our pleasure and comfort. We cannot be talking about each other like this. If you've got something to say to Raylene, say it. But not to me." Silence flattened spritzed curls and embedded a rule of no gossip.

Two missing members were Diane and Trent. Diane was a divorced mom with a daughter and a nowhere up job checking at a chain store. She didn't come very often. Trent was a lawyer and a cousin of Aaron's who had just started appearing. You never knew who would show up and only if you were absent more than a week, two weeks for Diane, would anybody call to ask.

Suzanne stumbled from bed Monday morning in the early June light. The windowless bathroom was dark so she turned on the light and was greeted by the bright gloss of Jamaica Kiss. For a moment she felt a rocking of water and waves hitting shore as she looked at deep red pink coral walls.

"Damn you, Mother. Leaving me to imagine you through coral instead of being here."

The dress she had worn while shopping in St. Thomas with Old John hung untouched in her closet. It still smelled of water, sweat and a perfume she used for seduction, but on that day, on the day she had bought the coral it was fresh. It had a raggy jagged hemline to flirt, a deep neckline and bodice draping her breasts. Soft lime green, the color of a vodka gimlet reduced by ice, is how Old John described the color as he leaned toward her. He had patiently been by her side as she walked from store to store observing an array of stones she didn't understand. He smiled. He was prepared to buy to gain memories of this week. She smiled. The women behind the counters forced business smiles. Then in the fifth store, Stones of Lore, there were legends above the showcases of endless gems. Poorly-typed, askew and on different papers the legends seemed an afterthought but they made the difference.

Malachite: Is often used to promote inner peace and hope. Use it in business to surround yourself with protection because it promotes inner security. She studied its dense green striped with black. It was almost what she wanted.

Ruby: An energizer to lift your spirits and express true love and devotion. It shows self-confidence.

Aquamarine: A true soother to your world worries. This stone will calm nerves and help you relax. Sailors carried it on voyages.

Suzanne read the legends looking for something that fit what she needed. Then she read: Coral is often given to children who lack self-confidence and seek love from parents. Parents give it to children they wish to protect.

"Don't you think coral has a beauty other stones don't match?" she whispered into Old John's ear. He asked for the larger cabochon cut on an 18" gold chain. He wanted a memorable week.

Now, it was Monday morning a month later - always a Pandora's box. She thought about what needed to be done as she put on shorts and a tee-shirt before an easy neighborhood run. There was a sales meeting at eight. That should be finished before ten. Then calls. Three appointments. Yes, she remembered three. An 11:45 at Overton. Two at Janson's Design Printing and a four-o'clock at Carroll's. After the run the shower water on her back felt good.

"I know, Mother. I know you wanted more from me." She stepped from the shower, took the cream-colored towel from the rack and began drying. "I know." Yes, the resounding coral on her bathroom walls gave soothing light.

Suzanne was a sales rep for Harkness, "Your Paper Goods Source," a major paper products warehouse distributor. Her geographic area spanned downtown Salt Lake City and the western industrial swath south of the airport, halfway down the valley. She and three other paper reps were supposed to make sure all printers and ad agencies in the area knew what paper was available, how it printed and what it cost. And p.s. Make sure it sold. She hadn't known there was anything besides notebook, stationary and toilet paper before she got the job two years ago, but now she could tell one brand's finish from another's and how it would print on a Kimori vs a Miehle press.

Working at Harkness was a way stop for Suzanne. She didn't know where it was leading. Scientifically laid out career plans from the foundation of a college degree had not been something she understood. Being a lawyer, architect, doctor was too disciplined and mired in convention and rules. The trenches of the real business world was where the opportunity really beckoned. She was trying to learn the lay of the land, the rules of the game, so she could carve out a place that was truly and forever hers. So she listened to her co-workers and boss, she read the memos from corporate in New York and Wisconsin, where trees must grow like fungus, and she was a very good employee. Her boss, Carter Holmes knew she was a bewitching mix of brains and body that numbed a printer's resistance and softened edges. That's the bet he took when he hired her. Several times he had stood behind her, even when she made a few unwise promises. In the long run it paid off. Suzanne worked more closely with Ron Karren, another salesperson, Shelly Amherst, who managed the paper sample room and Blake Martinez who ran shipping. Carter couldn't tell if he was jealous, annoyed or humored to hear Blake and Suzanne when they flirted with each other.

After the early Monday rah-rah sales meeting that too often ended in her boss relaying the boring details of corporate policy and strategy instead of better price breaks or a printing tip she could lure printers with, she began returning phone calls. Could she get the price someone wanted for a printing job? Would she give it for another? How much time and money was involved in shipping three skids of paper by truck or plane from Denver? At 11:15 she needed to leave for Overton's and wondered if it had been a mistake to make an appointment so close to lunch. But who took lunch anymore anyway? Eat and drive. Eat and work at your desk. Eat and run a press.

"Hi, Mary Ellen, I'm here to see Ken," she handed Mary Ellen a business card for easy reference.

"Is he expecting you, Suzanne?" Mary Ellen looked over her glasses suspiciously.

"Yes, at 11:45."

Mary Ellen rang Ken's office. "Suzanne Flint is here to see you from Harkness." She nodded as he answered and then looked up. "He'll be right out."

Suzanne watched Ken like she was assessing how paper held ink as he walked through the hall to the outside office to meet her. A bit hunched forward and walking fast, his shoulders lead him where he was going faster, sooner. On previous visits she hadn't noticed the power of that barreling forward walk into time and future. He looked to be just over six-foot, not considered so tall anymore in her generation but his energy was more contained and focused than the squandered hungry energy of men her age. His hair was dark brown and slicked back with gloss. A definite hint he thought about his looks and wanted to be young. It left his large forehead unprotected and almost an oversized target above the hooded eyes and straight dark eyebrows. His eyes were so hidden she had to look directly in them to see where he was looking. Only his open grin welcomed her. She was trying to read how busy and distracted he was by business or whether she could take extra time. She wanted to know this company's potential. Numbers had been up over the past year, but the higher the better.

"How have you been?" he stepped behind her as she led to his office.

"Fine. Fine. Very busy."

"I've got a new paper I'd like to show you. From Japan. Prints great."

He nodded an irritated yes.

She rustled a little in a carry bag and brought out samples. "It will make that 40 inch of yours sing," she paused to smile, "It has better opacity than what you just used on the catalog and we can sell it at a better cost."

"It's been busy. I'm hungry. I'd like to get away from this place. Want to go to Hammer's?"

"Well, yes, that sounds good," Suzanne knew when to take an offer. She left the paper sample swatch book on his desk, straightened, gave a bright smile and stood. "I'll drive."

The first time they faced each other they were seated in a booth at The Home Town Choice, Hammer's Burgers. Ken had a ticket in his hand with a number waiting to be called.

"You come here often?"

"No. Sometimes we order take-out, but I just wanted to get out today," he paused smiling. She hadn't noticed his teeth were almost all straight. At the most three were not perfect. "You were just the lucky one who walked into my office when it was time to go."

"So should I continue talking about paper?"

"No. I'll buy some. You know I'll need it. You'll give me the best price. You'll move me to the next price break. You'll take care of my account. Maybe not charge me for overnight on a job someday when I need it." He stopped. He had been watching her like a deer he was aiming at through a rifle scope.

Suzanne sat back. "Yes, I guess I will. The only one you'll have to work for is the price break. So what will we talk about? We haven't gotten our food yet."

The number was called on the loudspeaker and Ken got up for the tray. They didn't say another word while they moved the burgers, fries, ketchup and two drinks to comfortable eating positions.

"Tell me about the paper show you've got coming up." He watched his food as she listed the details of next week's Gallery of Fine Printing Papers. Reps from the major paper manufacturers were flying in. There would be food, drinks, door prizes, inescapable workshops, demonstrations of pre-press products and printing presses showing direct to plate. Maybe Ken would change to that soon. "Think of the money to be saved in pre-press," she finished.

"If you can afford the $100,000 press first." Still, Ken said he would be at the 'genuine paper extravaganza' in nobody else's words but Harkness.

Suzanne did all the talking during the short return to Overton in her Cherokee. Ken only talked when she turned the last corner, "That's quite a necklace."

She told him where it was bought and, "The reason I like it so well is it's impossible to get in Utah. The color is so different. There's no water with coral reefs here." Old John was never mentioned.

Suzanne pulled in front of Overton Printing and before she could turn off the car Ken had the door open, nodded good-bye and was barreling shoulders first to the front door. "See you at the paper show," she called toward his back.

Sometimes encounters weren't worth analyzing and this was one of them. The man was a little odd today, everyone is allowed a few odd days in life and well, she had learned a few odd days were necessary for printers to keep an emotional equilibrium of sanity. He promised to buy paper, she'd had lunch, maybe made a friend and noticed he was more good-looking than she had thought. It was time for her next appointment.

CHAPTER THREE

"Catalina, I named you after an island for a reason," she was reciting a childhood memory to Joel as he cut her hair. Her mother was sitting in a lounge chair in the backyard, holding a glass of iced tea and trying to hold her daughter's attention. She had just informed her mother she wanted to drop out of girl scouts and didn't want a motherly opinion.

"Catalina dear,' she paused to crunch ice in her mouth. "I want you to know how much I love you."

Sometimes her mother was slow to the point. "Yes."

"I told your father you were named after Catalina because that is where we had our honeymoon. But there is another reason." She had heard the reference to Catalina Island off Los Angeles a hundred times

"You are an island. I could feel it in the womb before you were born."

"And this is what I remember, word for word, Joel," Cat repeated from history's tunnel of changed perception. "I gave you your name for recognition. So you would know yourself. You isolate yourself my daughter where it would be better not to. I'm afraid for you. An island is lonely; though sometimes happily unto itself."

Joel referred to an island in the Great Salt Lake, "Well, at least she didn't name you Antelope or Philippine."

"Or Prince Edward."

Cat didn't think she was an island. Boat was a better description. She chugged between islands, always visiting. The island of marriage to Ken, motherhood was another, then there was Shiner's Island, Cancer Care House, the island of talking to her mother on the phone and Overton Island. And the Inside Herself Island that didn't often get visited. The way she wanted. No, it wasn't that either. It was only the way she had dreamed. Who can tell between wanting and dreaming? Unless her mind wandered onto itself as she gardened, she

34

seldom thought of that. One of the few times her mind was not deliberately occupied, it loosed sunken thoughts, surprising her that attention was not on the children, Ken or Eme and what their lives needed from her.

The only other time she was startled by curiosity about herself was when she read lurching words in a book demanding recognition of something she didn't recognize. The last time that had happened was Sunday after the children had been put to bed. Ken was watching TV and she was on the couch beside him. *"Come in if you wish. I have some whiskey."* The book was *Good Morning, Midnight* by Jean Rhys and the scene was of a cornered woman who felt beaten by life. Cat didn't know why the scene was compelling. The circumstances had nothing to do with her.

"I've got it," MoMo had returned from school after her visit with Joel, and yelled as she raced for the ringing phone. "Hi, Dad. Ya," She nodded her head to something he said. "Love you. Here's Mom," Cat had been walking toward her since she nodded.

"Hi, Ken, how are you?" Cat felt her brow knit. She didn't want him to be gone tonight. He hadn't been gone to often in the last weeks, but tonight she had looked forward to seeing him. Remembering her mother had reminded her of life's fragile moments. Tonight she wanted to be with the man who held everything together for all of them.

He wasn't coming home until nine or so. There was trouble on the scheduling for the second shift and he needed to be there. How about if tomorrow night they all go out for dinner together? Like MoMo she nodded, said yes and I love you before hanging up.

"Well, MoMo, I guess it's just you and me before Justin comes home. Want to go look at swimming suits?"

"Sure," her eyes brightened and she bounced up, a sprite out of water, ready to go.

"Maybe we'll stop and pick up something to eat for dinner to bring home."

They headed for the car and then to the mall, to wander happily in girls swim suits. Two suits were impossible to choose between so they bought the red, white and blue stripe in her size and the rose, yellow and princess lavender swirl in one size larger. Now that money was more available that was Cat's nod to frugality. Though it wasn't her turn to pick the kids up from soccer practice they were early enough to stop by and get Justin before dinner.

"Hi, Mom, Trouble Kid Sister, what's up?" They didn't often pick him up out of turn.

"Nothing. We're just on our own and thought we'd include you in the dinner plans. Want to bring Walt?"

"Nah, he's already with Mrs. James." Mrs. James, or rather Cindy as Cat knew her, was picking up this week.

Pizza was the dinner by a two to one vote. Cat voted for Chinese but was happy if her children were happy. They spread out in front of TV on the glass coffee table. Two milks and one wine to the sides of plates.

During the evening the children went to their bedrooms for an hour of reading, computer homework and calling friends. Trained from early childhood they each changed to bedclothes, brushed their teeth and then wandered down to finish their day watching TV on either side of Cat. Carefully, she led each one up to their rooms with sitcom laughter behind. The silver light falling through their bedroom windows to land on their sleeping heads allowed tears from Cat. She didn't understand the generosity, the healing stillness of night that urged her to bless her children in moonlight.

Cat was on another glass of wine. The children were sleeping and it was past nine. It was moving by 9:30. Half an hour had the palpable tick of seconds in a husband's absence. She poured a next. They had all been small glasses, she thought. She needed to loosen thinking.

There was a chair by the glass door to the backyard that could be turned to watch TV or to see the garden. She opened the door to know if the air was warm enough, this June evening, to sit outside. It was early roses, wet grass, dying tulips.

"She was crying because she was at the end of everything." That is what she had read in the next line about whiskey by Jean Rhys. There wasn't a discernible reason why that sentence stuck with her. In fact, seemed to mesmerize her to a point of silly attention to trivials; as though she needed to understand mosquitoes in December.

Where was Ken? Usually when there was trouble at the plant he called a few times as though he was bored with the conversation and demands of hired help and needed the infusion of love or there

was just plain time to spend and he knew he was too tired and distracted to work on bids, figures, columns of numbers that would matter
when costs had been subtracted from a total. It was quiet. She sat in a
chair, looking at her garden, trying to see through moonlight. It was
so quiet she thought she could hear the breathing of her children.

The stove clock said 10:20. Holding her glass she moved forward on the chair to stand and go call Ken. With that decision Cat
knew Ken would not be at work. The glass in her hand was light but
it felt like she was raising lead against gravity. She could not lift her
arms. Her arms were water dowsers for truth since she had been ten-
years-old. It was a secret she kept to herself and wanted to ignore. The
first time she felt it she was with friends playing by a stream. Water
was running high and strong from the winter to melt. Six children had
wandered away together on a hot July day after a church meeting.
Glen and Cat were a few yards away from the others when he turned
to her, his eyes probing searchlights.

"I think Julie likes me." Air quieted for Cat while she listened. "I want her to like me," the need in his voice made the background laughing of their friends a cruel taunt. Cat's arms fell like
young limbs from oak trees struck by an ax. She knew it would not
be. Glen followed Julie in shy loyal footsteps through their school
years and she politely acknowledged his friendship, while leveraging
greater opportunities. Glen left on a South American church mission
with tender hope, but never returned. He was hit by a car in Lima.
Julie, well, there were many young men who believed in the eternity
of her youthful beauty.

At age fourteen, before her father was told he had cancer Cat
knew something was very wrong when she tried to hug him and her
arms fell away, tired and too weak to hold the only man she loved.
When she first kissed Ken there had been an unexpected surge of life
that streamed through the tips of her fingers to hold tighter, hold
tighter. The strength of her arms had surprised them both. It worked
on its own, without Cat's intention and was sporadic and seldom.
Until now, she had also been able to accept what she believed it
meant.

Maybe she should call Eme. Was she with a man? Had Ryan
been successful? Would Sheldon be by her side? Cat would not have
welcomed a call after ten if she were with Ken. But there was no one

else and she was afraid.

"I'm sorry Eme," Cat thought before she dialed, to excuse the social faux paux.

The phone rang four times before Eme answered it. Feeling guilty Cat was about to hang up.

"Hello."

"Eme, hi."

"Cat. What's the matter?"

"Are you alone?"

"Yes."

"Good, well, I'm alone, too. Ken hasn't come home and I'm worried and I've had four, maybe five glasses, small glasses of wine."

"You don't need to apologize."

"Yes, I do."

"Yes, you do."

There was a pause. "I'm still here. Drinking my wine."

"Where's Ken?"

"At work. He called earlier. The children and I had pizza and I haven't heard from him at all."

"You're in the wrong business. Printing never was a good match for you."

"I'm not the point. Ken's life is."

"Well, call the place. He's probably just busy."

Cat paused. To call was monumental and she felt tired beyond the wine. "Yes, yes, I will." Her voice was weak and beaten. As though she were at the end of everything. "Let's meet for lunch tomorrow." Small talk relieved her.

Cat dialed Overton Printing. The first time she misdialed and quickly hung up before pushing the speed dial code. It was 10:40 and the small second shift should be singing like an early robin as Ken said. She should hear the melodic beat of a printing press that held the bank loan of her children's security.

"Hola, Overton." It was Miguel the night shift printer.

Cat cleared her throat and felt unsure in her ankles. "Hello, Miguel, I'd like to speak to Ken."

"Hola, Senora Overton. Por favor, Senor Ken is not here. He leave early," he was apologetic.

She said good-bye and hung up. Early. What did early mean?

A half hour ago? Four? She regretted she hadn't thought quickly enough to ask.

The wineglass was inexpensive and could have been put in the dishwasher but Cat's hands needed something to do. She pumped soap on the glass and rubbed with her fingers and a little water to a full froth of bubbles. For a tiny minute in a lifetime she ran hot water to clean the bubbles while staring ahead. Not much productive thought was going on inside that very busy head. Real thought but not earth productive thought. The concepts were so large they were granite boulders trying to move through one ear and out the other. Marriage. Belief. Trust. The children. Unexplained phenomena. Connections to herself were not possible; only solid heavy rocks in pictures before her mind; not words, not simple comforting words. Knowledge too disconcerting and laughing at her for that. The heavy thought strokes were not at all like the pebbly, sandy thought of grocery lists and garden plans that could be arranged, rearranged and controlled.

She reached for the towel, dried the glass, replaced it in the cupboard and stood at the door to leave the kitchen before turning the light out. The clock said 11:03. The children were too deeply asleep to know their mother did not check on them. She brushed her teeth, washed her face, changed her clothes and pulled the tie on the robe closer than usual before she sat on the bed holding her knees.

"Ya wanna rumble?" she heard her husband's Expedition approach like a late night man fight on TV. The approach was seconds before the garage door lifted at 11:28. Cat stood in the dark, removed her robe and slipped between the sheets still sitting. Ken stepped lightly when he came in the house darkness. She heard him walk to the kitchen sink, open the cupboard for a glass, turn on the water and, fill the glass to drink. There was silence as she supposed he drank and turned to look out the window as she had. His steps were slow and steady up the staircase and still she didn't know whether to be silent or say something when he entered the room. But she was sitting up and could not find the peace of body to lie down or pretend sleep. Ken's black shadow body outlined in moonlight silently walked from the bedroom door to the bathroom. His eyes were not as clear in the night as hers and he did not see her sitting.

"Hello, Ken," her voice startled him. Once more she was

frightened by the small unnerving events of this night. Her voice in the night's dark had never startled him.

"Cat, you're awake."

"Of course I am. I've been waiting for you."

"This evening went on too long."

"Where have you been?"

"I was at the shop, making sure the paper got cut right. They cut one wrong earlier and I was nervous. There's too much tied up in paper on that job. Then there was trouble with scheduling. Everyone wants their job by the end of week. What's so magical about Friday anyway? Are they working Saturday? No, but they make me perform like a seal to show them what I can do." Cat listened with a deeper ear, held to dirt, held to life, while Ken went on about the evening. One problem after another, but his voice wasn't in it. It was hollow and reciting routine answers. His feet hadn't moved from his hello. A smell of waning liquor reached her and she was smothered. Tired, a muscle heavy leaden tired that wouldn't let her move at all.

"The people from the agency came for a press check on Miguel's job. It was hickey, registration, color, one thing after another. When they finished nitpicking the hell out of it I offered to take them for a drink to make them happy. The bill's on the credit card." Only now did he sound weary. The day had been trying.

"Where did you go?"

"Ginger's. You know. 'Where friends meet,'" the sarcasm was real.

She recognized the name as a bar in a hotel not far from Overton's. Since they had moved to the growing web of industrial parks on the city's westside under the boom of airliners coming and going from the airport, two chains of hotels had moved nearby and brought convenience to business visitors and a faint ambiance of city to people who seldom go to the city.

"You didn't call."

"I know. I'm sorry. I got busy, distracted with the agency people," he rubbed his forehead, his fingers squeezed his head.

The evening seemed explained. Somewhat. If she brought up she had called it would sound nagging. As though she didn't believe him or wanted to prolong an already too long day. Perhaps it would hurt his optimism or question their trust.

"I'm sorry, Lina," he whispered in a near prayerful voice.

Cat waved at Eme from the patio in front of the restaurant when she saw her coming. Cat knew Eme would be a little late because she was moving offices from a small basement windowless room to a small side ground level windowless room. In academia it was a move up and she was encouraged her health science career of teaching and nutritional community study of new immigrants put her in line for dean when she was seventy-two.

"Love you, love you," Eme said from her walking portrait of thick bouncing curls, bright colors and tender red lips. Cat knew her friend's words were true and spoken as a vacuum to absorb last night.

"I love you, too, Eme," she paused, "you're my dearest friend." There was almost a catch in her throat.

"Well, that's a poor testimony," and they giggled at the reference to local theology of testimonies. The waitress looked them over. She hoped they wouldn't order wine, take too much time and tie up the table.

"I have something to tell you."

"It wouldn't be fun if you didn't. I hope it's naughty."

"Cat, you need a better word than naughty. How about fucking good? I hear it from the kids all the time," she referred to her students. "Old married women need to hear that life has more than naughty."

Unsure, Cat rolled her eyes. An improvement from the first time Eme had said it and Cat shuddered. She understood the word and didn't. Marriage should be an answer, warmth in life, not plaintive swear words.

"I've made progress with Ryan."

"Oh," Cat was not surprised.

"I was looking at the carrots on Saturday. He came up to me. Deliberately. Almost using my space. I moved a step just to breathe," she waved her hand in front of her face for air and her curls jostled.

Cat watched.

"Well, he started to talk. Just small talk. How do you like the carrots? We're expecting a shipment of raspberries tomorrow, a little early, but they will be beautiful."

Cat lifted her wineglass.

"I know what that means. Talk to me," and she motioned with her hands toward her body in a waving welcome, "Talk to me until your own talk seduces you."

"What did you do?"

"I listened. Best thing to do. I figured a produce person has been told to sell and needs to report about people like me on Monday morning."

"Makes sense."

"So we talked for a few minutes. About carrots, radishes, whatever. He smiled. Brushed my cart and arm like an awkward donkey as he left."

Cat waited. Silence. "What happened?"

"He went to the potatoes. I finished bagging carrots. It's a work in progress. I think Ryan is shy. I went out with Sheldon for dinner."

"How is Sheldon doing?"

"How can a Sheldon do? He wants to go camping next week but I don't know."

"He's been mighty steady."

"Yes, and near boring."

Cat looked down at her sandwich that had just arrived, "That shouldn't be boring. That should be well, maybe reliable. Not a bad thing really." Before continuing she brushed her mouth for crumbs. "I've got something to tell, too."

Eme's eyes brightened. The darkness of cave black-brown let a shaft of light fall through. Cat was encouraged. Before she talked she took a long sip of usually forsaken lunchtime wine.

"Ken and I are going to Snowbird for the weekend."

"Wow. Wicked. Or fucking good."

"Well, I'm happy. He suggested it this morning before he went to work. Said it would be fun and I'm certainly happy. The kids are going with Mother."

"Good. A weekend at a resort 30 minutes from home. At least he thought of it."

"He's been busy."

"At what?"

"Work has just been crazy. Last night there was a huge catalog job. Pewter, can you imagine? Where did that come from? It was an ad agency. Anyway, he said he needed to get away. He's been so busy. Last week was the paper show downtown. It didn't start until afternoon and both nights he didn't get home until after eleven. Tossed all night. Then he was up at five. Ken runs like crazy. He needs time away."

"Well, I'm sure you'll soothe the savage beast."

Cat laughed. "Ken is just the tired, distracted, overworked beast."

"Here's to Ken," Eme lifted her glass.

"To Ken and Sheldon," Cat replied knocking her glass against Eme's and noticing the disapproving eye of the waitress. Decadence as a wineglass.

That evening Ken arrived at exactly 6:00 and they went to a sit-down, menu-ordering, drink in a real water glass restaurant where hamburgers and steaks could be ordered. Conversation started in casual family tradition. Everyone told of one thing that happened that day and the other three were expected to react as though they had seen that exact story on TV. It had been Ken's idea when they started a year ago. TV had nothing to do with it, but he used the idea to keep the children's interest. He was sick of the "Oh, what a hard day you had," reactions that people said with forced politeness. He wanted his children to understand the variety of responses idiots and thoughtful people had, and to laugh or rant a little when it was necessary; to make things slide off their backs instead of fall heavy on their hearts.

MoMo talked about lunch that day at the school's summer classes. "I was eating lunch with Steph and Trista and Trista started talking to people at the other table. Girls I don't know. They are a year older. She just got up and went and sat at the table with the other girls. That left Steph and me. That was okay with me but then Steph got a funny look on her face," MoMo looked down and fiddled with a French fry in ketchup. "I think she wanted to cry, her face got so ugly. I didn't say anything." MoMo looked around the table and everyone was watching. Even Justin. He knew who the girls at the next table were because she had seen him talking to one of them last week.

MoMo's face scrunched to keep away tears. "Steph just got up and sat at the other table, too. By Trista. I was alone." In fourth grade it was understood a person did not want to be alone at lunch.

The silence at the table distanced the clatter of silver to plates, talk, laughter and whirl of the restaurant around them.

"Oh, MoMo," her mother said.

"What did you do?" her father's voice was strained and strident as he looked at Cat for silence.

Momo looked around and shuffled the fry again, "I took a bite of lunch but then I got up and left. I saw Annie by the door and I talked to her." All three of the audience took a breath at the same time.

"Good tactic, MoMo. You met crises well," her father's voice was softer. "Stand tall, be reserved, resilient and cool. Steph is a cowardly jerk."

"She can stink. She's okay in soccer, but she's always sucking up."

"Bag her," was Justin's advice. "I'll watch her," he ended.

"Well, dear, no one likes that kind of treatment. I'm sorry you had that happen, but I'm sure you learned," Cat added. It was understood they could all give sympathy, but it had to be mixed with useful words to meet life head-on, head down, nostrils flared, horns ready. So Cat added, "Females too often split company for personal benefit."

"Oh, hell, Cat," Ken shook his head, "so do men."

The weekend at Snowbird sat before Ken and Cat like a well earned certificate of appreciation. Neither Ken or Cat had mentioned Monday night though Cat had a few restless nights sleeping. She woke Tuesday at three and jumped out of bed before thinking. Her thin nightgown waved above her knees and the strap fell to her elbow. She went to the bathroom. A dream of Ken awakened her. He was laughing, calling her foolish and silly. A bit of a girl. A snip of a girl. A wisp of a girl. Barely a breath of a girl. She woke feeling accused and deserted. When she returned to bed he was sleeping the steady peaceful pace of her children.

As she packed Thursday evening she considered what they would be doing. June was off-season for the ski resort so entertainment was self-centered and gentle. Walking. Riding the tram, reading, the hot tub, swimming, drinks before dinner, pleasant meals. Sleeping in. Two nights and a day-and-a-half alone with Ken. She wanted it in a way she hadn't admitted; a way she wasn't sure was okay.

In a linen cloth bag she had been given at a printing convention two years ago, she packed three bras, four panties that matched different outfits, thigh holding hose, and two frothy nightgowns. She paid attention to socks, walking shoes and a backpack. On the bed she laid out choices for Ken. He would make his final selection, perhaps change a shirt and add shorts before stacking them by the suitcase for Cat to add. Her final task was packing an action reading book and a learning book for each of them. There would be board games in the room if they wanted to eye each other over dominoes. Wine, an opener, gin and tonic were packed just in case they wanted a drink before they went to the bar or when they returned to the room.

Snowbird was only thirty minutes from home, but Cat's trip to her mother's in Logan to take the children began at ten o'clock on Friday so she could be back for Ken by four.

"Have a good time, dear and don't worry about the children. We'll have a ball," her mother's eyes sparkled. She was happy to have the grandchildren spend the weekend with her and then spend a night in Cat's guest room before returning home. "We'll plan on being at your house by seven Sunday. But don't plan on us for dinner. We'll stop somewhere on the road before." Cat smiled and hugged the children and her mother good-bye. She wouldn't have to worry about them this weekend.

"It feels good to get away, Lina," Ken stretched his shoulders as they sat at a restaurant table that evening.

"Yes, it does. Its been a while since we've done anything like this. Why did you think of it now?"

"Work has been hell. I needed to get out from under it so I could manage it better. I knew things would be in control this weekend. People are finally getting their jobs down."

"How did that job turn out?" she had not brought up anything all week that had to do with Monday night.

"What job?"

"The ad agency job."

He sat up and moved his drink toward him. "Fine. Miguel handled it and everything got out Wednesday."

"The pewter job?"

"No, a brochure for a candle company. You'll see it come through next week."

Cat felt queasiness settling over the talk; nervousness. She wasn't sure if it was Ken or her editing her words before talking, but there was an edge she knew needed rescuing for the weekend. Conversations that gravitated toward strong feelings or negative emotions made her retreat to safer ground.

"You've certainly worked hard lately. Overton hasn't any choice but to succeed," compliments softened edges.

"You're great, Lina," his light brown eyes glistened yellow with an unexpected look close to gratitude, "you've been a great support."

Cat watched a waiter go by with plates that left steam in his wake as they fell into a silence. Ken swept up her hands in a move that was as surprising as compelling and she looked at him to see him staring at her. "I love you, Cat." Emphasis on the word love created the evening's bridge between Ken and Cat. The week was forgivable.

After dinner they walked on the grounds holding hands under moonlight before returning to their room. During the stay they had two dinners, one breakfast, one snack, one brunch before checkout, a tram ride and hike down, a visit to the hot tub, a walk through the stores for two small purchases for the children, three hours here and there of reading on the balcony, uncounted drinks and sex five times, if anyone needed to fill out a time card for a production report. Cat used only half her underwear.

Ken considered the weekend a success because he was away from the shop and he had been an excellent, ready and responsive husband.

Cat thought the weekend a success because she believed a small opening of earth in her close and comfortable life had been filled in with richly given and received love.

CHAPTER FOUR

The only man in her life Suzanne had never told Michael about was Sugarloaf. She was not sure why. Since high school she reported dates: whether they were good to her, how they acted and reacted, if they were entertaining. She never repeated in great detail how she spent time with men or what she considered intimate. She told funny things that happened. As a teenager she mimicked googoo eyes or retold stories of how they convinced her it was important to drive above the city, along winding new streets of housing construction and park to 'see the lights.' In later years, she reported dopey hungry looks when they threw their clothes off or the boring times when they bragged about money. Suzanne considered herself an expert on discerning how much money a man was worth. A man didn't need to sell it any more than her beauty needed to brag.

Except for Sugarloaf, Michael knew who she slept with and who she refused. He was a generous, goodhearted listener who admired his sister's flirting powers and he believed she had been up to any boy or man she had ever spent time with. What he had learned from his experiences with women he was glad to teach her for her protection or happiness.

"Let them see your ass before falling in bed. Hardness will improve ten-percent," had been his most recent offering. As a journeyman carpenter he appreciated practical application supported with numbers.

Friday afternoon Michael called at her office to ask if she was meeting everyone at the dance club, X-Cess. When she hung up, Ron asked "Where are you going tonight?" The wistfulness in his eyes made her sure he was asking to vicariously remember his own freer years. Blake and Shelly were standing nearby, ready to say goodbye until Monday.

Suzanne turned from her desk, pushed her breasts together

from her shoulders and glistened her lips in exaggerated comic puff, "Where you 'put that honey down,'" she answered and winked. Ron and Blake stepped back from the wind of her deep animal sexiness.

Shelly gave the grand laugh, "Good, Suzanne, good. Have a good time at X-Cess. Tell us about it Monday." She turned to leave while Ron and Blake stood flatfooted before slowly turning away.

X-Cess was starting to come alive. Raylene came with another new odd boyfriend whose name no one wanted to know. Michael, Trent, Aaron, and Sierra were also there. Only Diane and Eddie were missing. It was understood an interesting invitation of any one could mean a disappearance, but it was also understood one person in the group needed to be told. Suzanne didn't want to look tonight. She had decided to be casual, have a drink or two and go home early. At half-past ten she called Sugarloaf. He didn't like her calling on a cell phone that was easily traced to her so she went to the basement restroom and stopped at the pay phone.

"Hey," the less said the better.

"Well, hi," his deep voice brightened to the density of sustaining redwood.

"What do you say?"

"One-thirty," he was pleased.

"I'll be there."

They hung up.

Sugarloaf was her heart's secret and her mind's delight. Last November she had been racing from printer to printer because of overbooked scheduling. Everyone wanted paper samples, better deals, her attention and she worked to accommodate them all. It meant more money and she needed it. Late in the afternoon she still had two more appointments and at least an hour of paperwork back on her desk. After blowing through the stop sign at 13th South and Third West, she heard a siren and looked into the rearview mirror. Fuck, she thought. After pulling over and mouthing more swear words, she looked in the rearview mirror again and saw the visage. The spare lines of an artist's first suggestive promise walked toward her radiating life and sureness. She needed what he had. The chin was relaxed, unnerving in its ease to accept peace in tragedy, and tragedy in humor. The shoulders were straight with a slight lift, swaying from side to side. The hips held music. That's all she saw and she wanted it all.

Suzanne didn't object to the ticket. He was surprised she didn't say anything. Out of habit, just before he wrote it he held the pen high, pausing to listen to objections as a polite ritual to errant children. Still, she didn't say anything. He handed the ticket to her through the window.

"If you go to traffic court you can plead your case," deep tones resonated inside Suzanne waking her to a long remembered dream.

"Are you busy?"

Women often talked to him and he was often glad to continue the conversation to whatever end they had in mind but this woman had been silent and he wasn't sure what she meant.

"I'm on duty."

"Next week then," she nodded to persuade him.

He paused and then answered, "Yes?"

"Next Wednesday at six, at . . ." She stuttered because she didn't want to be seen with him and didn't know where to say.

"Terry's on 33rd?" he answered gently. "They have a sign that says, 'We like everyone.'"

"Terry's," she said softly while running a hand through her hair.

He saluted her with fingers to his forehead and went back to his car to wait for her to leave. It was his duty.

During the weekend he loomed larger, ever more perfect. The man was a fairy tale knight of legendary wisdom and strength. Unleashed fantasy and her sexual body response to this pathetic teenage charade in her head was so great, surprising and humiliating, it had stopped her from telling Michael.

Suzanne had never been in Terry's. It was a shabby bar set back from the dirty street behind a parking lot. Cars were parked at odd angles in front or discreetly hidden by the dumpster in back. Neon beer logos were framed by closed curtained windows. Obsessively on time Suzanne drove by a few minutes before six. She didn't know his car and didn't want to be first. She drove from 33rd into town, turned around and went back. Fourteen minutes passed.

Nerve almost gave way. Perhaps a first for Suzanne. But the pull to that chin, those shoulders and hips was stronger. Curiosity needed answers.

He recognized her as she walked in the door. A halo of street-light from the back illuminated the short spiky blonde hair he remembered and the slight but very female body he had looked down on. He stood up.

She saw the movement in the dark and began walking toward it. It was him. They were both surprised to find each other a week later at Terry's. A man at the table with him picked up a glass and walked away. There was a pitcher of beer on the table and a nod from the man she was meeting brought her a glass from a server. She sat down, let him pour a glass and for the first time looked fully into his eyes. They paused, for their own purposes and sat back in their chairs. Now they could talk.

Suzanne described her work, which was done from her car as much as from an office. She explained why she got sloppy about stop signs. She hated cooking. Loved dancing. Wondered what it would be like to be a geologist. Liked rocks and read how mountains moved. But she didn't like school and had never fit there. So she was in paper, a result of earth somehow.

He talked about police work, idiot people who try to outrun him, hate for the paperwork that her business encouraged. He liked to watch sports. Especially basketball. He worked out at a gym. Police work was what he always wanted to do. His father had been a policeman, but if there had been anything else in his life, it would be a mortician. The slimy fingers of what people do in their biggest moments of life meeting death was his interest. Police and morticians understood each other.

That's what they knew of each other when Suzanne suggested they leave. "I've got a few beers in the fridge." It was enough. He nodded to the waitress.

He followed her the three miles to her apartment; keeping an orderly traffic presence. Mr. Crichton ran out the apartment's front door as they entered and Suzanne retrieved two beers from the refrigerator. She handed one to him and he pulled the tab. The room was quiet, only breathing between them, the sound was shaking. He gave the open beer to her and she gave the unopened beer to him. They sat on the ends of the couch and drank in the silent darkness.

"Why are you here?"

"You asked me."

She drank again. He noticed the moonlight across her face. It was younger than him, beautiful, more intelligent than he often saw.

"Why are you here?"

"To fuck."

Honesty was paid well by Suzanne.

Out of duty to resources they finished their beer and did not talk. They did not hurry. They looked at each other. Suzanne turned to face him and lifted her legs to rest her feet on the couch. Her skirt slid up her thigh to show three lady bugs following a lavender and silver dragonfly. He put his empty can on the floor and waited. Perhaps three minutes later she finished and put the empty can on the floor.

Suzanne stood and began unbuttoning her blouse. Turning from the moonlight she walked into shadows toward the bedroom. The blouse fell from her wrists to the floor. He followed without sound. In the bedroom he looked for traces of man. Clothes, shoes, watch, briefcase, it could be a spoon in a drying cereal dish on the bedside table. She watched him with the light from the window behind her outlining his shadows.

"Only I live here."

He began unbuttoning his shirt.

They stood on either side of the bed with twisted sheets and a head worn pillow at a wrong angle. The morning had been hurried. She was annoyed, as though a boring beige slip were showing at a business meeting. Relief followed, allowing her to breathe deeply and fully for her enjoyment. A made bed was a woman's invitation of selection and desired choice, admission of preparation and primping. She needed to show power with this man to take what she wanted. He shouldn't feel too special. She needed to meet his strength.

Not very many men, and no boys, could make the circle connection. This man did and it had been a long time. From first sight in the rearview mirror, Suzanne knew she wanted this man and his body but she had told herself all week that it was only sex. Only a lube job. Don't expect too much.

That hour, in moonlight, in careless sheets, with a man whose name she had first seen on a ticket, she was soully satisfied. It had been too long since she had felt the flowing circle connection of light between breast, vagina and brain. This was a seldom enjoyed path and she was grateful. She would be pleased for days and she knew this man could not be lost.

"Thank you, Sugar," she whispered when it was over. "I'll call you that, Sugar." Only to herself did she think of him as Sugarloaf.

She did not call often. It was November when they met. Now it was June. Perhaps eight times. She was respectful of him. Of his ability to give to her. Yes, Sugarloaf was a true find and she only called when it was important. If she was interrupting a life of family and obligations she didn't want to know. It needed to be convenient and easy enough that he never said no. She hadn't said no to him.

When she returned from the call Michael was dancing with a blonde she had never seen, but Aaron, Trent and another unknown woman were sitting at the table talking. She saw Sierra on the dance floor. The atmosphere of movement, talk, music, shifting light patterns was comfortable to Suzanne. She liked its alive cohesive energy feeding on itself through each person in it, but at midnight she said goodbye and left. Suzanne wanted the ringing of the crowds' noise to be out of her head long before Sugarloaf arrived so she could hear his voice in words that carved air.

The tap on the door was quiet. Three clipped short knocks. From the darkness outside he entered her apartment's angled reflections. Once she lighted a candle but when he saw it he smothered its with two fingers.

"Hello, Suzanne."

She nodded, "Hey,"

They embraced and for the first time there was a gentler affectionate touch. "Thank you, thank you for coming," she whispered into his cotton shirt, not knowing if her words were heard. For a flash she thought, what would a man who had cheated on his wife on Monday do with her on Friday?

"My pleasure."

They stood holding each other until Suzanne shifted slightly and his hand moved delicately, without shyness to the under curve of her breast. Her mind turned fully to Sugarloaf.

What they continued to do they both did very well. They were now familiar enough with each other's bodies to enjoy, savor curve, strength of muscle, hair, smells. When Sugarloaf moved at five she whispered, "Bye, Sugar." He leaned, kissed her neck and was so quiet she did not hear the door open or close.

There were three ways Suzanne experienced clarity that was calming, encouraging and supported the way she wanted to think. Running three or four times a week wakened her body with air and light. By recognized body need rather than pre-planning she would open her eyes and pick her running suit from the floor in one movement before leaving the apartment within five minutes of waking. The calculated route took her beside the rushing early morning, four lane traffic of Ninth East, down to 4500 South and around through a few side streets of fifty-year-old tract houses. At 3.1 miles it was not going to get her ready for a marathon, but it moved her blood and helped her think clearly.

The second way was succeeding in business. Closing a good sale, breaking her sales record, getting a new client were exhilarations. She expected to be top salesperson in the ten-state company within three years or be gone. The smell of paper could make her stand straighter and breathe in as though she was flirting with a handsome stranger. The sound of the delivery truck as it pulled from the dock to take a large order of paper to one of her clients was worth a trip down the hall from her office and out to the warehouse just to hear it. There wasn't competition with the other salespeople; they were merely benchmarks for her to watch and know how hard she had to work, how much to sell, how good to be.

The third way energy could feel as though it was coursing through her and cleaning out cobwebs, bringing in light and centering her being was to breathe in maleness. It was the small pleasures she enjoyed when she was around men. Hair on hands, the line of an ear, the rootedness of a walk could all fascinate her as she watched how they handled themselves, moved inside their bodies, watched her. She had learned a long time ago how to be an interested observer watching without apparent interest. Only when she wanted to meet someone or talk further would she turn her head, smile or look into eyes. Otherwise it was just too dangerous. But she could not stop and knew she probably never would. She needed each man she had ever watched to balance her female strength by the giving to her of just who they were. She was grateful to each of them. Her world was safer because she understood the rules of men. That gave her freedom to be herself in business and love because she knew where she could bend rules, where they had to be followed and which ones could be ignored. From men she had learned how to work and be good in sales. How to walk away from a bad deal or even a good deal that wasn't ever going to work. In business and in love. She knew they liked the admiration she gave and that she was a ready student. It was a square deal.

Four years ago and two jobs previous she had learned well that it wasn't smart to mix a career with sex. Sandwiches and potato salad were what she sold to a moving parade of people always hurrying to get back to work. She worked in a downtown restaurant shadowed by the less than twelve tall buildings of the city. Her biggest tipper started a flirtation that continued two months with ever escalating amounts of money left in her palm. At the time she believed it was the money in her hand that felt powerful but after the unpleasant too hurried one time sex she decided it was a primal sense of obligation that money directly in the hand represented. She left that job the next week and strictly wrote off involvements with men she worked around.

"If they have possible control of even one dollar of money that is mine or should be mine, they are off limits," is what she had told Michael. Men were easy enough to find other ways.

Temptation hadn't visited once in four years. So why had she fallen into bed so easily for Ken Overton five nights ago? He was good-looking enough but so were a lot of men. She had ceased to be impressed by looks alone long ago. There had to be a calling, a deeper need of another's insides. Sultry eyes hadn't been enough since she was twenty-four. The easy conclusion was there had been a heart attraction to him, but she hadn't been able to define it yet and that was driving her crazy because on the surface being with Kenneth went against her personal ethics. With Sugarloaf Suzanne knew precisely it was a maleness she had never met anywhere else and she wanted to claim some of it for herself. Old John represented a possibility of a promising future that needed to be flushed out and failed to be interesting when it was.

Ken's guyness was fairly common. His looks were a moderate B+, his intelligence high enough but it seemed limited to a few topics. Humor had not yet made an appearance and it needed to soon. Their one-time together last Monday after Ginger's proved he could manage in bed but he probably wasn't going to be stellar. In his favor was an intensity of purpose that probably supported his intelligence. If this had been some guy from an obscure place in life like the friend of a friend or a new face in the bar she might see him a time or two so she could size him up better and make a final decision. As it was he had two huge reasons to be immediately dropped. He could make a difference in her income and he was married. An outsider's opinion would help, besides letting out the built up steam in her heart.

On Sunday Michael brought a pizza and she supplied the beer. They were watching baseball on TV, each of their faces looking forward.

"I've met a guy, Michael."

"Ya," he switched it to a sitcom rerun.

"I don't know what to do about him."

"There's a first."

"No, it's not," she wiggled slightly, a girlish embarrassed shoulder twist that surprised Michael in its self-consciousness. Mr. Crichton jumped on her lap and she started stroking him. "Anyway, I could use some input."

"Okay."

"Straight off he's a printer, one of my accounts and I don't know why I even like him. And, he's married."

"Drop him."

"I know," the stroking of the cat slowed down. "But I don't want to."

"Why not? He's already a drag on you. So you hit a loser. It hasn't happened very often."

"Ya."

The word trailed, alarming Michael. "All right. It's a commercial. Tell me." He looked straight at her. "What's got you about this loser?"

"That's it. I don't know. He's really not so special. Average everything. But, I'm intrigued and I don't really want to stop. Maybe I'm curious."

"About what?"

She shrugged, "I'm not sure."

Both of them were silent, waiting for an insight while a car commercial played.

"So tell me about the blonde I saw you with last night." It was time to put a finger to his ribs. Her name was Carole and Trent had taken her out twice but she was too intense. She was in the greater network of their nightlife scene, drifting in and out like the bars and the bands. Sometimes she was there and other times not.

Again it was silent until Michael softly pushed, "He's married. That's trouble. You don't need that."

"You're right. It's a bad bet and probably not worth the curiosity."

"That's right."

On Monday she avoided the situation. Overton Printing was only one of a dozen accounts to report on in staff meeting and only one company of several that had ordered paper that would be trucked in by Wednesday. Wednesday morning the paper came and she saw the order go through to delivery for that afternoon. She was as irritated with herself for noticing Overton's order, as with Ken for existing. Other clients were just as important. A dozen others had the potential to be more important to her income and she called them, pleased they were pleasant and willing to talk about upcoming jobs and paper problems. Maybe Kenneth thought it best to pretend nothing had happened. And it was best even though the pretense made him a jerk. Given a little time if things weren't comfortable maybe she could casually suggest a client switch with another salesperson. It was already over a week.

Thursday the phone rang just as she was ready to leave for sales calls.

"This is Suzanne," She imagined the brightness of her voice softened the clipped words.

"Hello, Suzanne. This is Ken Overton."

"Oh, hey, Ken," she paused, "did you get your paper?"

"Yes, the job's printing this morning," this time he paused. "I called to say the paper is here."

"Yes."

"And, I appreciate it." Oh, god, she thought, it was almost the Utah equivalent phrase of the bird with the middle finger of, "I appreciate ya!"

"Yes," one of the rules she learned from men is never make the person you are trying to outwit comfortable. Uncomfortable disrupts focus and makes it easier to outsmart. His voice seemed to rush up and hurry on to his prearranged destination.

"Suzanne, I've got some paper problems. A few things I'd like to ask about. Now we've got the 4th of July coming up, but why don't you give me a call next Wednesday?"

"I'll put you on the list," they hung up.

What was that all about? She didn't know and now, this moment, she was angry she had let the chance pass. She should have just said, "Well, what's up with you anyway? Let's just forget it all happened and go about our natural lives." Now nothing was settled, nothing was in place and she was angry with herself for letting business politeness get in the way of killing the man. Almost a full week would pass with this hanging over her head.

A savage, hateful fear mixed with need, the deepest kind of soul cry made her body feel dense and light at the same time; as though hate, love and desire were a freakin' country-western trio. Without picturing the scene, but recognizing the feeling she knew it was what she felt as a child when her father came home drunk from work. "A day in hell," he barked hello and scuffled to the kitchen table where he ate hot food made with her mother's love. Ate it like a barn animal breathing it in while his wife and children watched afraid and on alert.

He slurped his food, usually burped and told the children when they grew up they had to work hard, harder than a whore's conscience. From there he headed to the living room to watch TV and fall asleep. He often sent Suzanne for the ratty vinyl slippers she delivered with the tips of fingers.

"You need to understand your father," Mom implored with stricken grey eyes. "He works hard. His work is very hard. All day he stands outside digging roadbed, leveling hot new roads, making it possible for everyone to drive cars on smooth, new black roads." His smell of oil, rock, heat, beer, sweat and the detergent her mother used to keep him clean, would make Suzanne stand away, observing him staring lifelessly into the TV until his head rocked and he fell asleep.

She sat on the couch, able to comfortably watch a man whose sleep was so heavy her thoughts could take form and fly across the room to hit him. Slash him. If only they could draw blood. Make him hurt. Make it painful. By age ten, Suzanne knew she needed men, knew that her ripped heart would use her father as a back wind - pushing her forward, toward the men she needed.

She was fourteen on that grey Sunday morning in March when the valley's clouds were playful, energetic children pushing and kicking each other to lift themselves over the Wasatch Mountains. Her father had not come home last night. Mom was in a bathrobe, standing in front of the sink, moving dishes too roughly, mumbling, her hair askew and oily. Michael and she were in sloppy old tee-shirts that were now worn, faded nightwear, stirring spoons in cereal when they heard the car in the driveway.

They expected their husband and father to lumber into the house looking like a dirty neighborhood dog who lost a bar fight. Instead, when he opened the door and walked in the kitchen he was a man ready for Sunday school. From gleaming parted hair to shaven face, pressed green and brown plaid shirt to new stiff jeans over shined boots.

"I came to get some things. And let you know. Say goodbye."

No one moved, hearing only the wall clock ticking hours in seconds until their mother's choked voice creaked in four notes, "What?"

"I know this isn't easy, Dorrie. It isn't easy for me, but you'll do fine and I can't live this way anymore." For the first time he looked shy, but his voice betrayed a happiness she hadn't heard since he had taken her for a picnic in a secret place miles away in the Uinta mountains, a year after they married. "I've just come for some money and smoke. You can give the clothes away and keep the rest." Time collapsed as Dorrie and her children stared without seeing one another, listening to the quick sounds he made gathering tobacco, a bottle of gin, and money from a Christmas cookie tin in the hutch that had been Dorrie's mother's.

"Well . . . is that man coming or not?" The whiny demanding female notes turned their heads from the living room door to the backdoor, opening to the driveway. Wild hair looking like a drawer of small finishing nails crisscrossed her head, circling a determined, overmade face. She wore tight jeans and a furry sweater the color of high mountain pond water feeding on falling leaves and insects. Breasts grew out of the sweater like emerging summer moons.

"I'm coming, I'm coming," yelled her father. "You don't need to come in and make things worse." Back in the kitchen he held his tobacco tin, the gin and a wad of bills. The sight of his clean, pressed happy body leaning toward the future and a new woman, cut Suzanne's heart as she saw her mother, worn, tired, sloppy in an old robe, beaten by love she would never receive. For the first time in years their father looked each of them in the eyes. Years later Suzanne told Michael she thought he wanted to remember what he wanted to forget. "I'm sorry," he whispered, and then he was gone.

From that morning Michael and Suzanne knew their mother would never recover and they nursed her to the end - eight more years. Their sadness and anger was never released, never given full vent; they knew their survival as children depended on not causing their mother more grief. They never heard from their father again.

Now Suzanne appreciated a straightforward emotional agenda, based on action and feedback. She toughened on the outside while Michael softened.

Oh, to hell with Ken Overton. She'd have a great week, a great 4th of July and she'd do just fine. She always did.

CHAPTER FIVE

Wednesday, July 3, Eme and Sheldon came for dinner. Eme drove her red Toyota onto the streets of Sunshadow Estates like a hovering wild mother showbird landing for a short visit to assure her wing-clipped flock of her always vigilant stewardship. Sheldon was an out shown brown feathered bird pleased to be warmed at the edges of his showbird's spotlight. From her parents' bedroom window MoMo watched them step from the car and walk to the house. With deft practice Eme swept a hand through her thick hair for lift, adjusted the fall of a yellow scarf from a straw purse, separated the several gold bracelets on her wrist, adjusted the ribbon on the wrapped lemon bars and stood taller. MoMo noticed the swinging breasts from the chest of her beloved Eme which were so unlike her ribbed and skinny body. Even small yellow polka dots on a purple blouse could not camouflage the swaying full bounce of Eme's walk.

Eme took Sheldon's arm to pull him even with her. Purple, yellow, fluttering radiance held the arm of white cotton shirt, khaki pants, clipped and thinning brown hair, steadiness, calmness.

"Eme, you're here!" MoMo ran downstairs and stepped from the door. "Hi, Sheldon."

"My little dove. Wonderful to see you. And where is that bird-brained brother of yours?" Eme bent to hug MoMo.

"He's upstairs."

"What will you have?" Cat yelled from the kitchen.

"Gin and tonic. It's been a day. I'm going upstairs with MoMo. Sheldon will join you." Cat heard them banging on Justin's door demanding to be let in. Laughter caught in Cat's heart. Perhaps she could hold it there and pull it from memory on a lonely day. Why did she feel she was collecting moments of memory and filing them away like bills to be paid?

From years of working in the sun, Sheldon's brown face had

wear lines coming down like welcome thin ruts left by a desert rain from his kindly brown eyes. He settled himself on the bar chair across from Cat in the kitchen.

"I'll have the same. And here are some lemon bars Eme made this morning."

"Thanks. How's work been, Sheldon?"

"Oh, fine. Tramping and flying over mountainsides and valleys keeps me happy."

"Future generations will thank you."

"Future generations will ruin this beautiful valley. All I can do is help plan for their eventual takeover."

"Well, I'm sure Sunshadow Estates would appall the pioneers."

"Appall the pioneers and break the hearts of Native Americans."

Eme came in, claiming her drink from the counter. "This looks great. You make the best gin and tonics. On the strong side with lots of lime."

The children headed for the TV, ready to be in the same area as Eme, but not wanting to participate in the conversation.

"Let's sit outside. It's hot but the umbrella's up. Ken will be here anytime."

"Only if I don't wilt. This blouse isn't made for the vagaries of sweat."

They seated themselves under the umbrella in the comfortable padded chairs with pink flowers and green leaves. Cat had put ice cubes in her wine to make it cooler. She swirled it and took a sip.

"Did you know that in some dictionaries the word vagary is right before vagina and you are using the word incorrectly," Cat winked.

"No. I didn't know. And what exactly does vagary mean then?"

"It's a perfect introduction to vagina. Couldn't be more appropriate," she leaned forward, Eme supposed so the children wouldn't hear. "Vagary means a capricious, whimsical, wild occurrence. Or perhaps odd or eccentric."

"Well, that is a perfect introduction to vagina,"

Sheldon laughed as though he were gaining life on women's

ready, self-enjoying laughter. Cat wondered if that was rare or common in men. When she said things like that to Ken he just shrugged his shoulders.

"Sorry, dear, your sweat isn't whimsical. Not even odd - a common body occurrence. So you'll have to think of another word."

"I'll do that. Well, I'm going camping with Sheldon tomorrow," she took a swallow of her drink and nodded toward him.

"That will be fun. You'll enjoy it. Trying out the new fifth wheel?"

Sheldon leaned forward as though he were talking confidentially to Cat, "Yes, Eme loaded her idea of necessities before we came over; a jar of artichoke hearts and a vase I'm supposed to attach to the wall." He leaned back and looked at Eme, "I tell her she'll be sorry if she doesn't help me experiment with the water system and make sure we know how the stove works."

"Sheldon, dear, you always take care of everything important. I'm meant to bring excess and beauty into your life. Not practicality."

"I think I hear Ken now," the garage door opened and Cat noted the time on her watch. She was happy and pleased. It would be a wonderful evening with the most important people to her.

Ken was always polite and kind to Eme, and now Sheldon. He respected the friendship between Eme and Cat that stretched from college. He thought of her as a sister to Cat that needed to be treated well and distantly. Waving at them through the windows, he paused for a hello to the children before getting a beer from the fridge. As he walked to the empty chair he passed behind Cat and patted her shoulder as token affection. His large familiar hand was comfort and sex; security and excitement.

"Hi, Eme, Sheldon."

"The Fourth getting in the way at Overton?" Sheldon's half statement, half question was Sheldon's hello to Ken.

"It's a damn pain in the ass. Everyone wants Friday off. We aren't too busy and clients are on vacation time, too, so I've let a few of them off."

"You let them go in the ring and fight like cocks to decide who got it off?" Eme asked.

"No, Eme" Ken was smiling, perhaps imagining a few bouts, "they trade as they want between this and the Friday after

Thanksgiving."

"We're going camping this weekend in Sheldon's new fifth wheel. Any suggestions?" Eme changed the subject.

"Which one did you get? The Coachman or The Wilderness?" Ken was referring to a conversation the two of them had several weeks earlier.

"The Coachman. It has a good feel driving. Sleeps four, has an awning and Eme likes it," Ken nodded, reflected and returned to Eme's question.

"Take a portapotty, plenty of beer and don't wear cologne. Attracts mosquitoes."

"Even I know a fifth wheel is not that rural."

"In that case take gin, wine and brandy, a sheer nightgown and make sure the thing is on good brakes."

"You give Sheldon a lot of credit."

"He told me he deserved it."

"He did not," she slugged Ken's arm and they all laughed.

"What are you doing on the Fourth?"

Cat answered Eme, "The usual. Go for a drive in the Uintas, maybe up around Mirror Lake, have a picnic and be back in time for fireworks. A good day."

During the second cocktail, steaks were put on the barbecue, the children joined the conversation and everyone ate together. Cat sat by Ken and felt the heat gently waving off his body as she also felt the sun falling behind her in the sky. Justin and MoMo returned to TV after dinner while the adults talked. It was nearly eleven before the conversation lulled, more from end of day than end of interest.

"Well, I guess I need to finish packing. Sheldon said to be ready at seven. I couldn't talk him into any later. Have fun this week-end," Eme got up.

"You too, Eme," Cat leaned to kiss her. As Sheldon, Eme and Cat walked through the family room the children got up from watching TV and followed Eme as though she were the night bell.

"Have a good time kids," Ken called after them. He stayed behind, carried in the empty salad bowl and two glasses on his way to the refrigerator for another beer.

Cat waved goodbye with the children, yelling, "Report any vagaries."

"Come on kids, time for bed," Ken said when they returned. "First one down gets two dollars!" The three of them ran upstairs. Cat poured a glass of wine, dropped two ice cubes in and walked to the backyard. She sat under the now unnecessary umbrella and looked at her yard. Light from the children's rooms dappled the grass but she saw through to the white petunias behind the light. They shone like path lights, luminous and full. They were petite sweetly smelling ladies that needed sun and night, excess and protection. The red petunias were dark in the night; only a degree more discreet and not a half-degree less needy. Each sweet blossom smothered one out beneath it to survive and looked at Cat with the innocent openness of a child.

This was a weekend of family and love. Two weekends in a row Ken would be hers without Overton Printing interruptions. She picked up the empty wineglass, took it to the dishwasher, turned off the stovetop light and went upstairs to run her slim soft fingers along his wiry, too tight shoulders that felt like tree roots bulging with sustenance to care for those around him.

"What's old man Shiner pushing now?" Ken asked behind the morning newspaper on Saturday while they each ate a different breakfast of cereal, frozen waffle or yogurt and fruit.

"I'm not sure what his favorite book is but there's a new Crichton book. Probably good."

"Let's all go down there. Buy a book, we'll get lunch, and go to a movie. Justin, it's your turn to pick." Justin popped up at his father's suggestion and rushed to look at the paper through his arms.

"We'll make a quick stop at the shop and be on our way." No one said anything but all three knew what that meant. Maybe they would be on their way. And maybe they would be there an hour or perhaps leave and come back for him. Anything could happen if things weren't going well.

"I didn't know you had a shift running this weekend," Cat said as she poured coffee. "I thought you said you weren't busy."

"Isn't it great? We got two jobs in Miguel had to run today. I need to make sure they're running right."

Like a wary fan club the three of them followed Ken through Overton's glass doors flanked by geraniums, afraid their focus of adoration might be snatched by onlookers. Their deeper fear was that he would ditch them for what they suspected he liked better. Justin and MoMo eyed Miguel and Todd, the only employees working, like potential thieves. The beat of paper off the press mixed with the radio's Mexican station of love lost and lost again. Their watch of husband and father was only ten minutes, a near record. "God bless second shift pressmen," Cat thought, "they know how to work without help."

At Shiner's everyone waved at El behind the counter. Perhaps every other month Cat brought her family, trailing behind like ducklings. Regular trips to the headwaters of reading was how employees passed their love of books on to the next generation. MoMo headed toward young reader mysteries, Justin went to sports, Ken trailed to business and Cat walked through to fiction, biographies and cookbooks. The children would choose their own not to exceed a stated dollar limit, Ken would continue browsing through management books until everyone came to claim him and Cat would appear with two books, one for her and one for Ken.

"I've got a book for you, Ken," Cat said when she returned thirty minutes later with the children. He nodded but didn't look up.

"It's *Travels* by Michael Crichton. You like him. It's not his new one but I'll get that later. It's an autobiography and you might enjoy reading more about him. Listen to this line," she held the book up and waited until he looked at her. "*I think the only true expression of one's beliefs lies in action.*"

"Ya?" he was putting the business book away.

"That's you, Ken. You live that. My man of action." A slight tightness in his neck twisted across his shoulders. He rubbed his neck. Nothing, Cat thought, it meant nothing.

Ken and the children reviewed the movie as they drove home in late afternoon dry heat of a long summer's day. The dull constant noise of the car air conditioner forced louder talking and expressive movement between everyone but Cat. Her silence was not unusual and they didn't always expect her to join in. They didn't realize how she used silence to listen to the music of their voices and lives. She was assured by their voices and her silence that life was well-ordered and bolted in place. By marrying the right man, a beautiful man, and being lucky enough to have two healthy and very good children she had secured a more comfortable enjoyable life than she ever imagined. It was her private self-respecting opinion that she wasn't too busy or distracted or selfish to enjoy life as it was now. When her fortieth birthday arrived in two years she would be ready and grateful to enjoy the forties like she had the thirties. She'd play golf, take up watercolors and she and Ken would have a good time being parents of teenagers.

Chapter Six

Suzanne was up with the sunrise on Thursday. She pulled on shorts, had a drink of water and headed out the front door. It was her guess the surrounding quiet neighborhoods didn't like the dirty gold brick buildings where she lived. They must have popped up like unsightly warts in the 1970s, bringing an unaccustomed transience. Upstairs a cement walkway along the front was braced by utilitarian lines of contractor grade black iron railing. Downstairs cars parked as if at motels, six feet of front doors and living room windows. At each supporting beam and at the building's end a love-starved and straggly thirty-year-old juniper sagged, forcing people to walk around them. Suzanne didn't need a calendar to know it was the end of the month. The arrival of U-Hauls and overloaded pick-up trucks announced when rent was due. The population shifting also gave privacy.

She locked her door on the top floor in the middle, looked around at her neighborhood and thought, if you want better you need to earn better. Once past her buildings she was on Ninth East. Her run was predetermined through the neighborhoods of modest incomes. It felt like the area in Midvale where she had grown up. Every current design of house was built from 1880 to 1980 without planning or order as farm fields were slowly changed to neighborhoods over the last century. Some yards and houses were Halloween faces of closed, sagging drapes, uneven steps, peeling paint, overgrown yards and dented cars. Others were military precision of clipped bushes all in a row, white siding with aqua shutters, duck wind vanes flapping on roofs and neatly swept sidewalks welcoming visitors. On the perimeters where cars whizzed to their working day were houses interspersed with strip malls, gas stations and a grocery store. Old trees were too often surrounded by asphalt from curb to trunk to accommodate parking. This wouldn't be home forever. Sales were good and she would make sure they climbed higher. But even if they fell, Suzanne had a savings account. She would never be dependent like her mother.

After returning from the run and having a shower, she reached for a plain white A-line linen dress in the closet hanging like a party favor. Ready for a prosperous day. Suzanne picked up the coral necklace. She bent her head, clasped it and lifted her head, to look in the mirror. Conscious of wearing it too often she told herself never to wear it more than two days a week.

"Thank you, Mother," she whispered, "thank you for protection and love. I miss you so much." Now she was ready for the day.

"Here, Overton asked for extra samples and had us ship an order overnight. Said you'd make it free," Blake explained, looking at his work order rather than her. He laid the samples on a chair by her cubicle. "He wants it this morning. Will you take it?" Now he looked at her. "The order's small and if you'll bring your Cherokee around I'll put in the back."

She didn't want to. She was sure she didn't want to do this at all. Pointedly, she avoided calling Ken since last week's conversation. But in the world of being an employee there wasn't anything she could object about.

"Couldn't delivery do it? I'm busy this morning."

"You're more convenient. And we've got bigger orders. It's only for business cards. Come on. We haven't sewn your name on a shirt yet."

She appreciated his sarcasm, "Okay. But I don't want to and you owe me."

"Don't want to. I don't want to do a lot of things either. Tell my wife about it."

Blake was a good man. He smelled of oil, soap and the near distance of security. Not hers. Another woman's. Suzanne gave him silent credit for being both faithful to his wife and appreciative of women. She pulled her Cherokee around to Delivery and the order was put in the back. It was an unusually small order for Overton.

"Bring the signed delivery receipt back or die," Blake tilted his head in good-bye.

Well, she thought, Blake had said, "this morning" so the

68

sheets didn't need to be delivered until 11:59 and it was only half-past eight.

Before leaving she reviewed her schedule, packed what she needed, made sure she had her cell phone, notepad, pen and calendar. Between the second and third visit she stopped at a gas station, filled her car with gas, visited the restroom and bought breath mints. She always kept extra in the glove compartment. It was a nervous thing to do for comfort like she saw her mother smoke cigarettes when she was a child. A nervous habit could keep hands busy and give mind time to plot.

She left Presson with a handful of swatch books and a brochure on direct to plate imaging she knew he wouldn't pick up. He was a kindly old man who didn't want to give up his prepress room for the ease, modernity and monthly payments of a direct to plate press. All he wanted was to sell his business in a year or so and retire in some comfort. He may be ten years too late for that.

"Has Overton decided to convert yet?" his eyes searched. He was asking the shortened version of changing from offset printing to direct to plate.

"No. But I think he will."

"He'll need to, but I want to just stay the course. Finish the only game I know."

"You've been a good businessman, Mr. Presson," he turned and smiled.

"For my day. Ken, he's working with today."

At 11:20 she pulled into Overton's parking lot. She felt out of her usual control. It was her habit to know exactly what to say and how to greet each company 'in her designated portfolio of responsibility' as she was told. Some liked her effervescent bubbly happy self. Some liked her warm sensual self. She knew the difference and played it; not to herself but to them. The game paid the rent. She understood and had fun.

Through the wide glass doors Mary Ellen saw Suzanne coming. She buzzed Ken's office to let him know someone was close.

"Hello, Mary Ellen," she couldn't say his name and give him victory of deference, "I'm here with samples and a small delivery."

"I'll ring Ken." Suzanne stepped back to wait and looked around the office. There was a new woman at a desk in the back.

"Who the hell cares?" she thought to herself. "Why am I noticing the women anyway? Every office has women." The woman's head was bent over papers, her hair was dark and she was absorbed.

Ken walked out. She looked at him and clutched. Hopefully, yes, she was sure, it was an internal clutch. She looked at Mary Ellen to be sure she was busy with a new phone call and had not looked up to notice her surprise. The Ken before her was not the Ken she had been imagining, thinking about, reviewing and dissecting this past week until he was the mental size of an earthworm. No. Now, here in this office he seemed, well, he seemed larger and more enveloping of every corner. This was his space. These were his women and he was coming out of his office to acknowledge and get. She reached her hand out but all her fingers were splayed like a cat in attack, ready to claw. "Hello," was all she managed.

"Hello, Suzanne, have you got the cover sheets?" his large hand closed her fingers.

"Yes, in the car."

"Okay. Before we get that, let me introduce you to my wife."

Suzanne now knew he was a bastard. Now she could be calm, "Yes." She had met bastards before.

"Suzanne, I'd like you to meet my wife, Cat," he watched his wife, not her.

Cat looked up. At first the look was startled, as though she hadn't heard a word. The notes of the calculator were all that mattered in the trusting universe where she existed. Then Suzanne noticed an expression combining kindness and idiocy. Suzanne knew she was a good and thoughtful woman, too involved in her kindness to be aware. Bright with school, stupid in the world.

"Hello, Suzanne."

"Cat does the book work. Keeps up on everything Overton is doing."

"Well, good," Suzanne whispered.

"Nice to meet you," and Cat offered her hand to shake.

Ken ended the conversation, "I know you have a delivery. How about pulling around back?"

Ken was standing at the open overhead door when Suzanne pulled around and stopped, facing him at twenty feet. He would have to walk to her, or one of his employees would have to walk to her. She didn't give a shit. Customer service had parked her Jeep.

Ken walked to her. She regarded him through sunglasses and the coral necklace. He didn't have the easiness, the slinky earth movements of Sugarloaf. He would never match that. He didn't have the solidness, the grounding security of Blake. There wasn't Michael's casualness and fun. There wasn't the gripping love-hate fear of her father. Ken didn't have anything. Maybe he was a younger Old John.

He leaned down, put his forearm that broke to pale muscle at the edge of a dark blue golf shirt on the open window and looked at her. He was silent.

"I have the order in the back. If you'll move I'll get it."

"You didn't call," he sounded like a cranky boss spliced with a three-year-old child.

"There wasn't a reason. Your orders were taken care of." Again it was quiet.

"I want you."

His stark words were Sugarloaf's ghost without sustaining resonating lust. It sounded like a declaration of picking an outfielder for a baseball game. Suzanne was quiet. The enemy needed to explain himself.

"I want you," he said again.

"And . . ?" Unsure what his motives were she was torn between his ability to excite her and that he was a bastard who had just introduced his wife.

"And," he touched his finger to his nose as he looked at her through the open window. Silent again.

Instead of finishing the sentence he looked down and opened the car door for her to step outside. As though she were on display to the employees beyond the garage door she stood straight and walked with distance between them. They went around the car and she opened the back. They were hidden from employees behind the Jeep.

"Here's your paper."

He bent, and his back lowered, his shiny over-combed hair was below her where she could hit, shake, scream at him if she wanted. Why can't men sort their feelings out any better than women, she thought. He doesn't know what to do - this notion gave her only a second to decide if she was still curious. Pity, god dammit. And her need, more god dammit.

71

"I'm going to be at Ginger's after work."

Awkwardly, he stood back up with the order in his arms. He sounded relieved but his eyes were dark. "After work. For me that would be six."

"All right. Six." She got in her car, didn't look at him again and backed up a few feet before she turned around and drove away.

"Damn!" she didn't get the delivery receipt signed. Before she walked into Harkness she pulled out a pen and signed Ken's name. The scribble wasn't his, but it wasn't exactly hers either. Blake wouldn't say anything.

At half-past five she sat at her desk staring at the padded blue backing of her cubicle. What was she doing with a married man? They were dangerous. Not even a lot of fun really unless a woman had a reason to do dirt to her own kind or was hard up for sex. No one else was on the horizon. Since ending it with Old John two months ago there hadn't been anyone for dinner or to watch TV. Yes, she had turned down guys, but only because they hadn't been interesting. Their too easy looks and grasping need of what she gave instead of having anything to offer was not enough. If they grew to be interesting she'd see them again. Salt Lake was just too small. The guys who rotated around her social circle were plain too young and their brains unformed.

Last month, on the night of the paper show Ken at least provided a little conversation. It happened he was at her booth when the show ended. Maybe he planned that but she didn't think so. He looked too tired and distracted. Printers often did. He helped her gather the remaining paper samples and box of notepads Harkness had imagined would be in demand to people already loaded down with paper. They took them to her Jeep in the basement parking lot.

"I'll bet you didn't have a chance to eat anything," he said and invited her back to the coffee shop. They talked for over an hour before it stalled. All of it was about business - his end of printing and her end of providing the paper. They looked at each other and laughed. An easier camaraderie than the lunch over hamburgers. He walked her to her car, shook her hand and said goodnight.

It was the stupid Monday night at Ginger's two weeks ago that messed things up. She was there with Ron, Shelley and Blake after work having a pitcher of beer. Generally, they were complaining about work, the sales expectations, slow orders that couldn't seem to make it across the Mississippi and demanding clients.

Ken walked in with three agency people she recognized. Most of the active people in the industries knew each other by sight if not by name. He led them to a table by the right wall and was seated a few minutes before he looked up and saw her. Both nodded. She explained who he was and everybody already knew the agency people. They were known for their popular design and meticulous detail follow-up.

Time passed easily in the comfort of work friends before she looked over and caught him watching her. She smiled again. The next time she looked the agency people were walking out the door and Ken was walking toward her table. Shelley left first to pick up her children at her mother's, Blake was next. Only Ron was left at the table with her. They were talking about a new grade of paper a mill was introducing in the fall with, of course, couture colors. Suzanne introduced Ken who sat as easily at the table as if he were part of Harkness. They told him about the new line of pretentious promise in a paper with Jaspar Blue, Cotillion Pink and Chablis Natural. A couple of beers made it funnier than in the morning staff meeting.

Ron left when he finished his glass with a big wave that included two other tables where he knew people. The table became quiet. Suddenly, there was little to say. The noise from around the room was a crashing sea of voices, falling on them and neither one knew how to swim away.

His eyes were sword-bright-light, darting about her as if he was consciously trying to call it back to himself with information. She couldn't tell how much of it was brought on by the drink, excitement for life or for that matter, her.

"So how was your day?" she asked.

The day unwound from when he arrived at the office until he brought the three dicks from the ad agency. Six jobs were delivered today. One of them hadn't been plated by ten, but that was a small job. Telephone calls to customers who barked at him, vendors who wanted more time to deliver, the small squabble about telephone etiquette between Mary Ellen and his treasured but easily distressed day pressman, Darrell. And the pizza delivery kid who must have dropped the lunch pizza because all the pepperoni, sauce and cheese were on one side and bare slimy flat pizza crust was on the other. When she laughed as he finished, another glint of light sprang from his eyes to read information from her. Suzanne felt warmed and attended.

"How was your day?" he returned the conversation.

Ron had reported the staff meeting so she started after that and listed the printers she called or visited. A few were direct competitors of Overton with press size and capability, but she noticed his eyes didn't seem to change to business, didn't seem to care at all that she might have information on them. Lunch was spent with her friend Raylene at a beer house where they had good hamburgers and she had a Mountain Dew because she was on duty. The frustration of the afternoon occurred when the order department made her spend an hour on the phone tracking down three skids of paper for one of her customers. It was somewhere between Wisconsin and Salt Lake. It was their job to keep track of orders but they thought she should do it because they were busy with other things and she had been spotted in the office not looking overloaded.

His eyes were dazzling she decided. And they were directed at her. Every time he looked at her his eyes lighted up and the corners of his mouth rose. Not at all like when he was in his office. Or at the paper show. There was something very mysterious and intriguing about this man that went beyond moderate to good looks of dark hair, too light skin, penetrating hooded eyes, a heavy chin and a strong lumbering, purposeful walk.

At nine, after dusk turned to night, they walked from the front door to the back parking lot in silence. The June night was broken only by cars on the freeway two blocks away and the crunching of pebbles beneath their shoes. He walked with her toward the Jeep. She looked up at him ready to say goodbye when he swept her up and kissed her fully, intentionally and without care that he received it back. Here was his gift. A man who appeared to give and not need back.

Now she was his. As the kiss slowed she stepped back and looked along his face and into his eyes. There are surprising, surrendering moments of recognition, with slight awakening nudges felt as though a fond and familiar dream is remembered. Friends become friends, lovers become lovers, by the smallest of touches, the barest of looks, sometimes for a lifetime and sometimes for an instant, until they disappear into the crowd. To step into recognition of a future that calls beyond your heart to your soul is as fearful as to step back, afraid of its heat and life - knowing you are less because you were afraid to become whole. Suzanne felt deep in the bottom of her belly a homecoming of anchored peace. By gesture of a gentle handhold he led her to his Expedition with tinted windows. They slid in, needing each other very much.

It had been two weeks. Going to the laundromat, watching the ten o'clock news alone, playing pool at O'Riley's, making sales calls, anything to put distance and sunlight between that night and her imagination. There had been time to think and obviously time for him to ignore her. She certainly wouldn't be on time for a man she shouldn't be seeing and shouldn't have hooked up with and was foolish enough to let him bumble his way into a meeting at Ginger's, and wasn't all that special anyway. Being on time was for business hours with over caffeinated wild-eyed people who always looked as though they had six other things on their mind and three places they would rather be. There was always paperwork to complete and calls to make at her desk so she would spend the time catching up.

At 5:10, she thought her private life could be re-claimed so she called Michael on his cell phone. He was working at a housing development in the south end of the valley. The moderate houses with linoleum kitchen floors, and a built in shelf for the TV were placed six feet apart and planned to attract the young families of Utah with a penchant for new houses with garages more spacious than bedrooms.

"The job has a deadline for the sheet rockers to come in so I'm here for a while."

"I'm meeting the married man."

"Bad news."

There was silence.

"Just for a drink. At Ginger's."

"Oh." Another silence. "After I'm finished, Eddie and I are going to O'Riley's. If you come I'll buy you a hamburger."

"Maybe I will."

"Besides, you need to go home and feed Mr. Crichton. You neglect that cat."

"That cat neglects me. He was gone for two days last week and came home with a 'Don't ask me any questions you don't want answers to,' look. That cat's had more excitement than I've had this summer."

"It's only July."

After they hung up she returned to paperwork. Half of it disappeared but time was passing slowly. It was a quarter-to-six and Ginger's would only take ten minutes in a zip drive through the industrial section of the city. She washed her hands, freshened the very small amount of make-up she wore and spritzed her hair. No perfume.

Finished with that, she sat at her desk, glanced through an industry magazine and clipped an article on a new direct to plate press being introduced in Germany. One of her clients could use it. There was still time to back out as she drove to Ginger's but she knew she wouldn't. Her curiosity didn't have a name. Nothing about him stood out and demanded her attention except him in general and nothing in particular. And now he was at least part bastard. Was it her or his wife he was trying to humiliate or torture with the morning's introduction? The woman didn't seem to have a clue, so the emotional drama was for her benefit.

At 6:12 she pulled in the parking lot. At the far end was his truck, sitting all alone and the size of her childhood bedroom; probably cost as much as the house too. It could have been closer with the other cars. Again he was a bastard. If he thought she was a sure thing he was wrong.

Even without Michael by her side Suzanne had a rhythm to walking into a restaurant or bar. It was her way to take several full steps in so she wasn't clogging the doorway and asking for an untimely bump, stop, give the barest turn of her shoulders away from the turn of her head and survey. She liked the time it gave her to assess the best seat, who she might know and to notice who looked at her. Ken was seated at a center table on a level three steps up toward the back. Good choice. They were reasonably away from the noisier part of the bar without looking like they were trying to escape from everyone.

He stood when she began toward the steps and waited for her to be seated. Men her age never stood. Age had its graces. For a few seconds they assessed each other as though the other were of related but still foreign species.

"You've had time to order a drink." There was oil gold liquid like scotch or bourbon with ice in front of him.

"Yes," he turned toward the bar and the server came.

"Gin and tonic," she looked at the female server and as she walked away Suzanne turned to Ken, "A good summer drink."

They were quiet.

"Thanks for bringing the paper this morning. It was a small job but for one of my better customers." She nodded a you're welcome.

"At least someone who pays on time and doesn't barter every nickel."

"That's rare around here."

He smiled, relieved she was talking. "Here comes your drink."

She was silent again while she sipped. He was forced to talk or listen to the silence.

"The internet and technology has changed printing completely. Turned it upside down. Along with the rest of the economy."

"You started as a quick printing place didn't you?"

"Yes. Overton Overnight. But I could see those days were closing. We would have been scraping forever with what home and office computers left us to do." They were on safe ground and Suzanne was a salesperson willing to wait. Men's motivations weren't any easier to read than women's, but she did know sometimes a better sale came from patience. As he talked about his transformation from overnight quick services to the presses and equipment he had today she realized how deeply his enthusiasm ran for his business. Along with excitement to see each day start there was worry, nervousness, fear and willingness to work. Now she could report to Accounts Receivable that she knew Ken Overton was dedicated to making his business succeed. There was the barest touch of humanity in credit terms when dedication was known. And he was interested in learning more about direct to plate and a larger press.

She nodded, sipped, set the drink down, waited and went through three cycles of this before he was aware of the time that passed while he shoved air at her with his business recital.

"So, how was your day?" After his uninterrupted monologue he caught himself with an obvious attempt to be interested. She gave a sanitized version that didn't include any thought of him.

She finished with, "And of course, I met your wife."

For the first time his eyes looked down. He was on his second drink and he took a swallow. "Yes. Cat works on Thursday and sometimes comes in when needed. She helps with tracking expenses."

"That's a good partnership."

"Yes." He shifted in his seat as though movement stopped his speech.

"Well, Ken, I thank you very much for the pleasant after work drink. I enjoy working with you and you have an amazing company. When I walk in I can feel the organization and dedication of everyone there," she said it all in one breath, trying to sound calm and businesslike.

His eyes searched, trying to look deep into hers, not to catch her attention but to see her heart. Suzanne turned her chest and shifted in the chair to stop the invasion. It was her decision who came close.

"But I have a date," she paused and the words were out without thought, "I'm meeting my brother for dinner." Why did she say that? She could have made it sound like a real date instead of a transparent announcement of genuine availability.

"Suzanne . . . " he stopped.

She stood and reached to shake his hand. "Thank you again, Ken. But I need to go."

When she walked out the door and off the short sidewalk heat from the asphalt scorched her face like she was opening a hot oven.

"That man is a standard fuc-king," she thought, "fuck upon command king. No thanks." The long stretch of summer sunlight demanded more day be lived before it said goodnight. She looked at her watch. It was almost eight o'clock. There was time to meet Michael at O'Riley's, *Home of the Mountain-Sized Beer*.

CHAPTER SEVEN

"All right kids, time to pack," Cat called them to their bed-rooms two days before camp. Justin would be with Walt at a hiking camp in southwest Wyoming and MoMo was going to southern Utah with her friends, Annie and Frieda, to ride horses and sing cowgirl songs. Cat didn't believe Justin would return any better prepared to make his way in the wilderness or that MoMo would master horses, but they still need durable clothes so while they were encouraged to throw what they wanted on the bed, she had final say on whether the clothes were a good choice.

Justin's carelessly tossed jeans and tee-shirts were fine. Cat added a jacket, a shirt, jersey and underwear. MoMo needed convinc-ing the pink satin blouse she wore Christmas Eve wasn't up to the rig-ors of outdoor life and was not right for the 'Cowgirl Happy Trails Party' on the last night. Both of them were required to go through the camp's packing list, checking it off with Cat. Heavy socks were added to a shopping list of toothpaste and wash-ups. She would need a few of those things, too.

Sheldon had given Eme lessons in driving the fifth wheel whether she wanted them or not and encouraged her to take it for a few days. Oh, why not, Eme complained. Cat and Eme were sched-uled to leave Sunday morning. Ken would take Justin to his bus ride Sunday and MoMo needed to leave early Monday morning. Cat would be back Wednesday, the children midday Saturday. After final check of three suitcases, Cat brought her book into in the family room on Saturday afternoon. Ken, Justin and MoMo were eating popcorn and switching the TV between a Jackie Chan movie and baseball. MoMo was in Ken's lap and Justin was slumped in the couch like a snail in its shell.

It was a good time to call her mother and catch up on daily events. Usually, they talked twice a week on an irregular schedule.

With a glass of ice water and her book she carried the phone to the patio and sat with the umbrella shading her head while the sun hit her legs propped on another chair.

"Hi, Mom, how are things?"

Her mother reported a visit to the grocery store, going out to dinner with a friend and how her rose garden was doing. Several of the bushes were on their third blooming.

"How is Aunt Betty?"

"Not doing so well. Her children took her to DisneyWorld with her grandchildren for a family remembrance trip. Gennie called before they left crying and afraid. We talked for an hour."

Aunt Betty's daughter, Gennie, lived next door to her mother with her family. She and Cat had been friends as children but since Cat left for college they had fallen away. The conversation turned to Cat and she reported the camp packing and how she was looking forward to a few days in the mountains with Eme. Before they said goodbye, Cat opened her book.

"What do you think of this, Mother? Mao wrote this." She held up her book, *Fresh Air Fiend,* by Paul Theroux and read, "*We must learn to look at problems all sidedly, seeing the reverse as well as the obverse side of things. In given conditions, a bad thing can lead to good results, and a good thing to bad results.*"

"I think, dear, you need to read Mary Higgins Clark. Lighten up a little." Cat laughed.

"You're looking forward to this, aren't you?" Ken said to Cat over dinner that night.

"Well, yes, it should be fun seeing Eme maneuver that thing and it's been a long time since I've been camping. It will be fun."

"Camping? That thing?" was he imitating her voice, "is an apartment on wheels. Nicer than the first one you and I had."

She nodded and faintly smiled, while looking down, unsure if she had heard his voice mock or gently teased her.

"That was a lovely apartment. I was happy there."

"I wasn't. Too small."

"It was small. But it was, well, close and sweet for those days."

His shrug dismissed sentimentality.

They overlooked the children sitting at the table with them.

"I better be in the same bunkhouse as Walt. You did put that down didn't you, Mom?"

"Yes, I did and I'm sure his mother did, too."

"Just make sure you're ready, Justin. You're on your own after your mother leaves. I don't pack."

"He's ready, Ken. No need to worry." She whispered. She couldn't read his tone. It was neither his usual kindly father rough-housing aimed to steel his son softly into manhood, an accusation of her skills or a defense of his inability to pack.

"We're picking up Walt, Dad."

"Yes, you're picking him up to take him to the bus, too. I promised his mother."

Again Ken shrugged. Neither interested or disinterested, like an insolent teenager.

For weeks he had been distracted, on the tip of dangerous anger with nothing to direct it toward but the three of them where it had been landing with a thud of unhappy meals and silent evenings sitting before TV. None of them seemed to understand what was happening but it was as though a November wind was too often whisking along the ankles of their summer, unanticipated and foreboding. Cat ended the silence.

"I am looking forward to this since you asked."

"What will you do, Mom?"

"Well, MoMo, I suppose we will do a lot of talking, looking at trees, hoping Eme doesn't run into a few of them, hiking and roasting marshmallows just like you'll be doing. How does that sound?"

Two sets of childish shoulders shrugged. Ken didn't move.

Catalina Margaret Daniels Overton and Kenneth Mansfield Overton made love that night. Had sex. The two of them had their own definition but when it was over they each turned an opposite direction with their legs touching. Comfort lulled them to sleep. There was the warmth of a summer night and the peace of being with the familiar.

Cat had a dream, memorable only because others were not. She was packing and readying to leave a hotel and it was important that all she was to take was in the bag she was stuffing. Someone, neither male nor female, was sitting in a chair, kind and patient, waiting for her. There was a knock on the door. Cat did not answer. Time passed in silence while she packed and the kind person watched. After several knocks Cat answered the door. A woman stood there and Cat told her she knew she had kept her waiting, but she was not ready. The woman answered she knew that. But had kept knocking anyway.

Cat woke to silence. Space and air felt empty and suspended. Rosy morning light slipped through curtains replacing the disembodied dream. Slowly she remembered. A beautiful, luxurious home surrounded her, twenty-five feet of grass separated her from neighbors, the sun was shining, her children were going to camp, there were a few wonderful days to be spent with Eme and she loved Ken. The man who was, no doubt, downstairs making coffee right now.

While they were drinking coffee in bed and reading the newspaper, the children wandered in sleepy-eyed and in pajamas. Each brought a box of cereal and snuggled between their parents to watch the smaller TV in their room. The only talk was an occasional phrase or nod between the parents as one mentioned an item from the paper and the other acknowledged but was too busy reading to want talk.

Cat's black weekend bag was packed and waiting by the door. The children's bags were ready in their rooms, left open only for toothbrushes and hairbrushes. The omelette pan, for Ken's breakfast, had been wiped and put away. The toaster used for frozen waffles had been wiped and returned to its keeping place. Cat opened the refrigerator to show Ken food possibilities she stocked for the next few days.

She went outside with scissors and cut a half dozen petunia stems in as many plants so discreetly the missing flowers would not be missed. They filled in, lightly growing in each other's arms and up their backs as they reached to be highest. Back in the kitchen, she pulled a small vase from the cupboard. Sweet delicate perfume drifted in the air. As she was taking it upstairs to the bedroom she heard Eme pull in the driveway. While the children rushed to greet her and Ken graciously welcomed her at the door, she placed the flowers by Ken's side of the bed so the largest blossoms faced him when he lay down. Good-byes to the children were generous and effusive as hugs and kisses were traded all around.

"Check the Daddy Food area. I stocked it up for you. Have a good time with Daddy to yourself tonight," she said to MoMo. The hug with Ken was stilted, a bit staged, but she hugged him hard to make up for the perfunctory kiss.

As soon as they were on the road outside of Sunshadow Estates Eme stated they needed to stop at the store. "I need to get a few fresh items. You know how it is."

They walked to the produce area where Cat stopped by the bananas and Eme left her to walk to Ryan. Cat chose a few items while never taking her eye off Eme. From her distance it appeared casual and friendly. It may as well have been a TV commercial. They walked to the cantaloupes, chatting and exchanging smiles. When they stopped Ryan put his fingers to several before picking one up. He sniffed the stem end and showed Eme how to touch the fruit to determine ripeness without damaging it. His fingers looked like a spider trying to curtsy. She took the fruit, smiled and sashshayed away Eme-style. Only Cat could see Ryan had already turned away to look at another woman in the lettuce section who was tall and thin.

"I think we have more than enough fruit."

"I suppose, but you need five servings a day, Cat. And it should be fresh and just perfect. If not, who knows if those vitamins will be damaged."

"We have cantaloupe, bananas, raspberries, two kinds of grapes and a papaya I packed. Ken won't eat them. That should be enough until Wednesday noon."

After Eme got the apartment she was driving back on the highway she appeared less intense, Cat continued talking.

"I still don't understand how you found Ryan in my neighborhood, ten miles away from your tree-lined street by the city."

"Remember when you sent me to the store before that party for Overton?"

Cat sighed. Eme had been a volunteer to help Cat on the logistics of a party for Ken's employees during Christmas. Now she knew this had been a long, simmering relationship that could be near the end or a real beginning.

"Was it okay to miss Shiner's this Wednesday?" They were heading up I-80 in Parley's Canyon, where they would turn to Kamas and then hook to highway 150 to the Uinta Mountains. Everyone was passing, while Eme held the wheel at ten and two o'clock, keeping a steady path.

"Elliott only shrugged. He doesn't care. I think we all seem like bothersome cousins to him. His father considers us pretend children, like in a novel," she paused. "I do enjoy it there. It's a working meditation to lose myself in the books."

"How's it going at Overton? Do you like that?" she sidelined a concerned Mom look at Cat.

"I do. It's so different. Certainly not something I would have chosen for myself but I've found I enjoy the satisfaction of numbers adding up, moving to columns, aligning themselves to become part of commerce and space again. It somehow seems a lesson in the movement of life."

"Cat, you're nuts."

"Maybe. Numbers are more soothing than books. I have to suspend my belief to enter their world. They are escape. People are unpredictable but numbers have a flow like music, never ending and comforting in their continuity."

Eme didn't answer. She waited for more.

"Besides, Ken likes me there. I seem to serve a purpose for him."

"I'm sure you do."

Cat was reflective, quiet, letting Eme pay all her attention to the traffic, "Do you think it is love or serving a purpose?"

"Between men and women or you and Ken?" A semi-truck passed. It was hard to hear.

"Between you and Sheldon."

"I don't know. I love things about him. The slow meticulous way he does things. Nothing he takes time to fix or do ever needs redoing. I admire that. I love his patience with me. When I can't be on time. He seems to truly enjoy my crazy love of color and my wild hair. But you know," she paused, "these are actions of his and reflections of me I want accepted. I don't know if I love the existential Sheldon. I don't know if I know what that is."

"You do serve each other's purposes." Eme nodded and Cat continued. "You are outgoing, he's not. He accepts your independence. Like this weekend. You give brightness, excitement to his life. What does he give you?"

"Besides what I've already mentioned? Let me think about that."

Talk switched to Eme's topics; jewelry, the visual joys of watching men and new restaurants. Up the winding mountain road by

Mirror Lake they continued toward the Wyoming border. Sheldon had reserved a spot for them in a campground of aspens below Ruth Lake. Parking took a great deal of laughter, body language, frustration and concern there should not be one hairline scratch on Sheldon's fifth wheel or a felled tree.

To get acquainted with the area they took a walk around the campground, veering off when they found a stream to follow. Eme made a note to buy Sheldon a book on Utah wildflowers and next time she would bring a camera. When they returned Cat became frustrated her cell phone didn't work in the mountains. Ken told her it might not and not to worry but it was still disappointing she couldn't talk to him and be assured. Assured of what she didn't answer to herself. Eme was watching her as she mixed two gin and tonics before dinner but she didn't say anything until they finished dinner and made a small muscled fire they wouldn't keep going long.

"You do a lot of worrying about Ken. At least it seems to me," Eme's face had the dances of firelight playing like a Picasso painting.

"Oh, Eme, you just have to be married to know. It's not worrying too much. It's taking care of each other." Eme saw the same dances on Cat's face with a bit more light as the last of the day's shadows fell behind the mountain. "Anyway, thanks for making the fire. This is great. Ken doesn't like to camp at all and I miss it. Remember when we went camping in college with all those crazy people?"

"Yes, I do. And you seemed like a little married lady then. Only you worried about everyone around you and whether they liked you."

"I still worry about that."

"Well, you shouldn't. Some will and some won't and most do. That's as much as anyone can ask."

Cat nodded, looking in the firelight, taking a sip of the gin and tonic she returned to after dinner, noticing the cold of ice on her teeth and the heat of fire on her cheek. Still thinking of Ken, she shifted in the camp chair. MoMo didn't leave until morning, so they were probably huddled in front of the TV. That would be a compelling black and white portrait if shot at the right angle. She would have to do it one day.

"What do you really think of Sheldon? He seems like a good man." Maybe a change of subject would lighten her heart.

"Sheldon's what your mother would call a good catch."

"In other words, you're bored with him."

"Not bored exactly. I realize how good he is. I guess," she paused, "I guess, I would just like it more earth shattering. More lustful and crazy with forgotten, timeless weekends and practical and honest so you could wake up happy and want to eat scrambled eggs and go earn a living with a decent nine to five job. Everything. Everything."

"There's nothing wrong with wanting what you want."

"I know. There's nothing wrong with wanting it. There's nothing promised about getting it either."

The fire crackled and condensed darker before Eme spoke. "Men have their niches. I've known them to be absolutely crazy fun that I wanted to go on forever. Remember Robert? And then there was Johnson the First. He was a steady, stay as you go guy. Wonderful in his way but not for me." Eme referred to two of her many lost loves.

"I remember. I remember with Robert you couldn't decide whether it should be rock or seashell but you wanted to hit something that would hurt you back so you wrote his name on a boulder and hit it until you were crying."

"Yes, it felt so good I went out and did it again the next morning." The fire crackled before Eme continued, "I think, Cat, I think men should be tradable commodities for a woman's moods and needs. Rather like a grand library in human form. It could work for both sexes." Giggles stayed within the heat of the fire. "We could check them out based on their book covers."

"Their loincloths?" Cat asked.

"Yes, and if we were late returning them, we would expect to pay a fine."

"That would probably subsidize their beer at the library bar. They would be happy living there waiting to be called."

"And certainly it would make them happy to have different women check them out."

"When they were fathers we could ask for extended stays," now Cat was enjoying herself.

"Hell, let the kids check him out," Eme waited, her voice softened. "Sometimes I would want stable and caring. Sheldon."

"Or brawny and hairy, like Ken."

"Could talk and cuddle. And Ken's not that hairy," Eme said.

"Were courtly and kind. I think he is."

"Intelligent and inspiring," Eme offered.

"Were fun. Could make us laugh."

"Were clever and could fix things around the house, like Sheldon."

Cat purposely looked at Eme and exaggerated a winsome, blinking schoolgirl, "Would look into us as though we were the only woman in the world."

"Or exotic, enigmatic. Just plain gorgeous."

"Could screw until our eyeballs fell out."

"They would never have to live their lives pretending to be anything to please us. Because we would know they were to be returned, used by others and cherished by memory."

"We expect a lot of men," Cat looked at the dying fire, burning white heat in the center, cold black burned wood protecting it on the outside.

"Yes, they're much smarter than we are. They know they're not going to find everything in one woman." They both felt the wall of cold forest dark behind them while their faces glowed red.

Cat shifted in her seat and regretted she could not call Ken at home tomorrow night. "The library could work for everyone. Who made up the system we have anyway?" Her voice was weaker, less buoyant.

"Our own bodies. Our library beer bar is the house and kids. Some of us are kept put. Gathering dust."

"Men would love your idea, Eme. I know it. Women would want each of them."

The next morning they packed lunch before heading up the trail to Ruth Lake. It wasn't busy on a Monday. At times they were alone, shoes on rock, breathing to the pace, outstretched arms rustling branches, their human noises an intrusion in this mighty cathedral of nature. Through glens of aspen, over smooth rock worn slippery from melting snows, along flat compact mountain valleys with flowers and areas of grass growing to their waist. Snowflakes from previous winters melted, sliding from the peak into the pristine, cold blue water of Ruth Lake. A two-man tent was on the other side, silent and waiting like a pitched doghouse. Amazing how simply humans can live in the vastness of nature if they are on their own for everything, Cat thought.

"It's lunch time," Eme began spreading out the simple lunch that nourished and pleasured foot travelers for centuries. Clear high mountain air, cheese, fruit, ham, bread, water and wine brought translucence and peace to Cat's eyes.

"Remember the summer we hiked above Brighton Ski Resort in college?"

"I sure do. We marked ourselves as women that day."

"Was it that official? All I remember is rolling in the dirt." She laid back on the grass and spread her arms like a bird, gathering a twig and a handful of grass in her hand. Protecting them with her cupped palms she laid them on her belly.

"Don't you remember what we said to each other?" Eme was staring across the lake, mesmerized by the sparkle of sun off the water; reborn glowing snowflakes flying to the sky.

"A little bit. But what I remember most was the feeling of freedom and the glitter of the aspens above our heads."

"We said, 'Good-bye cruel childhood. Good-bye puberty and silliness. We are now women with lives. Beautiful, true women and members of the Future of Inner Trinity."

Cat sat up, "Yes, I do remember. And then I met Ken. He was the man I could be woman with."

Eme was quiet.

"I'm worried about Ken, Eme."

"Whatever for?"

Cat told her of his late nights in June that didn't have the same cadence as normal. How in July he came home on time every night, but his moods were like a match; suddenly hot and mean and then as quickly small and cold. He seemed to purposely be angry, purposely pushing her away. When she questioned him, he just said it was stressful at work, which she knew it was, but it was more than that. Dangerous, spewing drops of hate and fear were falling on her and the children. Yet, there was nothing specific she could point to, only information that breathed warning from her insides.

CHAPTER EIGHT

Suzanne walked out of Janson's Design Printing and checked messages on the cell phone. The last was Overton. Since leaving the fuc-king at Ginger's three weeks ago she had not talked to him. All work had been through Mary Ellen or the telephone inside salespeople. Fine with her.

"Hello, Mary Ellen, this is Suzanne. I'm returning your call." She sat in her Cherokee, legs dangling out the door for sun, still in Janson's parking lot.

"It wasn't me, Suzanne. I'll get Ken." And then silence while she was on hold, suddenly also holding tangled thoughts.

"This is Ken."

"This is Suzanne." She could hear presses in the back. He wasn't in his office.

"Yes, yes, Suzanne. I called you."

She didn't answer.

He cleared his throat. "How about a nice dinner? Monday. Robber's Roost Steakhouse." He named a linen table-clothed restaurant with baby lamps on each table. It was also hidden away in a cavernous downtown hotel where local people weren't known to visit. People were easily anonymous among conventioneers.

"Suzanne?"

She didn't answered. Dark restaurant. Monday night.

"Why Ken?"

"So you won't think I'm a cheap jerk. Be friends."

"I'll call you back. Tomorrow." She clicked 'end' and threw the phone on the passenger seat.

The e-mail sent by Trent read he was going to O'Riley's. Whoever spoke up first with a group e-mail chose the place and was responsible to call Eddie and Michael. Michael always called Diane.

Suzanne was killing time playing pool with Eddie before she handed her stick to Aaron. She came to O'Riley's hoping Raylene would show. Raylene of the flowing red hair, milk skin dappled with sun kisses, as Suzanne called her freckles, and advice too old for Methuselah. If there was anything bad about her advice, it was that it was good. She had a center like the magnet on the North Pole, so why she only went with losers was something no one in the group understood. She wasn't telling Michael about Ken's call because she didn't want his advice. It was predetermined and unnecessary. New information would be more helpful; perhaps more approving. At least Raylene's advice would have reasoning, instead of Michael's thoughtless 'dump him.' Confusion was overrunning Suzanne's usually neat day timer thinking, making her aggravated and impatient.

Raylene had not come and she was frustrated. Michael was sitting with the blonde Carole he had dubbed Caramello in a dark side booth. Suzanne plopped down beside him as though she were a cocker spaniel needing a reassuring pet.

"This is my sister, Suzanne," he said a bit quickly to allay any misunderstanding.

"Hi, I'm Suzanne," she lifted her arm to shake hands.

"Michael said he had a sister."

"Ya, well, I'm the one," Suzanne sounded insolent. Michael lifted his chin to his sister.

"Suzanne, I'd like you to meet Carole. Carole Young."

She hadn't known the female's last name. Not that it made a difference. Young. Like Mellon or Rockefeller on the east coast, she guessed.

Suzanne tried for pleasant. From Michael's report of the last few weeks she realized this female was important to him. At least for the moment, which was long enough. Michael told her over hamburgers at Hammer's last week that this Carole person was good. Her lashes even talked to him. The curve of her throat. Oh, god, Suzanne thought as she chewed on a French fry.

"Michael, do men really notice the 'curve of her throat' when they want to screw?"

"I do."

"At least on this female," she wasn't going to allow any more respect than that.

"So what's your problem? She's great. Are you jealous?"

Without answering she did, "Name the best thing she reminds you of."

"Caramello candy bars."

Caramello became Carole's nickname because in Michael's words she was 'so rich and sweet with folds, softness, and a lushness that one little bite could satisfy.' How romantic was Carole when Caramello slipped off the tongue like warm caramel? Michael was now showing what Suzanne called dopey eyes.

Suzanne returned her thoughts to the evening's problems and watching for Raylene. Trent put this evening together but it was almost ten and he hadn't shown up either. Suzanne was finishing a hamburger at a table near the pool table when he walked in the door with a guy she didn't know.

"Suzanne, Arnie, Arnie, Suzanne." His arm moved like he held a baton. They nodded. Regarding.

"Greenhall," he finished the introduction.

"Flint," said Suzanne.

Trent didn't notice his imperfect introduction. "Arnie's new at the firm. Specializes in corporate law." Trent was in real estate, "He's our answer to diversity. A curly-haired white guy from Virginia."

"Hey," she said, stretching her hand to shake.

"Hello," he looked into her eyes searching for an answer to an unasked question. He was a tall good-looking guy with dark-blonde curly hair that reminded her of August moon shimmer. He had an admirably slinky walk that pivoted from his hips. The only thing she thought was humorous and a small reason to be wary of him was the way he raised and lowered his eyebrows. It could be unconscious expression or conscious sarcasm.

As they left her table, Raylene finally walked in the door. With her was the least butt-head boyfriend she had brought the last two years. Carson Whitney followed her like a trained chimpanzee watching territory and smelling his own balls for assurance that he was succeeding in polluting the world. Or so Suzanne imagined. Actually, the guy wasn't that bad. Just not munificent - her mother's one big word. Generous of self and spirit. She would say it like it was her single friend against her husband. Carson defined and protected space as he looked around O'Riley's and stepped aggressively beside Raylene to claim. Maybe Raylene needed that. The presence of someone like Carson made it possible for her to spend time giving to people who received well, instead of protecting herself from ungracious takers.

Looking at Carson, Suzanne felt braver. Considering her own bad choices, Raylene would be more munificent with Ken.

"Ray, I really need to talk to you. I need an opinion."

In a sweep Raylene motioned Carson to the pool table and she and Suzanne walked to a far booth. Suzanne gave a shortened version of the last two months. Good customer, one night stand, silence, seems to want sex about as often as wife might be on a period. Monday night invitation to dinner. What should she do?

"How much do you like this guy?" Raylene was steady, her eyes spun sugar, bright and watching.

"Enough to ask you about him instead of just do it."

"Strategy is important."

"I guess," she looked down at the table, realizing how weak that sounded. When she looked up she decided to plunge through and give Raylene a closer tale, "I don't know what I want. I just know I'm intrigued."

Suzanne shifted her hips. "He's married."

"How married?"

"I don't know."

"Does the wife look like a player?"

"No."

"So. Suzanne has itches. Man has itches. Wife is stupid."

Michael hit a ball, cracking the air.

"Sounds like a good, easy set up the way it is," Raylene suggested. "It may wear out and be an incident for you and a memory for the man."

"I won't suck the air out of a marriage for sex. I get that somewhere else."

"Then tell me the real reason you like this man, Suzanne." Raylene's voice was so soft and caring Suzanne answered.

"I'm not sure." Starting with a disclaimer sounded less cunning,

"There just feels like a connection of energy. Like we're on the same

92

path. But I'm not sure. Not really. It could be all wrong, but when I'm around him I feel like I'm at home in a way I don't understand." Suzanne straightened in her chair and spiked her hair with a tug from pearl red fingernails, "But, he's married and I don't share."

"Then I suggest, Suzanne, that you say no to the dinner. I suggest you flush him out. But say it with an opening to him so that there is barest hope. Wait and see. Home always comes."

The next day Suzanne called Ken of Overton Printing, and said to his voice mail, "Ken, Monday will not work. Perhaps another time."

CHAPTER NINE

The petunias looked like awkward girls learning to dance; their stems showed bent knees where blossoms had been lost. Their perfume was too light, too innocent, too sweet for what a woman should know in the September of life. Away from the tendered pots, the marigolds were absorbing the fall sun, opening tight petals and glowing orange red to the sky. Their small round faces looked directly to the sun and their sturdy stems never wavered for water. Nights with lacy cool edges and warm days with the soft, silky feel of the barest breath of fall urged marigold's greatest blossoms. It is a sensual month of finally being mature enough to enjoy life. Day takes its time to become light, without rush, like the full measured stretch of a pleased woman after sex. Cat was not aware of how the sun of September pleased her, warmed her, and did not demand the attention of July or August. She did know it was important to notice happiness, so she was consciously noticing how it felt in her body at this moment.

Frost had not tempered the garden yet but she knew any late September night could swiftly kill. Lucky gardens lasted through October. Her fingers were muscle hot from the pruning she completed around the perimeter of the house. Stiff short stems from five bushes were in the wheel barrel that was now heavy to push. She leaned and chose five branches to take in for a vase. They would make an interesting study on the dinner table. It was likely there would be three settings, two if she were lucky. A stark arrangement of branches would be artistic for whoever was eating, whenever they ate.

Since her trip with Eme, Cat had decided to be happy, assume a happy position and she would be happy. After all, she really hadn't proof of anything. August had continued well. Ken's schedule was routine and expected. When he was cranky it felt like a hailstorm in summer, unexpected, fleeting and even if it soaked deeply, it was soon over. She gave wide berth to a man she knew was emotional and under daily pressure of a dozen deadlines and demands.

Kathleen, Ken's mother had pulled her aside at a family back-yard picnic when their engagement was new. She was tall, imperial in her manner and when Kathleen put her arm around Cat to guide to a quieter corner of the yard, she felt both honored and reduced to feeling like a child.

"I can tell you love Kenneth. You have a lovely look in your eyes."

Cat cleared her throat and squeaked a yes. Kathleen's household was run by declarations and posture. She had seen all four of her children stand taller when addressed by their mother.

Kathleen was nodding, "And I believe Kenneth loves you. He certainly has been happier lately and therefore, his father and I are also happy."

Cat smiled, large and like a little girl.

"I've trained my children to be good spouses. Told them their duties and what was expected. Robert and I invented the wheel. We don't want our children to." Kathleen motioned to a chair, "Here, dear, let's sit in these chairs under the tree. I had Robert put them here before everyone came." For the next half-hour Cat heard what Ken had been like as a baby, a child, and a teenager. Stories from a mother's view of the always busy, planning, self-demanding, sometimes petulant, endearing Kenneth. "He is a good man, Cat, and I believe he will make you happy, but he is my mercurial son. His emotions are sometimes too large for his chest and it seems steam needs to come out from time to time. It does not lessen the great love and integrity he also has in his heart."

Through the years Cat remembered that afternoon and been grateful to Kathleen for information that made it possible for her to seed understanding instead of fear or anger. Only on Labor Day was the happy disrupted. The family of four spent the hottest part of the afternoon in a movie theatre watching an overrated 'family block-buster.' After a late afternoon barbecue, Justin walked to Walt's and Trista's mom picked up MoMo for a few hours to visit. Ken leaned back in the patio chair, looking pleased with the day and dinner. Cat had planned to work in the garden but his informal invitation to prolong a pleasant meal was better.

"What do you want, Cat?" It was a gentle voiced question and he seemed lost in reverie.

Unalarmed and curious what he was getting at she asked, "What do you mean?"

"I mean, what do you want with your life? What do you think is next?" Sitting in the lengthening shadows of sun, after a busy pleasant day, it may have been a college student's vague philosophical question to entertain the evening.

The question surprised her. Life was a given with children and home and responsibilities. She started slowly. "I suppose, this is it. Right now the house, children, you, Overton. That is my life." She felt Buddha-like living the moment.

"So you haven't thought beyond that?"

His phrasing made her blink, but she didn't move. Buddha disappeared. Ken lifted the almost empty can of beer and finished it. When he looked at her again, it was eye to eye. "I look further. I have to. To run a company is to always look ahead."

Again she nodded. Yes, she thought, that makes sense.

"But looking forward like that makes me see things. Some of it I don't want to see."

"What do you mean?"

"Oh, Cat, it just makes me look at what's really happening. Priorities and making a living. For example," and he shifted in his seat, "your priorities are here. In this house."

"Yes."

"Do you think a priority could ever be Overton?"

He was questioning new territory in their marital talks. "Overton is a priority to me. I know it needs to succeed. As much for you, as for Justin, MoMo, and me. We depend on it."

"Yes, but could you put yourself into it?"

"I do. I work there."

"Lina, the children are getting older. They're not babies anymore. Could you put more into Overton?" His light brown eyes were unhampered, clear of malice or intrigue as he watched her and patiently waited for the silence to end. She had seen this look in his eyes as he waited for an employee to come up with the obvious answer to a question he thought simple. After a full minute, he softly, very softly said, "I'm going to get a beer and I'm coming right back. I want to

96

hear what you think."

The beer was popped open when he returned. In fact, the clear snap of the can's lid also forced Cat's words through the very small space of thinking that was making sense in her head. The sound seemed like a warning bell she couldn't comprehend.

"Do you mean, you want me to work there, everyday?"

"I want to know what you want, but I want to know your commitment to Overton."

"I see my first commitment to you and the children. In this house. Overton is a place where I support you because you have chosen it and I believe in it. But it's a world I don't understand and one that is yours."

"Are you going to work one day at Overton and one day at Shiner's forever?"

"I don't know." This talk was not casual. "I haven't had a chance to think of that."

"I need more support, Cat. I need your help. I can't do this alone." His words were spoken so evenly, so clearly, that she knew they had been rehearsed many times.

"I will think about that, Ken."

He nodded. For the first time she saw a glimmer of not quite malice and not quite revenge. He got up and went in to watch TV.

The children were back in school, Cat began preparing the garden for winter and she continued her schedule with Shiner's and Overton. There wasn't another talk with Ken about her intentions with Overton. The thought flitted in and out of her mind, but she wanted the whole idea to just disappear. During a soaking long bath one evening she closed her eyes and imagined a schedule of working forty hours a week at Overton. Claustrophobia and dread came over her and she sat up from the bubbles to shake it off. If Ken was overworked and needed help, they needed to hire another person. Perhaps he needed a partner in the business like old Mr. Presson could have been.

Halfway into September she received a call from Cancer Care House to begin weekly Friday morning meetings on the fundraising dinner dance to be held the following spring. She felt lonely for Ken and wanted to share the news. He liked her to work on charity projects. "Get out of yourself and show off Overton and your natural organization skills," Ken said. She liked to see him happy.

After her quiet lunch at the counter with a magazine she reached for the phone and called Ken. She needed to know she was still in his heart.

"Hi, just thinking of you."

"Oh," he was distracted. Her timing hadn't been good.

"I won't keep you but I just thought I'd say hi and let you know I got the call from Cancer Care House. Meetings are starting." She paused, "And I miss you."

"Ya. Oh, Cat, I'm probably going to be late tonight. Don't expect me at dinner."

"I'm disappointed." And she was. "What is it?"

"Just work. I've got to catch up. You'll see how busy we've been when you come in."

"Okay. Well, love you."

"Love you, too. And by the way, Tomorrow I've been invited by the main guy at Harkness to go fishing. He goes to Fish Lake and asked me to go."

"Well, that's nice. You haven't been fishing for years."

"No. It should be okay. I need to go." Goodbye. Civil and sweet for a twelve year marriage.

It was true the company had picked up its pace recently. Dan's sales efforts were paying off, plus it was also moving into a traditional busy season so she would do well to be grateful for the work. Still, he was gone a lot. Last Saturday he even disappeared in the middle of the day for an odd hour.

The children managed to be at the table with her at dinner. She made a pasta something that would keep and warm nicely in the microwave for Ken. Whenever he came home.

Cat got a glass of wine when MoMo went to bed. Justin stayed up. It was Friday and he was allowed a little later. Cat and Justin watched TV, switching back and forth between two movies so they could talk about both of them. One was a teenage movie of drinking, girls and avoiding school. The other was High Society with Grace Kelly. Cat pointed out dating differences and how girls liked to be treated. Justin nodded and said little. Partly because he didn't want to talk about girls to his mother, though he was eagerly listening, and partly because she was drinking more wine than usual and her voice sounded a bit rough, a little threatening.

At half-past ten, they heard Ken's car pull in the garage. He and Cat looked at each other and then both, for their own guilty reasons, looked straight ahead at TV and waited for him to come in. The door opened quietly. Until then he wouldn't have seen the lights in the family room, wouldn't have known anyone was up. As he opened the door he heard the TV.

"Anybody home?" his voice was a soft inquiry. Neither of them answered and they both wondered why. When he stepped in there was a clear quiet second when the three of them looked at one another.

"Yes, we're here." Cat said.

"Hi, Dad."

"It looks like a mom and son movie night."

Cat put her glass down and stood to head toward the kitchen.

"Here's your dinner. I'll warm it up."

"I'm not hungry. Todd went for hamburgers."

Under the glaring light of the kitchen his eyes were glassy and unreadable, not close to family or this house. They weren't warm or comforting. Ken straightened himself, pulled away from Cat in a slow military correctness that was official, an unquestioned distancing.

Justin got up and started to his room, "G'night." He disappeared and the soft step of his feet on the stairs were intertwined with the voices of Grace Kelly and Bing Crosby.

"Where have you been?" Her voice whispered. She swayed slightly on her feet, as much from the wine, as the release of gravity as Ken leaned away and reached for the phone.

"Don't believe me, Cat? Here call Miguel. He's still working. Want me to dial?"

He watched his prey, calculating threat and put the phone down. "I'm tired. It's been a long day." Cat waited for further words. There were none. He simply removed his lumbering, beautiful self and disappeared up the stairs beyond the light. Cat went to the kitchen to pour more wine and watched TV without seeing.

Hostility was in the open. She could not name what part of her it was directed at but she knew she was the target. Dislike she did not understand was coming from Ken, the man she loved. She hadn't enough clues and little understanding. How men operated and their motivations were not what she was taught. She was only taught to be good, available, keep a clean home, be loyal and honest and clean-living for godsakes. How was she ever to know what to do with the heart of man? That did not match her training.

Another glass of wine helped her to stare without blink into the changing, flashing screen. She wanted all of this to evaporate like a bad dream and be unimportant. But she knew life was altering beyond a simple, "I'm sorry."

An hour later she went upstairs and fell heavier than she wanted to the side of Ken. He did not move. It would have been so nice, so very nice, if he had moved to hold her and say he was so sorry that he had been detained against his will at the office. Of course she was more than important. She was his life and the center of his being and he needed her nourishment to live. It would have been so nice to hear that.

At 5:30 he leaned and kissed her good-bye before going fishing.

CHAPTER TEN

Suzanne thought Michael was spooky. There hadn't been one mention of Ken in over a month, but Michael seemed to read vapors of thought patterns. Last Friday when he stopped by the apartment before they went out he started with, "Are you seeing that married man?" He tried to sound casual but Suzanne knew his voice and it wasn't a casual question.

"No, not since June, really. Just talked to him once in July and August." There, she told the truth without giving away feelings. He nodded and reached for a handful of stale popcorn in a blue Corning Ware bowl that had been their mother's. Suzanne slid a beer to him across the kitchen counter and poured herself wine in a water glass.

"Not beer?"

"It's too filling. I need something lighter with as much punch."

"There's only red punch in Utah."

"I'm thinking of developing a taste for scotch but I can't decide. It sounds old. Vodka sounds too young. Gin is degenerate. Rum too trendy. Tequila too dangerous."

"You could always not drink."

She nodded and petted Mr. Crichton who jumped in front of her on the counter.

"I could but then what would you and I do together?"

She was quiet for a few seconds while Michael watched her before continuing, "I'm thinking of finding where Crichton lives. Maybe we could meet."

"He'd be better than a married man."

"You've never met him and maybe he's married."

"I don't have to. Married people are trouble. Remember Mitzi?" Michael winced remembering his short overheated affair. Standing in a familiar beige apartment kitchen with a newly opened beer and two years of intervening days, he still felt the enclosing days with Mitzi. April wet snow piercing long and hard like fingers that want too much, black short shiny boots on thin heels and the rose wind smell of her hair against the soap in her pink pillows. He was hers the moment he looked into those crazed blue eyes that should have been in a mental hospital. For a week he lost himself in her every day. She was air and exhilaration. His mind shut down. Until the night there was a key in the door and Mitzi's husband who had been out of town came home. She was shoving him out a sliding glass door with his pants thrown ahead of him when the husband came in the bedroom. A bellow of pain and anger was so echoing from the bottom of the man's soul that Michael felt almost as much hurt for him as he did fear for himself. He didn't know she was married until his white backside was the last of him the husband or Mitzi ever saw.

"I remember Mitzi but it's not the same. Besides, I'm not seeing him."

"What did you like about him? So we can avoid this mistake in the future."

"Everyone asks me that and I'm not sure. I think Mom even asked me that in the shower the other day."

Michael smiled. He knew of Suzanne's imagined conversations with their mother.

"Something about where he is in life. He's stable. He's got something. He's not scratching like we are."

"Yes he is. You just don't see it." He had been a man long enough to know this was all men's inheritance.

"He works every day but he's further. He's got something. I like his ambition. His force."

"You just want dad."

"No, I don't just want Dad. Dad's ambition was greed. His force was meanness," she leaned and shook her head at him and took a swallow of wine like it was beer. "I want a future and I don't want to start at Go holding an iron."

"Maybe you should see where Mr. Crichton lives."

"He's too old."

"You want everything. Age. Money. Stability. Give me a break. At that rate no one should want me."

"And looks. You forgot. I want looks. And plenty want you

102

for the same reason I like Ken. You have stability and looks. Age and money will come."

"Now I have to hear his name. I'm glad he dumped you. Hear that? Dumped. Get him out of your head."

She bristled, "I dumped him, Michael. And it's not a bad name. But his last name is stupid. Overton." Suzanne's cell phone rang. Mr. Crichton went to Michael's arms, "Hello."

It was Sugarloaf.

"Hey."

"I'd like to see you."

"Yes?" Her blood weakened. This man undid her with his voice.

"How's one?"

Suzanne turned away from Michael but she knew he heard every word. "Yes, okay."

"See you."

"Bye."

"The married man?"

"I told you, I haven't seen him."

"Good. I'm glad you've got another on the string but disappointed you haven't told me about him."

"He's a new guy. I don't know him much," she hadn't felt this guilty for a long time. Michael was not who she wanted to deceive. In apology she continued, "I call him Sugar." Adding loaf seemed demeaning to a man she would never demean.

"My sister. She can get any man. Now she's got Sugar Ray."

"Except Michael Crichton."

"You could get him if you wanted."

"His pictures do look good. Maybe I should try."

"God help the real Mr. Crichton."

A lanky man with long hair in a flannel shirt was strumming a guitar to celebrate Friday night at O'Riley's. "When did O'Riley's start caring about ambiance?" Trent whispered. He brought his work friend, Arnie, again and Sierra and Eddie were already there. Suzanne stuck with the wine which everyone thought was worth a few jokes but she teased back about their lousy pool playing. The evening was casual, easy enough and even a little fun with Arnie looking at her and shifting hips every time he shot the ball. He was the only holdup to an easy getaway to Sugarloaf. When she got up to leave he came over. "Suzanne, when is it time for you and me?" An eyebrow shot up.

Generally speaking, she liked all men so it was easy to be welcoming. Besides, he was good-looking and interesting enough. "Maybe another time, Arnie. I'm tired tonight." Before he could say anything she headed for Michael. He was busy with a brunette with thick hair cascading like frozen waves down her back. His quick sidelong nod acknowledged she was going and he didn't want to be interrupted. She would have to ask about Caramello.

Thinking of Sugarloaf was good. The quickening and excitement was an invigorating pull to life. She needed the male strength she pulled from him. After eleven months and perhaps twice as many meetings, she still didn't know if he was married, where he lived or much about what he liked to do or eat or watch on TV. Long ago she learned not to ask questions you don't want answered.

When the soft three raps came she opened the door, he was a lurking shadow growing from moonlight. He didn't step to come in but watched her as she held the door to beckon him without movement.

"Come in." he didn't move. They looked at each other openly without expectation. "Come in, please."

"I like looking at you in moonlight."

She waited.

"Perhaps because that's all I see you in." A few moments passed. "It seems natural to you."

"As a policeman you would know that."

His head lifted in question but he did not move away from the door where he leaned. There was a breath intake of power. She wondered if he used his air and substance to intimidate on the job. "I mean you notice people. You see them. I do belong in moonlight."

"You do." His voice softened like she confessed to a crucial piece of evidence. They looked to each other through shadows once again under lowered eyelids for protection.

"Please, come in." This time he did.

The understanding between Suzanne and Sugarloaf was fulfilled need without apology or expectation. They didn't know what the other was suffering, was facing in the lonely world they each imagined for the other and they didn't want to know. They wanted to heal each other and themselves in the time they had.

"I'm glad you called tonight."

He nodded, pleased. "Then you won't mind if I touch you."

"No. I never do."

At four, after an hour's dreamless sleep Sugarloaf woke fully simply by opening his eyes. Silver light outlined Suzanne's body now turned away from him. As though he were feeling silk for the first time, he ran two fingers from her hair, to her shoulder, along the rib cage, up the hip and down her legs to stop before her knee. He leaned to kiss her ear before saying good-bye. Suzanne nodded, stretched to her back for one last full naked hold from the length of Sugarloaf's now dressed, buttoned and buckled body.

Saturdays were odd lots of time she didn't fill efficiently. There weren't tasks of duty that stepped her forward in life, as in the workday world. Sometimes she spent them alone which she didn't like. Sometimes with Raylene. There had been other friends from high school but through the years they had fallen to friendly fire of steady lovers or husbands. Trent called her a few times to hike around the foothills or a few of them dared each other to bowling. Today, she called Shelly from work. They'd done a few things together.

"Can't today, sorry. I drank too much last night, I'm recuperating, the kids are running wild, and then I've got to get ready for a date tonight."

Enough of the girl talk. She called Michael. She thought it was going to end at voice mail when a groggy Michael answered.

"Yes."

"Well, hello."

"Suzanne."

"Thought we could go to a movie or something."

"No movie. I'll be over at noon or one or something like that. Have food." He hung up. At half-past one he arrived. Dutifully she had microwaved frozen potato skins and fresh popcorn. Favorite foods.

"You don't look any too healthy." It wasn't his looks. They were perfect, it was his demeanor, the slant of his shoulders that were not taut, not rightful. "You better sit down and watch something quiet like golf." Michael was angry when he had too much to drink and it wasn't worth an argument to tease him too directly.

"I'm going to the gym later. Right now I'm eating these and popcorn," he pointed to the potato skins and lifted one.

"Well, I don't have anything to do today and I'm bored and I'm feeling sorry for myself and I don't know what to do. Where's the Damn Prince anyway? I'm waiting, dammit." She fell to the couch alongside him and they silently watched TV.

"Arnie could be one," he slipped it in like their mother would slip lettuce in a sandwich and didn't look at her.

"Ready for a beer?" she asked a little later.

"Not yet."

"Well, how was she anyway?"

"Huh?"

"The brunette with the cascading curls that would take till noon to appear natural."

"She followed me home."

"So, did she show you how to really hold a hammer, Mr. Carpenter?"

Michael's words were funny but his voice was not. "No, but we drove a few nails."

"Now tell me the real story."

"The woman was great. Well, you saw her," as though that absolved. "But when it was over all I felt was bad about Caramello."

"And?"

"And she left me her phone number and this morning I burned it so I don't know how to get in touch with her."

When the doorbell rang their shoulders left the couch. Only Mr. Rogers rang a doorbell. On the second ring, Suzanne got up and went to the door. Through the peephole she saw Ken. She looked at Michael to calm his curiosity and opened the door. Ken saw her eyebrows were raised and forced a bit apart. Her body was stretched and ready, lean and near feral.

"Hello."

"Hello." She paused, "Come in." She didn't know what else to say.

Ken was surprised to see Michael. By the time he looked, Michael straightened and turned to directly watch the person entering.

By his sister's slight step to hide what was behind the door he knew attention needed to be paid and stood up.

Ken nodded, immediately aware Michael was younger and not as big as him.

"Ken, this is my brother, Michael," Suzanne said, "we're watching TV. Just Saturday."

The two men stared at each other; assessing what a next step would be and what the other meant to Suzanne. Ken offered a hand and Michael reluctantly took it.

"What would you like, Ken?"

"A beer."

While she was in the kitchen the two men held their positions.

"Here you are," she handed him the can. Three people sat down to stare at the television.

"How did you find where I live?"

"Ad club directory."

Silence was split between the golf game, Ken's beer sipping and the silent listening by Suzanne and Michael to each other's clues. At five minutes Michael stood.

"I'm going for more beer. I'll be back in ten minutes," he didn't look at either of them as he headed toward the door. They heard his red truck back up and leave. Alone for ten minutes with the woman who drew him near without seeming to want him, Ken knew he had to make it count.

"I want to see you again." His voice was steady and quiet.

"You're my client."

"That's not what I mean."

"Why?"

"I need something you have."

"The world does."

"And especially me." Ken was frustrated, Suzanne intrigued as they silently rethought strategy.

"What do you need, Ken? You've said that before but it doesn't mean anything." Suzanne whispered and stared at the TV. A commercial for beer, shaving cream and insurance went by. They didn't have much time left. "I need something I don't have. And I think you have it and I'm lonely. Very lonely."

"The world's very lonely. That's what you want from me.

What do you have to offer me?"

He took a last swallow of beer. Suzanne automatically got up to give him another. He stood, worried the brother Michael would return before he asked her. She held the beer in front of him but when he didn't take it she put it on the coffee table and waited.

"What do you want, Ken? And what do you give?"

A polite applause broke on the eighteenth hole as the game was won and they stared at one another. His eyes were unfocused, afraid, knowing the next words would cast a die he didn't want to see, didn't want to read but was inevitable; already in the future.

"What do you want, Ken?" Her voice whispered from dreams.

"I want a woman. A woman beside me. A partner. In business and all life."

The commentator began talking about the players, their talents and deficits, while Suzanne Flint and Kenneth Mansfield Overton looked into each other's eyes for truth in a boring beige apartment, with a coral bathroom, a fridge with beer, yogurt and apples and an unmade bed where two people had been very happy last night. They could smell greasy potato skins and popcorn.

"I want to see you, Suzanne. I can't promise anything but I'm here because of you." His voice cracked in unsteady words, "I'm here for you."

Ken's words opened a frozen winter stream of icicles jutting to melt her heart. Her mother's voice startled her. Instinctively Suzanne reached for her neck to touch the necklace, but it was not there. When she was fourteen Suzanne and her mother were stopped at a red light, on the way to another doctor appointment. During her last years their mother spoke in frenzied phrases at odd times, stuffing information down their reluctant throats. Staring ahead as though the light deserved all her attention she said, "When a man walks out of his way for you when it is not easy for his life, Suzanne, he is serious and it will be good he cares, but you must be careful. His passion will either help you flourish more than you ever imagined or it will take you away from yourself where your true self will die trying to please only him."

Michael's truck stopped in front and they heard the door close. Ken stood and faced Suzanne, bending to see further into her.

"Will you come with me next Saturday? You said you like coral. Have you ever seen the Coral Sand Dunes in southern Utah? We'll take the day and drive there."

"What time?" He had remembered her comment about coral.

"I'll pick you up at six," She nodded, still surprised.

Ken and Michael passed each other on the stairs with a bare glance.

"I can see why you're attracted to the married rat," Michael said as he put the beer in the fridge. Suzanne stood motionless, her eyes frozen in question.

"Oh?"

"Yes. He looks like the real Mr. Crichton's ugly cousin. You must be desperate. How slicked back can an old man's hair be?"

It was Friday when she told Michael she was spending Saturday with Ken and she hadn't wanted to tell him at all. She called only because of their promise to keep reasonable knowledge of each other's unmarried lives. Michael could be relentless with questions if he didn't think he was getting enough information. He told her he was taking Caramello on a real movie and dinner date and Suzanne slipped in she was going to spend the evening alone in the tub with bubbles and watching TV to fall asleep before going on a drive with Ken tomorrow.

"The ugly Mr. Crichton?"

Suzanne sighed, was he really right? She thought quickly and didn't want to answer, "Ken is his name." Mr. Crichton was in her lap.

"You're spending the whole day with him?" the tone was accusatory.

"Yes. Whatever time it takes."

"Married men have families on Saturdays."

She didn't answer. She recognized bait.

"Let's go to X-Cess tomorrow. 'Let that honey down,' isn't that what they say? And you can tell me all about the day with the married man." Saturday nights Michael liked the warehouse turned dance house in an industrial area that was popular for drugs, sex and careless eyeballing. It was a point of reference on the planet for confrontation of the basest good kind.

"I'll be ready," she answered.

"Suzanne," Michael whispered, "take care of yourself. Hell

with the married guy."

She understood. When they thought they were giving each other survival notes they always talked in direct short sentences. When she was eighteen and Michael was sixteen, Marcie left with another date when Michael arrived to pick her up for a high school dance. It was Suzanne who stopped the ringing in his ears with, "Girls like that suck nickels in front of mirrors, Michael. Wait for the women who know sterling." They didn't talk for English teachers, only for each other.

On the way home from work she stopped at the state-owned liquor store and bought two 32 liter bottles of wine. That should be enough, she thought. Enough for what she hadn't thought. At the grocery store she bought containers of yogurt, frozen rice bowls, a quart of milk, a few pieces of fruit, sweet rolls and beer.

Suzanne liked living alone. The small living room separated by a breakfast bar to a postage stamp kitchen would fit in a trailer, but it fit like a familiar sweater and kept her warm and safe when she wanted it. The bathroom separated the living room and bedroom where there was a window shaped like a dining table for six. She could lie in bed and watch the stars in the southern night sky. When she pulled up the blinds and lay on the bed the stars bathed her in silver.

The bathroom was insular. A womb of nowhere when she was in water. The feeling of enclosure was relieved only by the striking coral color of St. Thomas. She lit a candle, ran water, poured wine, gathered a robe to put on after and caught her reflection in the mirror. She was lovely. A slim silky trophy shaped to win. There was satisfaction knowing she was a currently idealized shape. It enhanced marketability and should be used to reach goals. Through the warm, rippling water her belly reflected an underwater world of promise and pleasure. Without the feel of surrounding clothes, life was freedom and lightness. There was also a great fear. That life would not have enough freedom and lightness for her. She was on edge. Near an abyss. Suzanne Flint was afraid.

"Help me, Mom, to get what I want. I don't want to be alone. And neither does Michael."

The next morning when the doorbell rang at three minutes after six Suzanne was ready.

"You're late." She locked the apartment, turned and led Ken down the stairs.

"Yes." Combined surprise and humor considered her gruffness.

She opened the Expedition and reached for the overhead handle to pull herself inside. He saw her swing high and sit low. Ken imagined her as a puppy dog excited for a ride to the park; but seeing her dressed in a white sleeveless cotton blouse with six silver buttons and navy blue shorts, he knew she was not. And no innocent puppy dog girl wore those fuck-me platforms that made her a good three inches taller. It was the tap of the very same sandals against the heel as she settled in the seat that reminded Suzanne it was not Monday morning before tasks were attacked. Instead it was a day of observance.

Ken had coffee, donuts, an orange and a full tank of gas. A thank you for the food and a few sips on hot coffee was all to be heard before they started south on I-15. Suzanne noticed his well ironed cotton tan pants and the button down collared plaid shirt of red, brown, green and white. His sleeves were rolled to below his elbows. A slight wind of cologne was in the air, but she wasn't sure if it was a clean car or him.

"Not much traffic on Saturday." He ventured.

"Saturdays are quiet."

They rode another ten miles, proving Saturdays are quiet. Suzanne began gentle talk about scenery and the growth of houses and businesses along the freeway in the past few years. She moved words gently to break the stiffness of their beginning. Perhaps he would not bother to talk. Some men entered private playgrounds of game warfare when they drove. Silence was expected while they maneuvered, cursed, out distanced and barely saved the lives they gambled as they dodged traffic. This man's driving rhythm was lyrical, cognizant of space. Ken drove 80 miles an hour through Spanish Fork as the conversation paced.

"I had an uncle who lived in Spanish Fork." His head jerked slightly to the right.

"Oh," she answered, wondering if the jerk was natural or a quivering response to fear of what this day meant. Every movement needed assessment.

111

They passed Nephi. "When I was a kid, my parents would always stop at a hamburger joint here."

Suzanne watched him, and decided to be more encouraging, "Sometimes we stopped for gas."

Ken sat straighter. Common ground found with Nephi, Utah. They were 80 miles from home in rolling farm country bordered like a cereal bowl with scraggly mountains.

"There's music in there," he indicated the glove box.

"I don't need music." She didn't want to listen to another woman's choices.

"How do you like your work?"

"My work?"

"Well, yes," Ken defaulted to comfort and what he understood. "Do you like working at Harkness?" Suzanne gave grace. She talked for the next few miles about Harkness, the Monday sales meetings, Wednesday rallies and Friday wrap-ups interspersed with sales to customers like Ken which made it possible for a few old men controlling paper in New York, Wisconsin and Connecticut to be rich. Like she wanted to be some day. It was a routine she understood, one she enjoyed for the purpose of sending her ahead in life. Three years is what she vowed would either show a step up or a step out. Ken felt her sliding hip movements in the seat as she talked and he imagined them in front of him ghosted through the semi-trucks, vans and cars on the highway.

"If something doesn't pay off in a certain time, there's no use staying," she finished.

Ken thought of Cat when they passed the turnoff for Fish Lake. He had been there enough times to report a make believe day. Right now he was involved in conversation that jolted, hit and backed away to silence all the way to the Cove Fort turnoff. Ken hadn't worked so hard for small talk with a female since high school.

At a restaurant in Panguitch, Suzanne had a chicken sandwich, and diet Pepsi. Ken had eggs, bacon and potatoes with coffee. Suzanne talked easier with the grey formica tabletop and the solid feel of floor separating them. Twice a summer, her father would pile the small family in a station wagon with a tent that smelled of oil, sleeping bags, hotdogs and drinks in a cooler, potato chips, a box of cookies and no change of clothes. Off he would take them to drive Utah's or Wyoming's old highways. "But, we never came to restaurants. It was too 'peoplized' as he would say, but I think he just didn't have the money." She didn't tell him about the years that followed those fuzzy sweet memories. Ken didn't hear of his drinking or her mother's ever more vacant eyes and slow anguished death.

As they drove south on highway 89, Suzanne looked up at the clear pulsating September sky and saw airliners fishing across the sky. They were silverfish in water, leaving an arcing trail that left her behind. It was almost noon when they finished the last 12 mile stretch off 89 to The Coral Pink Sand Dunes State Park. Ken parked in the visitor parking lot; a man feeling his blood rush for the woman beside him with almost 300 miles under his belt and another 300 to finish that day. The West is a big place with room for big dreams and very long driving days.

"Look at that!" for the first time her voice was naturally animated. Before the key was finished turning Suzanne was out the door; walking toward the dunes. He followed her over undulating baby girl pink waves on the visitor steps to an overlook. When she stopped it was so sudden he lifted himself on his toes and held back to give her room. She leaned down to undo the straps and take off her very inappropriate sandals.

"I'll see if the sand is too hot or if I need to suffer these shoes." She led Ken down a boardwalk for real sand walking, wriggled her toes for a deep grip and started walking again. Ken saw her toenails were a deep black purple. MoMo had wanted to buy that color, but Cat said no, "It's too old for you."

Yuccas, ocatilla and broom dotted the waving landscape as it rose and fell. The fenced area for foot visitors kept them away from the sweeping large area ahead and below for sand buggies. Only half a dozen could be seen racing like tiny ants in the dunes beyond. Red vertical cliffs rose as a frame bordering the dunes to the east.

For half an hour Ken worked to dance step smoothly next to Suzanne's erratic walking to discover, touch, view from over here and over there. Shoes were off and on and off again as she led in and out of sun-soaked sand. He nodded his head to her exclamations, said yes it was beautiful and quite surprising to find. Her voice was a soothing sound of clear, bubbling water and it washed over him, through him, watering cells he hadn't felt in a long time.

"We should have a beer to celebrate. This is great."

"Sorry I didn't bring any. And none for sale here," he looked around, shrugging his shoulders, lifting his eyebrows to imitate a child looking for sweets. Her smile to his answer, to his gift of this moment swayed inside him. He steadied himself by moving his feet apart to stand more solidly. They sat on a rise of sand and looked beyond to the Joshua trees and desert surrounding this odd land form sprinkled in the background by camping spots with ponderosa pine, grasses and the fading petals of wildflowers.

"This would never make your necklace, but it is coral color." His voice touched a chord of clear need in Suzanne. He understood coral and its blessing.

"It's coral color anyway," she looked over at him with eyes the brightness of reflecting crystal. "I really like seeing different parts of Utah. I'd like to see more of the West, more of the world really, but it's always been important to meet bills and make a living. It was wonderful seeing St. Thomas and we took a ferry to St. John. Beautiful."

He nodded, not taking his eyes from her; not asking who she was with.

"I suppose you've been to a lot of places."

"No. Only a few; not a lot. The business is difficult to leave."

"You have a good business. Your paper sales are up."

Ken laughed an open big release of happiness. He was a cheery Saturday casual men's clothing ad in lunar landscape, "Here we are in a place you seem to like and you switch to business."

"Behind pleasure is business. There is no pleasure like this without business that puts at least enough money in your pocket to visit it."

They wandered at the Pink Sand Dunes State Park over an hour, walking the sands and the paved road through campgrounds to stretch their legs. The day was heating up but the boiling point of July and August had softened with September. Still, miles needed to be retraced and they walked back to the waiting courier Expedition of mighty hunger for dinosaur remains and computer readiness to return north. Conversation was easier and trivial. They talked about paper, printing, people they knew in printing and advertising, clients around town everyone wanted, who paid, who complained.

It was past five when they were a few miles south of Nephi. "You must be hungry. I am. Want a hamburger?"

"If you show me where you went as a kid."

It was dizzying when they slowed to 35 miles an hour in the wide quiet main street. Ghosts lived on Main Street. There were boarded up shops, one restaurant with a dirty front window, two motels with drawn curtains, and a block-sized city park. Ken spotted the corner hamburger stand that didn't look like a day had passed since he was fourteen. He ordered at the outdoor walk up window and Suzanne headed to the back restroom. To wait he stepped away to lean against a cottonwood tree that he remembered having a kick contest on with a cousin. Out of his pocket he pulled his cell phone and dialed.

"Hello, Cat."

"Oh, fine. No fish, though. What was caught was thrown back."

"We're heading back now. In Nephi getting something to eat."

"Okay. See you later. Go ahead and have dinner. I'm eating plenty of junk."

"Love ya. Bye." He did love her. It hurt to feel it. He loved the idea of Cat; the memory of her. The children of her.

At the window he ordered two double burgers and fries. Suzanne came back before they were ready, her lips freshened, he was sure. She leaned against the car door to wait. Ken saw a flickering scene in a Paul Newman movie as he walked to her.

The smell of greasy meat and potatoes exploded in the car, "I don't remember it being this strong."

"It smells great. I'm hungry."

"I thought we'd get some beer and gas," Ken didn't look at her as he pulled into the gas and convenience store parking. She shrugged not commenting. Suzanne listened to and watched the rhythm of his movements while he undid the gas cap, pulled levers and waited. Through the rear view mirror she saw his reflection. There was steadiness, forward timing on a measured beat, no startling or disrupting syncopation. His walk away from the car to the store was a more measured easy swing than at Overton where he rushed from duty to duty. Today his stride didn't call attention, but it took all the space and time it wanted. On his return he put the beer on the floor in the back and opened the front door, lifting himself up by leg action and rocked when he sat heavily in his seat. Or maybe it was her heightened imagination that felt rather than knew what was coming.

"Where will it be? City park or motel?"

Suzanne turned and plumbed his eyes. Heat fell with the desperation of a July rainstorm from her heart to her vagina. His voice echoed to silence. It was up to her. A truck pulled in on the other side of the gas pump and they heard talking of a man and woman followed by the double clap slamming of car doors. They walked to the store and it was quiet again. Ken watched Suzanne's chest rise and fall through silver buttons on cotton.

"Motel."

Twenty minutes later Ken opened two beers and set them on the round table by the window before sitting down on the vinyl chair. The late night traveler's motel was accredited by no one, and updated to 1984. Suzanne was seated in the other chair, her face a checkerboard of late afternoon shadows showing through the sage green curtain. Ken noticed for as many times as he looked at her that day the deep cut of the blouse before the first silver button. Freezing his eyes on the sack of food on the table he didn't look at the U curve of Suzanne's shorts between her legs where there was nothing to see and everything he wanted. Freeway traffic from three blocks away was a low soothing sound, mixed with a dirt bike contest on the television Ken had turned on without noticing. The bag of food was between them, smelling up the room as it had the Expedition.

"I think we'd better eat this food before it eats us."

"I remember it as good."

"I'm sure it is."

She took a long swallow of beer and set it down before turning to the food. Rather than open the food bag Suzanne tore it down the side until it was a placemat with the heaped fries and ketchup. They reached for hamburgers.

"The reason I like my work is because it is different every day," she seemed to be saying to the walls around them. Ken listened for undertones. He had employees. He knew undertones were undertows that could sink an unobservant boss.

"I like that, too. I never know what to expect." She nodded to his words.

"I also like the words."

"The words?"

"Yes." Again she paused. "Laid."

"Paper words?" he knew the texture of laid paper.

"Paper and printing," again she prompted him, waiting for a move; a flicker of humor.

A commercial was on TV but they weren't listening. "Gripper."

Suzanne smiled, took a swallow of beer, a bite of French fry dipped in ketchup and countered, "Felt."

Ken leaned back, happy and relaxed. Again she had named a paper. He knew printing, better, "Hickey."

"Good. I knew that would be soon. Hot spots."

"You're turning to printing."

"Yours are better."

"Work and turn."

She laughed music to his heart, "Score."

"Spread."

"PMS." She referred to standard ink colors in the Pantone Matching System.

"I wouldn't have said that. Gripper."

"You've already said that. Work and tumble."

"Tail in."

"Haven't heard of that," she put a last bit of hamburger down. Her meal was finished.

"It means to put different sheets on the end of a run to see if something works on a different paper. Sort of a freebie or experiment to see if something is possible."

Light was changing in the room. Late September was lengthening shadows and planes of light broken by fully leafed trees in their grandest beauty before undressing.

"An experiment to see if something is possible. Sort of us right now." Suzanne lifted her purse from the floor. She took out a lipstick and swirled it open. Ken watched as she glistened her top lips, her bottom lips; a movement demanding acknowledgment she was with this married man. Holding the lipstick under her blouse from the bottom she lifted her arm to the top opening of the shirt. While watching Ken she drew a line from where her breasts started to a place he couldn't see as she curved to his left under her shirt and swirled her nipple. She pulled the lipstick back, closed the lid and dropped it in her purse.

"Where the hell have you been since June?" Business in her voice demanded he look at her face.

"Seeing if I could live without you." He dropped his eyes like a kid who doesn't want to confess, "I can't."

"It's your move." Suzanne was surely the more comfortable. The prey was hit and wounded. It had only to fall.

Ken stood, walked to the TV and turned it off. Suzanne was sitting, her body outlined by diminishing light diffused through drapes. Ken sat at the end of the bed, magnetism pulled between them. His face was resolute and wild; seeing the future he wanted and walked toward; knowing he could not look back at the destruction he would leave behind. Inching as a spider, he moved his fingertips to the bottom of her open fingers. Slowly, as though they were alone on a dance floor for a last sad love song, he played within them, intertwining his fingers along hers, around hers, tickling her palms and moving by invitation of her hold to her wrists. He lifted her right hand and kissed her palm.

Supplication was not in Ken's vocabulary. He didn't know its meaning and would have considered it an old woman's word if he'd heard it. So, it would be better to say he was pure in motive; a man who understood the power of love and was willing to seek it. Ken had been good. He had stayed at bay all day, circling ever closer in his mind, ever careful of the best way home. Now he pulled her softly toward him onto the bed, as a gently lured treasure until he was the caught one, laying on his back with her kneeling beside him. A car's light swept through the window, lighting his face. Suzanne saw he was consumed by what this was meaning to him. Whether for his wife or for her she didn't know, but it was a good sign. Lust was securely ribboned with depth.

Wriggling her wrists away from his light hold she unbuttoned her shirt. The lipstick mark led from her belly and around her breast as a swirling seashell. A pink-red trail named Sha-Na Boogie connected to her heart and sex.

Inhaling after sex was how Suzanne read meaning. Leaning

on his chest, she slowly rubbed her open palm on his nipples and soft-ly breathed in his skin, sweat, hair. So she would know. Who was this man now laid bare? Was he worth her time or not? She needed to know. His breadth was good. Probably from workdays of walking from his office to the press, lifting paper, making himself part of every job in his shop. Very good. Dark hair shadowed the chest. Age showed in a layer of girth that was strong, not youthful. Full of controlled venom, not showy, useless stride. He had been a man now longer than he had been a boy. Today's 600 mile gift had shown he could caress and not smother. Overall, Suzanne and Ken had successful fishing trips.

CHAPTER ELEVEN

Justin leapt from the couch to answer the phone before MoMo. He sank back down into the soft pillows in front of the TV before talking.

"Oh, hi, Dad," pause, "ya, we're watching TV and having pizza," he paused, "any fish?" Another pause, "You threw them away?" His voice rose, "here, Mom wants to talk to you." Cat was standing with her hand expecting the phone.

Her head bobbed. "We'll be waiting for you. And Ken, I'm glad you're having a good time like this. It's been a long time since you relaxed."

"Dad's friend wasn't feeling well and they stopped in Nephi. They're on the way back." Her voice was toneless; the children didn't notice. As she walked away to stare at the backyard her brow furrowed deeply under the thick brown band of bangs. Colors were lost in shadows of grey, silver, black and white.

Ken worked hard and was gone enough during weekdays. She didn't like Saturdays to be claimed by the ever larger and looming Overton Printing. It was also true it had been a long time since he had taken time to do anything casual and fun with a friend like she did with Eme. Maybe it was good he was fishing. His pole had been leaning unused against the garage wall since they had moved into this house. That it was gone today when she and the children left to run errands and go to a movie was a sign of middle American normality.

Overton Printing was an overbearing visiting relative who didn't know when to leave. She kept that idea to herself since it was Ken's relative. He complained about jobs being late, presses not working and customer demands but he never complained about owning the business. For every ounce of energy it pulled from him, Cat knew it gave two ounces back. Remembering her father's years of weary heartless trips to an office he only tolerated, Cat was glad her man's work touched his heart. Overton was a vortex of demands, emotion, money, energy and time; but it was their vortex and a chosen one. Upset and feeling ignored, she couldn't blame Overton for this evening. She felt guilty she wanted Ken home. She should be glad he was happy. There was nothing to do but have another piece of pizza and watch TV with Justin and MoMo. Both children were up after eleven, holding personal bowls of popcorn when the garage door opened.

"Everyone still up?" Ken's voice questioned in monotone; not a usual booming hello. Again the children were oblivious, but Cat was startled. Why didn't he sound pleased to be here? He must be tired. The day had been long. MoMo ran to him and he lifted her, twirling her in a hug. Justin waved his arm and Ken walked over to toss his hair. Without a word to Cat, without a nod or a wink as he did when the children insisted on attention, he walked to the fridge for a beer. Cat walked to him and put her arms around his middle, squeezing hard, her head resting on his back.

"Okay, I'm home," when he turned from the fridge, he put a hand through Cat's hair, flattening it for the seconds his hand held it.

"Yes, and I'm glad. We missed you."

"Then I'll watch TV with you," he settled in his chair.

"What happened to your friend? Tell me about it." Ken thought she sounded like a left out mom questioning her daughter after the prom.

His eyes were on TV, "Not a friend. The guy from Harkness. Had an upset stomach and couldn't take the drive till it settled. Maybe it was the sandwich he brought. I'm glad you had the chicken for me. I didn't eat his food."

She nodded, watching him. Still he had not made eye contact. "How is he now?"

"Fine, fine," there was a quick look, then he drank beer again.

"Where did you go fishing?"

"I told you. Fish Lake. He has a little fishing boat. My knees are killing me from sitting in it," he glanced at her again and his head twitched to the side slightly.

"Did he get any fish, Dad?" Justin asked.

Ken cleared his throat, "He did. I threw mine back."

"MoMo, you look tired. Why don't you head up to bed." Cat

was gentle with her daughter.

"Not till Justin goes."

"Then please look like you are watching TV instead of sleeping."

"I'll carry her up if she falls asleep," Ken didn't look at her. They all watched a trailing few spots of news, sports, Mel Brooks in Frankenstein and a cop show placed in Los Angeles.

Before long, Justin lifted himself from the couch and walked to his mother for a kiss before starting upstairs. Ken got up to carry MoMo. Alone in front of TV Cat noticed the coldness of the air, the coming of fall, the removal of her family from a circle united around the television leaving her alone. She got up for a glass of water and returned to the end of the couch. Upstairs she heard Ken place MoMo in bed and walk to the bathroom. A water pipe became background sound to the television until it ended. A commercial came on but she was listening to Ken's movements. She decided to be pleased. Routine cadence was returning to life, Ken had a good Saturday with a friend and she had a pleasant day with the children.

Ten minutes went by, perhaps fifteen before she was sure Ken had quietly gone to bed. Later, she didn't know how much later, she turned the TV off and went upstairs to change in the closet where she would not disturb and stepped lightly to the bathroom to wash her face and brush her teeth.

Sunday was a day of quiet solitude. Everyone was involved in the private music of a day of rest. Each person was a solo note standing alone. MoMo played with dolls, worked in a science book and walked down the street to play with Steph. Justin was on the computer in his room, did some homework, sent e-mails to Walt and two friends and watched TV. Ken straightened shelves in the garage, watched baseball and football, and took the Expedition for a car wash to 'stretch sore muscles from fishing.' Cat felt out of rhythm. Unmoored, too busy. Her movements were not as languid, not as sure or relaxed as everyone else's. She felt caught without knowing what bars surrounded her. A kitten in a trap, clawing with nothing to complain about. Something under her feet was giving but she didn't know what. Maybe it was seeing the children grow so quickly. She vacuumed, cleaned a drawer, straightened Justin's room, trimmed marigolds, read three chapters in a book and cooked a fall dinner of pot roast.

"Ken, I love you," Cat spoke as they nestled in the dark. She was not sleepy but she needed to be in bed with Ken. Her mother would say it was what a wife should do. She would say she wanted Ken. His lust. Him.

It was fabric brushing against itself that she heard first. His arm reached around to caress her head. Awkwardly finding her in the dark, his lips kissed her head and he whispered, "Lina. Dear Lina." He leaned away and slept.

Again she dreamed of someone knocking at the door and she didn't know whether to answer or not. Whether to recognize or not.

Eme was posturing. Cat didn't know if it was sincere or melo-dramatic. "It's not going to work. It's not going to work." Though they were separated by telephones, Cat could see her friend's hands and arms flailing as she talked, wiping dry cheeks with tissues for effect. "It's not going to work," she paused. "I want it to." Her voice trailed in high drama.

"But Eme, dear," Cat consoled, "You really don't know him. He's imagination. He isn't worth your time. He's, he's," she gave a female cliché, "he's not worth it."

"Every man is worth it." Eme's heart swelled in romance.

Cat shrugged. She didn't have enough experience to assess that one.

"He never played straight with me."

"How about dinner tonight? We'll talk about men. I know one. You know a hundred. We'll meet in the middle."

Eme laughed, "Okay. But Ryan is out of my life as of now. Maybe we won't talk about him at all."

"Maybe not," Cat liked the idea but doubted it.

Cat called Ken at the office from Shiner's. "Ken, Eme's got a problem."

"Eme's always got a problem."

Her problems were a running joke and she appreciated the genuine kindness he always showed Eme. "Well, tonight is another one and we're going to dinner. Can you get the kids?"

"Yes," he paused, "I can."

"Good. I won't be late. She just needs to air out."

"I know. We'll be waiting for you."

"Thanks, Ken. Love you."

"See you later."

Over a pasta dinner with salad, breadsticks and wine, Eme began. "I was talking to Ryan and he was absorbed, just absorbed. We're talking about fruit and dancing. I know it sounds crazy but somehow in the middle of talking about grapes from Argentina, dancing comes up and it seems he's taking salsa lessons. I'm almost ready to invite him to dance at Rafael's Worldorium, the Latin Rhythm Emporium and I swear, Cat, I swear, we are that close, and this tiny redhead the width of a toothpick walks by and he says, 'Have you got your grapes?' and he fades off to her!"

Cat was not sure whether Ryan was to be discounted and removed to history or just temporarily set aside. She waited for clues. Nuances were important. Eme took a bite, so Cat ventured, "So is he worth the agony or not?"

Eme was a pouting four-year-old staring at her food, "No. When I got home I wrote his name on an old stinky abalone and crushed it." In the whole restaurant all Cat saw was Eme stabbing a mushroom.

"Ryan is out. Is Sheldon still around?"

"Sheldon. He is always Sheldon. He wants to get married."

"Congratulations, Eme. Is that proposal number 45 or one thousand?"

"Maybe ten, but who's counting."

"Speaking as an old married lady, me."

"Why?"

"I can't imagine the romance, the wonderfulness of being wanted by so many. Me. I live by the demands of one."

"Demands? Does Ken demand?"

The waiter hovered, filling water glasses, "maybe not demand exactly, but marriage expects. It is a game of anticipated and expected fulfillment. Or else."

"And not being married is a game of unfulfillment." Eme sat back in her chair.

"Maybe they are the same," Cat's eyes lighted, "want to hear something I read today?"

Eme was accustomed to Cat's small flights to literary safety.

She picked up her wine glass and waited.

"It's from *Without Stopping* by Paul Bowles. *'Relationships with other people are at best nebulous; their presence keeps us from being aware of the problem of giving form to our life.'* What do you think of that?"

"I think, how can you have a life without relationships? Does he mean form a life without other human beings?"

"I've got something I want to show you." Cat's eyes waved in joy, "On the way home we have to take a drive so I can show you."

"What do you see?" Cat had the voice rhythm of free and happy taps on solid wood floor as she turned her head to view the valley's expanse. They were pulled to the side of the road with the Audi still running as they viewed the valley.

"I see a wonderful place. My city. A twinkling city that is mine and I am grateful." Eme stared straight ahead at the flickering lights teasing night's blackness over Salt Lake.

"It is a wonderful place isn't it?"

"Yes."

They were on Chandler Street, a residential mountain road facing west. Late dusk shadows reflected blue black hues tailing the sunset now beginning Hawaii's cocktail hour.

"Look Eme, I want you to see this." Cat turned the car off and moved the seat back. "I have come up here before. Only a few times, but I love it. It gives me a new friend. Just below on the mountainside is the cemetery. Dark, foreboding, of death and darkness."

Her hand swept across the windshield at the city cemetery, surrounded on all sides by valuable city land. The cemetery was the largest in America, the land laid aside by shortsighted pioneers who thought it more important to live by their growing crops in the valley and who lacked any vision of the monetary value of seeing across a valley in generations to come. Cat's arm lifted and the tip of her pointing finger became a paintbrush, "Then the city is bright, glowing, vibrant. You can hear it from here. I love it. See where we live, travel everyday, laugh, dance, go to work and school, have parties. Cry. I felt it all." Cat was suddenly quiet. She retrieved a bottle of wine, opener and two Styrofoam cups.

"The blackness of the cemetery is a swath below us and

before the city. Cat said with excitement as she handed Eme the wine bottle and opener. "An artist's brush. The city. The lights. It's almost impossible to tell depth from up here. You have to study how depth and perception fool you or you will never know. Did you know that?"

"No, but I believe it." Eme was turning the cork; almost ready to pour.

"And look, Eme," she glanced up as the cork popped.

"See across the valley?"

Eme looked, trying to see what Cat was talking about.

"There is Yearning Woman." Cat stared ahead.

In deference to something she knew was important to Cat, Eme was silent before she said in equal tones of acceptance and reverence, "Yearning Woman."

"See?"

On the Westside of the valley, perhaps twenty miles away Eme looked to the serrated horizon of the Oquirrh Mountains. Cat's finger outlined a woman's reclining head. Hair cascaded toward the Great Salt Lake, a nose, mouth, throat, nipple with a small light, perhaps a radio tower she thought, reclined to a slim waist, and the hips of a woman. All of her was resting above the valley as silent symbol to female life. She needed night shadow and imagination to reveal herself. Daytime would never see her. Cat held her cup out and Eme poured. They regarded Cat's artist canvas of Yearning Woman.

"Are you going to marry Sheldon, Eme?"

"I like being with him."

"That counts."

"He's good to me, smiles a lot even if he doesn't always laugh."

"You laugh enough for both of you. He thrives on your laughs."

Eme stared ahead, her voice serious. "I always wanted everything, Cat. Every man. Everything. I wanted tall, skinny, short, big, dark, blonde, sexy, serious, adventurous, reclusive. Now I would be settling for part of that. One person does that."

It certainly did. But in her librarian voice she urged, "It doesn't mean you stop talking to men. They don't disappear in front of you. You just don't sleep with them. That's all." Catalog that statement, because in the end the only ones who don't question that are women who don't observe their men.

"No, and Sheldon doesn't like it when I talk with other men when he's around. That's the only time he huffs."

"Talk or flirt?"

"I don't know the difference and he knows that."

"You don't want to be alone, Emeraude Collins."

"Sheldon is a good man. A trustworthy one. That's important. And the sex is good. A time or two it's been excellent."

"Well, what could be better?" Cat shifted in her seat. Lately, hers had been unconnected and cool. If she gave her fears air by talking to Eme they might fly away. The words stuck in her throat. They hadn't been named and they couldn't be recognized.

For the last two weeks Ken was cold and official. There was a strain in his voice she never heard before, not even when Overton was too busy to breathe anything but ink or paper, or too slow to sustain itself. Even with the children he was abrupt and didn't meet their eyes. The sex on one night was automatic and remote. She felt used and moved aside, curling her knees when it was over.

Then suddenly, without reason, he came home one night warm and huggy like he hadn't been for a long time. He insisted they order Chinese food for dinner, but didn't want it delivered before eight because he was going to dance with MoMo to her favorite music in her room before playing on the computer with Justin. Then he would make gin and tonics to have before dinner arrived.

Pleased at the change in atmosphere, the children were relaxed enough after dinner to take themselves off to bed, happy to leave their parents smiling at one another. Ken and Cat talked for an hour about their first years, when the babies were born and for the first time Ken was caught up in the gauzy, not always accurate picture of that time's simplicity, true love and a young couple's purpose. He was nostalgic and dear and the sex that night was a mending of close heeled yesterdays Cat hoped would not return.

"What could be better is what you and Ken have." Eme's words were pinpricks.

Cat started the car, "Marriage is a long time, Eme. There are ups and downs."

"You mean Ken's not perfect."

"Even Ken is not perfect."

Eme turned smiling, "Are you?"

She shook her head, "Especially not me. But I do try to hide the imperfections. Only you and Ken could come up with a complete list."

"Oh, I'll bet you keep a few imperfections to yourself to savor. Or perhaps Yearning Woman knows them."

Eme was a sweetheart.

When Cat was home she opened the refrigerator door, poured wine, sat among her petunias and marigolds and then went upstairs to slide under Ken. Awakened for sex. His scrubby face and heavy hips were comfort, his hands were home.

CHAPTER TWELVE

Suzanne was walking toward a client's door when her phone rang. Automatically, she stepped to the side of the walkway as though traffic needed accommodation. The sun blazed in the first days of October through green, orange, yellow and red leaves before falling through a prism of angel light around her.

"Hello, Ken,"

"I can't make it tonight. I've got to pick up the kids."

There was nothing to say.

"I'm sorry, Suze. I'll be there tomorrow night." He stuttered.

"Maybe I'll be busy."

"I'll be there tomorrow." They raced to hang up before the other.

Damn married men. Tomorrow's the showdown. Life was too short and too long to be weighed down with a married man who wasted time. Either he had something worthwhile or he didn't. Old John hadn't been treated any different. Nor had he treated her any different. Give or I don't buy. She gave and he bought. Their wordless contract had been show me what you've got before I give. He had taken her to dinner, had a preview lay in a beige apartment and then bought tickets to St. Thomas. They were even when Suzanne called it quits. Old John acknowledged it. "It was a good week Suzanne. Think of me when you wear that necklace." No, Old John she thought, I think of my mother. Mother. She watches over me with that necklace, not you.

Twenty minutes went by with the client. Half of it spent talking about paper and printing and half of it spent talking about children she would never meet who were excellent soccer players. Behind all her business and complimentary words was anger that Ken put her on hold to other loyalties. Anger she was made a party to deception for the convenience of a man who cared for a woman who should be smart enough to know what was going on with her own husband but was apparently too stupid to recognize the last few weeks. Her eyes blazed as she shook her client's hand good-bye. The over-worried, underbidding printer who operated on fear fumes imagined for a flickering moment she was flirting with him; she seemed so alive. But she turned too abruptly and he was disappointed and then disappointed with himself that he wanted it so much.

As soon as she was outside she called Michael but it went to voicemail and she didn't leave a message. Before she unlocked the car door she knew she wasn't going to call him again tonight. He would be too happy to hear her anger at the married man, who he called the ugly Mr. Crichton. No, she didn't want agreement the situation was working out as predicted. She wanted prerogative preserved.

Before her next call she moved the seat back to give legroom to easily stretch across the passenger seat. The hem of her dark blue dress slid up her thighs but she didn't close her knees. Appreciatively, she noticed her own body beneath her and arched before leaning back and resting her head on the window. As she dialed she licked her lips.

"Hi," she practiced languid. Sugarloaf was now a friend who understood silly.

There was a pause before the deep, cavernous, wonderful voice resonated for her to fall into deeply. "Hello, Suzanne."

"I'd like to see you tonight."

Again there was a pause. She didn't know if he was maneuvering traffic or thinking through his answer.

"That could be arranged."

"I want Chinese food."

Sugarloaf gave a three note chuckle. His body heat came through the phone. He knew he was being used, "I want beer."

"We'll exchange at nine-thirty."

When Michael's number came up a few minutes later on caller ID she didn't answer. Her evening was arranged and private.

Between five and seven Michael called three times. On the fourth call Suzanne relented and answered. She said she was tired and needed to sleep. Oh, and by the way, she was busy with some things at the office tomorrow so she'd talk with him on Friday. How was it going with Caramello?

His voice turned into warm marshmallow and she was angry with him, too.

It was six-thirty Thursday, and Ken hadn't come. Mr. Crichton didn't know if he was being petted or disciplined under Suzanne's hands, but he received attention so sporadically and emotionally that he was willing to suffer the uneasy pleasure a little longer. If cats are as intelligent as some people think, he knew what she was thinking. Who did Ken think he was? Clogging up her life like a bad cold. Something to be endured, not enjoyed. She needed better. More permanent. More inclusive. More giving. It was him who said he needed to be home by eight or there would be problems. Every minute counted and now that it was 6:32; at that moment she made up her mind.

At 6:38, Ken tapped at the door. Mr. Crichton stepped out when she answered, knowing he was not part of this alliance. His back hunched as he passed Ken. The shadows of October slanted through the ends of the drapes, filtering the room in yellow greys. Ken leaned forward and then back. Instinct said not to move quickly. He needed to be allowed.

"Ken." She took a large breathe. Over the last two days she thought and rethought her next move. At noon today she called Raylene.

"Sounds like the man is feeling a steel trap around his ankle."

"Then he needs to bend down and take it off. Either for his wife or for me."

"You move fast and you are unmerciful."

"What would you do?"

"I don't know the man. I don't have your problem."

"Raylene. You know what I mean."

"Right now he's lost in your body. That could go on for a lifetime. If you want him to notice anything between your ears you need to call his attention to it."

"What? Start reading the dictionary in bed?"

"No," Suzanne's anger let sarcasm in the door. "I mean give him a piece of yourself he has to respond to. Make him choose an emotion other than sex. You'll see a little more of him. Maybe, if Michael's lucky, you won't like him at all."

"Michael talks too much." As she over-petted Mr. Crichton she thought about what to say to Ken. Now as he stood at her door she hoped the words would be right.

In Ken's defense, his eyes now watered from keeping his sight on her face while he felt her chest rise and fall. Her lovely soft chest. He nodded, urging her to talk so he would be allowed to touch. From his mother to Cat to his employees he had learned sometimes women needed their words to hit the air to evaporate and male interruptions only slowed things down.

"Ken, this isn't working."

An already deflating balloon, he wilted further.

"Ken, this isn't what I want." Silence amplified the sound of a car driving down the roadway. He felt air leaving his body.

"Ken, I need you, all of you, or I don't want you at all."

They watched each other in ghostly terrible pantomime. What one did to shift from one hip to the other, the other did on the opposite side. They neither gave nor gained as they watched, knowing this was the moment of their story.

Since returning on Saturday night a month ago from the Pink Sand Dunes they met over a dozen times. Five times during lunch, once on a Thursday while Cat added numbers back at the office. Three times he paid cash for a motel room; twice in the Expedition. Suzanne wouldn't let him come to her apartment during office hours. Let him be inventive. It was inspiring to watch a man who truly needed.

They met in Suzanne's apartment only on off hours. Usually it was a soft wake-up call before seven, between Ken's home and Overton Printing. A time no one noticed. He had a key Suzanne warned would be replaced if he didn't call first. Other times were on the way home. Time in fuzzy increments counted by a wife and two children; allowed and watched because they trusted and needed his shelter.

"Ken," she stopped. "I need a beer Ken, and then I need to tell you something." She sat on the couch and waited. Ken stood dumbly before realizing he was to get the beer. He returned with two and sat facing her. Time had density that was settling under his heart.

"You remember my coral necklace?" Ken nodded. She decided to begin mercifully, laying any fault on her before she turned the table. Using the necklace as an opener made it easier. "There was a reason I chose coral," she cleared her throat for direction and force. Suzanne was unafraid of what she wanted, but she was always careful how she worded it to men. She had not found a man who understood and it was in talks like this that she had lost others. Ken was ignoring his beer.

"I need my mother's protection. A working single world is full of danger. We never really got along when she was alive. Constantly, we fought and she always disagreed or argued with me even when she agreed.

"Yet when she died, I knew I lost the one person who wanted my happiness as much as I did. So, when I learned that coral was worn by children as protection, I knew it would be a way for me to feel a little bit of my mother still." She took a gulp of beer and looked at Ken to see how he was listening. While she talked she darted her eyes away from him, giving them both privacy, but it was now time to see if she should proceed or he was lost and angry at being pulled into a female world he did not want to understand.

His full eyebrows were pulled inward and his eyes stared at her. He was forward on the chair with his elbows on his knees, his hands resting together in front of him.

"My mom made me think. She never wanted me to be ditzy and she always expected me to have reasons for what I did. I thought she was easier on Michael than me. He was expected to just 'be' like some primitive man presence. But then Michael was always good and I was always…curious." She caught a smile from him.

"Maybe I don't need to go on longer. What it comes down to is this." She set the stage as gently as she knew how. The coral was preamble. Now she was at the showdown that sent others away. She felt drunk, as though her words were unable to stay inside where they belonged. "I do know what I want and I'm looking for it now. I want a man. A man who can be a true partner, that I don't have to ever 'try to make happy' just because he's the man. I expect to give unconditionally, mind, body and soul, but I expect the same. I believe you and I could build a life," she shifted uncomfortably. "We have the parts. You know printing, numbers, running a company. I know people, paper. I'm not afraid of work and I want it to pay. I sell. Clients don't leave me. Or complain. Harkness knows that. I like your strength and power and I expect to whack it around from time to time. On some things I don't bend. And that turns me on about myself, so I don't expect to change."

She paused and then stuttered to start again, "I am attracted to you. I like the way your eyes can look mean, but I know they're your curtain from the world. They'll get me what I want." Again she paused to silence until she spoke after a swallow of beer.

"We could fuck a few more times as a good-bye if we both want. This could be the end of us." Pleasant exit alternatives helped make male answers genuine.

When Ken was sure Suzanne was not going to say more his voice rumbled like loose stones over boulders. He hadn't known he was going to say them.

"Or this could be our beginning."

Suzanne went to the kitchen and got a match to light the mango scented orange candle on the kitchen counter. She set it on the coffee table before sitting. The flickering flame, standing straight at 2 inches became the focal point.

"Ken, you have a lot of obstacles. A wife and children and the life you have is very settled."

He nodded silently and she saw a river of feeling was weeping through him.

"I want you, Suzanne."

She nodded, waiting to hear what that meant. It occurred to her to walk over and put his hand on her breast. That is what she had done twice before. First with Darren and two years later with Beese, as he was called, short for Beesley. She received the sex she wanted, she also received months more of indecision being played from their power. Yes, she would have liked to be touched and satisfied, but what she wanted to hear was his head's decision, not his dick's.

"You're something, Suze," he looked at her as she looked at him, except it alarmed her to see the slightest smile on his lips. "I'm on the ropes. This is buy or leave time. I recognize it at the office, but I've never heard it this way."

They sat with nothing to say. What was required was a move. Suzanne got up for another beer. She didn't offer one to Ken. She knew he had to be leaving and she didn't want to make things easy.

"I need to think, Suzanne," the whole idea was so overwhelming he repeated it, "I need to think, Suzanne."

"I understand, Ken, you've got a life and I want one. Not one borrowed when you can find the time." She stood for him to go. At the last moment she couldn't help herself. Suzanne slid against him, urging him to kiss and touch her with hands reaching for life and closeness as fully as he could through linen before she opened the door and sent him away.

CHAPTER THIRTEEN

Thirty minutes later Ken smell the basil, oregano, tomato, beef filled air when he walked in the door. Cat perfected the lasagna after Justin was born and it became a signature dish. It kept well in the oven, made leftovers, wasn't expensive and it greeted him when he walked in the door once a month for ten years. This fragrance greeted him more than a hundred times, not counting leftover nights.

The television was playing to no one, so he walked to the French doors. A shadow of Cat reflected on the patio as she knelt on the dirt to plant. Puppeteer light angled from her ending in night's darkness, seeming to pick her up with strings of light.

"I'm home."

Cat jumped to walk to him, smiling, ready to kiss. Her arms started to extend and then fell away, flattened to her sides against desire and will. She stood by him confused she could not reach up, afraid, telling herself she must be wrong. Must be wrong. Bodily response was not predetermination. The man she had fallen into years ago with dowser arms now kept her away with the same strength. Ken turned away, not noticing.

She whispered, "Good. I was planting the few last bulbs and it isn't very cold though it is almost dark. MoMo is upstairs reading and Justin's still at Walter's. I'll call him." Her voice continued behind him as they returned to the house, "You know that meeting for Cancer Care House last week? I forgot to tell you. I'm working on the silent auction. So plan on donating."

"Pick something out. Haven't the kids eaten yet?" His voice pitched.

"I gave them Daddy Food to hold them a bit. Dried apples and pretzels. I want a family dinner." She dialed Walter's and when it was picked up, Cat turned away. "Hello, Cindy. How are the boys?" Pause. A nod. "Well, please send Justin home, thanks." Cat replaced the phone and walked to the flatware drawer.

"He shouldn't be walking home in the dark."

Cat looked up, surprised. Justin was half a block away, 700 feet, at seven forty-eight in sanctified suburbs without previous problems; secured with illusion that money buys on a quiet dusk in October. Was a sudden protection of a son he often chided for living a safe and overprotected life a barb at her or genuine concern for his son?

"I'll go look for him," Ken headed to the front door.

Chastised without knowing why Cat took the lasagna out of the oven and continued setting the table. Ken gathered the children in front of TV while Cat finished fixing dinner. When she called, they sat at the table, with a background of canned laughter and stilted lines.

Cat held up her hands and they all joined in Ken's quick blessing. As their hands pulled away Cat gave private blessing to the head of each person at the table. Ken's boot brown hair slicked back was earth, mountain dirt, life sustaining. Justin's had golden swath through caramel, youth, freedom. MoMo's was honey silk and fall sunrise. Hers was bark, reaching through cavernous depth hiding light and unrealized, unacknowledged truth.

"How was your day, MoMo?" Cat began.

"Annie wouldn't sit with us at lunch, so it was Alicia, Steph and me," Honey red hair beamed light. The continuing story of girls growing up.

"I see," Cat nodded, "when you're older girlfriends won't be this way." Ken was not listening. Distended brows hid his eyes and himself as he stared at lasagna as though he were being forced to eat at an endurance trial. Cat put her fork down and smoothed her hair behind the ear. She needed to hear. Justin seldom began talking without urging and it was usually Ken who prompted him, but tonight Ken was silent.

"How did the math test go?" Cat asked.

Justin shrugged. School was not his big concern.

"Okay?"

"Okay."

Forks hit plates without resonance or melody. Cat tossed between concern and irritation. "How was your day, Ken?"

Hearing his name, he looked straight at her, his eyes suddenly visible and staring as though to a dart board. The children sank in shadows, "We're rerunning two jobs that could amount to a loss of $3500 in paper alone. Mary Ellen disconnected a call from the German people I needed information from on the 40 inch press and Rhonda left early because the boyfriend couldn't watch her kids another half hour. I need a new pressman but they want another five dollars an hour than I've been paying, which translates to eight dollars with taxes and god knows what I'm supposed to give in benefits."

The children looked down while Ken and Cat looked at each other. Justin got up, carrying his plate to the kitchen, rinsing it and putting it in the dishwasher. MoMo looked confused but she followed.

"Can I have ice cream?" she said.

"Yes, you both can,"

Justin looked in the freezer, handed his sister an ice cream sandwich and they headed upstairs. Ken and Cat listened to their children settle. Only one door closed. MoMo had gone into Justin's room.

"You had a stressful day." Her whisper was a statement.

Ken nodded. His lasagna barely touched. Cat got up and walked toward the kitchen. She did not turn around as she spoke, "Would you like a drink, Ken? I could enjoy a glass of wine."

"A martini."

"You'll need to make that yourself. I'll get the olives." Their voices held steady.

He went to the kitchen to begin the slow, lovely, inviting recipe of martinis. Six to one he liked them and he didn't do this very often. Cat put three stuffed olives on a plastic skewer. She hoped he would give her one to enjoy. A custom that would show he was irritated at life, not her.

"I'll check on the children." Cat went upstairs to see what they were doing as Ken shook the aluminum shaker until ice fractured in crystals on the outside.

"Goodnight, Mom," Justin wanted it over. He said his words and moved away. MoMo leaned into her mother's arms, urging Cat to envelope her.

"I'll see you in the morning," she said after kissing MoMo's forehead. She left wondering if she had dispensed love medicine to those who needed hope or she was being sent as lead warrior in protection of the innocent. Before returning downstairs she went into the bathroom to prepare. Cat smoothed her face with cream, brushed her hair and held the cologne a foot above so it would fall in sweet desire, just heavy enough to knock out the lasagna. Lipstick added shine to her lips. Her lips were still full and soft she assured herself, they hadn't hardened in old women's judgment lines.

"Is the third olive for me?" Cat was afraid to leave the olive's fate to chance. She walked to the family room of chair, table and couch, lighted in the shape of an igloo by silver TV light.

Ken leaned forward, "Here, my little Lina, it is yours." She lifted the olive between her fingers with dainty show and breathed out. He must have rethought his brusqueness. Always he could quell her fears with the right words.

"Lina."

This man's emotion always made her feel beautiful. Youth had been kind but not abundant to Cat. As a young woman she was neither remarkable nor unremarkable. What fullness of cheek and gain of weight had marked the passing years, was a surprisingly nurturing kind beauty that invited people to warm themselves in her acceptance. The mental island she kept herself in was losing shoreline to the warm harbors of welcoming eyes. Strangers, store clerks, people on her silent auction committee felt kindly and fully accepted by Cat's gentleness.

Ken could not look into her blue eyes of heart-centered caring. Cat, he ruefully thought, had simply become more of what she was when they met. The promise of unquestioned love and true acceptance that attracted him in the beginning now felt like a heavy coat keeping both of them away from themselves and each other. She had played steady with duty, obligation, and responsibility wrapped in affection. It was him who now needed a rough and tumble comfort and hard knock conscience she could not offer. He married believing love had one meaning. Now all he knew was his heart ached into stone and cried without tears until Suzanne touched it.

She waited for him to continue.

"I'm tired, Lina. Things are closing in on me. I'm not sure anymore," his voice was lost life.

Watching his face, she remembered the words from a book she read last week, *"Note that the tips are atrimble even on the stillest days when men of duller sense feel no movement of air. So should a true scout be - ever more alert and aware than others."* Waterlily, had been written in 1948.

"Lina," his voice was quiet. Reflective. The six to one martini was working. "I'm making another martini. Would you like more wine?" She nodded yes. It was important to be part of the group to gain information. He didn't speak until he made the martini, poured the wine and brought the drinks back. "Please leave a big tip for the cabana boy who brings drinks."

Cat smiled. He was a dear cabana boy. But how was the man? He settled as an oversized tired dog into his TV chair across from where she sat on the couch. Cat noticed his shoulders, the stiffness of his lip, the straightness of his hair slicked back to meet the world on Ken's decided terms, perhaps not his heart's desire. She always wondered if he did things for himself or programmed expectations.

"What do you want, Cat?" he uttered from beneath his usual voice. The notes were a hunter's fair warning. Alarmed, she looked at him. Danger filtered the air. Cat knew the sound of a pulled trigger before gunfire.

"What do you want, Cat?" again the voice was guttural with liquor, insisting.

"What do you mean?" She spoke for clarification, time, in hopes this was not a return to Labor Day.

"What is your life's desire?"

Quicksand was beneath her curled feet on the couch. The absurdity of his question laid bare the overwhelming abundance of their lives and made her angry. As though life's desire was even thought of by 99% of the world's population. She took a drink to gain time and began slowly, knowing she lived in middle America where such stupid questions were given serious consideration, "I suppose I want peace. Happiness." Did she sound like Miss America? "Our children to grow well. You and I to be happy." Ken looked at her in unmeasured sadness. She had not answered correctly.

"You can't have all that. It's impossible. What do you want? We can't walk around happy every moment of our lives," The denial of wanting happiness with her and the children was so startling Cat didn't answer. "You've always wanted everything, Cat. Everything. It's impossible, Cat."

Cat listened; not understanding. She remembered wanting

love. Life. She did not remember wanting everything. The fancier house, the better clothes, the bigger cars, those had been Ken's. Now she felt blamed for them. She had been a teacher, ready to gain on life inch by inch. She had pulled behind his driving force in support, not as a leader. Yes, she enjoyed all of it, but she thought it fallout of being Ken's wife, not a result of being Catalina. Did accepting all those things mean she wanted them?

"I don't understand, Ken. What do you mean?"

"I mean," he paused and leaned forward. She leaned back away from his aggression, not loving interest, "that you are confused. You are not ready to meet the challenge."

She leaned back further, "The challenge?"

"Life is a challenge, Cat, didn't you know that?" His eyes blazed. He gulped the martini like punch. "Where have you been? Shiner's? Hiding in a bookstore?"

Cat's chest shook. She held her breath to keep it from shaking twice. It might invite anger. She listened for the children but could not tell if they were asleep or listening by the stairs. Her left hand gripped the couch.

"I don't think you are ready for the challenge. Not many people are." He turned away in disgust. Silence was punctuated by TV. Ken turned back to face her.

"Lina. You and I married a long time ago." He waited like an overly patient, overly strict schoolmaster until she nodded. "Do you think you can live up to Overton Printing? The demands of business and life?"

Cat's eyes widened, watching. She nodded to appease and keep the house silent for the children. The banker's daughter wanted peace and order.

"There's a lot to it, my little Lina," for the first time in fifteen years the word Lina was a weapon, a sarcasm greasing his lips. From their first date until now it had been an endearment. "But you," his head moved slowly from side to side. Cat couldn't tell if it was gin or hate that slackened his cheeks so slightly, "you will not be up to the task."

Ken stood, in holy understanding of Cat's failures, moved his lips in reverent knowledge and walked up the stairs.

Cat did not move. She counted his drinks. Wine at dinner

while she drank milk. Three martinis. It could be blamed on that. Cat heard without movement when Ken got up at 4:50, showered and dressed. She heard him through the master bath door and closet. He was dressed and ready when he turned out the light, opened the door and walked to her side of the bed. Cologne was around him like a shield of power. He touched her hair and patted twice, "Good-bye, Cat. I'll see you at the shop."

"Yes," she whispered. He left in darkness, as sure of his steps as if they were in morning light. He walked downstairs, out the door and opened the car door. The rising of the garage door shook house timbers, like a house skeleton now transparent and lonely in pre-dawn darkness. For an hour she lay without moving, her mind blank. She didn't know what to think and what came next, she didn't want to think. Life should be pleasant. Her parents' lives had been pleasant. Days followed each other in comfortable routine, toward years that slowly added to life's dowry of simple pleasures. Thirty years ago a small town banker's life provided a quiet but secure home for a book-ish daughter and a woman who enjoyed making cookies and polish-ing furniture she inherited from her own mother's house.

Ken's excitement and ambition for life and Overton had been a foreign aphrodisiac but had happiness been the cost? There wasn't any reason not to be happily contented every day of life when they had as much as they did. They worked. They were honest. They had two healthy beautiful children, a wonderful house, food, everything. They should be grateful and happy. To want more was obscene and selfish.

Mary Ellen and Rhonda were sitting in their office places when Cat walked in Overton after taking the children to school. Rhonda began telling her about having to leave early the day before and how she would make it up through the lunch hour. Usually the three of them talked for a few minutes when Cat arrived. The time provided a break for Mary Ellen and Rhonda and Cat enjoyed hearing the harmless office gossip, what movie was worth seeing and the superficial entertaining details in each other's lives. As she sat in her chair she saw Ken in his office across the way. She waved, hoping he would accept it as a peace offering. He shrugged back.

Todd came from the back holding a box with a thousand

brochures and put them on Rhonda's desk, "You need to take this to old 'we press on'."

"You mean Presson's?"

"You know I do, sweetie, I'm delivering the rest of the order to UPS, but I need you to get this to them so they don't have a heart attack."

Printers often trade work behind heavy curtains, hiding sleight of hand. They get the job done on schedule and in budget, but who puts the job on their presses and keeps the profit is between printers. Presson's subbed a good size five color job they couldn't do effectively to Overton. They needed the thousand samples now to take to their customer before it shipped to a convention in California. Rhonda walked to Ken's office for the keys to the Expedition.

Mary Ellen was still first on phones with Cat second. She turned attention to her computer and answering another call and Cat turned to the stack of jobs and invoices neatly stacked for her to rearrange for billing.

With a handful of papers in her left hand she headed to the back shop. Anything she wasn't sure of matching correctly or questioning amounts, she would ask Ken or whoever in back was involved in the job. Cat stood at the door of Ken's office first. "I've got a question about this job." She stepped to his desk and put the paper in front of him. "Would it be correct that you ran the paper on 80-pound when the order was for 70-pound?"

He answered clearly, as though he were onstage projecting his answer for Mary Ellen to hear, "It was cheaper to run it on 80-pound and we called the customer and they approved it." His eyes were lifeless and unseeing. Cat nodded, picked up the paper and backed out to find the two other people she needed to question. She was back at her desk when Rhonda returned.

"Here Cat," she walked briskly to Cat. "You must have left this in the car. I found it wedged by the seat when I moved it. You probably thought it was lost."

She put the lipstick on Cat's desk. The case wasn't familiar. The color was bright, shiny, not the soft deeper shades she liked. On the bottom it read, ShaNa Boogie. "This isn't mine, Rhonda. Has anyone else been driving the car?"

Before answering a ringing line she hurried an answer, "Not

that I know of." Cat set it on her desk and watched it like it was about to germinate.

Pizza arrived just after noon and was placed on the table in the kitchen. Cat got three pieces on one plate, napkins and two drinks.

"Ready for lunch?"

Ken looked up. "I guess so. That time, huh?" His eyes were heavy lidded and puffy. Last night had worn.

"You've been working in here pretty steady."

"My ear's starting to hurt from the phone calls."

"Maybe you need help. Another sales person with you running production."

"For now Dan's all I can afford. He's keeping the presses going and I need to connect with our major customers."

Cat lifted the lipstick from her pocket and put it standing between them on his desk, "Rhonda found this in the car. It's not mine. Who else has been driving the car?" Her voice was neutral beige without expectation but what she saw was a body shudder from Ken's forehead, down his face, neck, shoulders and chest. It was a quick gulping sound while he was chewing that caused her to look and see the shudder and his eyes dilate just in time before they were normal.

"Where did you find that?"

"I didn't," she watched closely, heartbeat starting to sound in her ears. "Rhonda found it and it's not hers or mine."

Ken looked at pizza and shook his head, "I don't know where its from."

The lipstick stood as a shiny bullet between them during lunch; each of them unwilling to touch it. The steady beat of the press in the back room, the choral sounds of people laughing, talking, yelling, the ringing phones all covered their silence. Ken made a show of finishing his lunch by crunching his napkin and putting it on the plate where a full piece of pizza still lay. Silently, Cat gathered the plate and lipstick and left him to his telephone calls and the thoughts she could not read.

Ken and Cat didn't speak to each other for the rest of the afternoon. The usual string of phone calls, and people walking in and out, up from the press area and back continued. Because of her whirling mind Cat worked slowly and had to back up and redo several columns of numbers and re-question on two purchases. The gold tube lipstick stood by her calculator all afternoon. Purposely she stared at it; trying to read history. Wondering if it mattered; afraid to let all thoughts take shape. It was past four when she finished and she wasn't sure how to make an exit. First, she said good-bye to Mary Ellen and Rhonda and then walked to stand at Ken's door.

"I'm going now, Ken." The crooked half smile on his lips held a secret or a sneer and Cat didn't know which.

"I'll see you at home." There was nothing to say. Cat turned to leave. Once in her car she leaned back and closed her eyes. For two minutes she tried to calm herself and not allow the stabbing fear run through her blood. When she opened them her head slowly turned to look at the dark green Expedition hovering high in the next parking stall. Ken's pride and joy. Overjoyed and cocky happy the day he drove it off the sales lot, he turned to look at the children and her, "Let's take a first ride now!" They took a freeway trip up Parley's Canyon toward Park City. At the discount mall everyone was given $10 and ten minutes to find something for themselves. MoMo got a purple shirt with boa feathers on the neckline. Justin got a CD of Metallica, Ken said he gave his ten dollars to a passing ski bum and Cat got a discounted pie pan imported from France. They drove to Park City for a late lunch and ate only Daddy Food for dinner in front of the TV.

The children were home when she arrived, eating pretzels and watching TV.

"Homework finished?" they looked at her and she knew her tone was grating and starched. She didn't know the emotion with it. "Have you finished your homework," she repeated in measured tones. Yes, MoMo, nodded. "Most of it," Justin said.

Ken was home at six. Early for him. "I'm taking the Expedition to have it washed. Want to come, Justin?"

"Sure," the question hadn't been finished before he was up and on his way.

"I want to go, too!" MoMo whined.

"Okay. Come along, then," they were all out the door leaving Cat staring. When she consciously heard the TV's canned laughter after a bad joke she walked over and turned it off. Sitting at one end of the couch with her back against the armrest, her legs folded up and her arms around her leg, she hugged herself to feel calm and happy. Trying not to think she looked out the large window French doors to the yard. The marigolds were blazing in a row along the grass. Leaves were changing in the young trees in her yard and behind the fence in the neighbor's yard as well.

Maybe it's just the pressure of work. Maybe that is why he is short tempered and distant. Maybe he needs relief and more what? Affection? Sex? Understanding? How was she not giving enough? Certainly he is entitled to have emotions and feelings. Now that they're in the open the steam is relieved. Everything will be fine.

She smoothed her forehead and ran fingers through thick curly hair. Where did that lipstick come from? It must be simple. One of MoMo's friends? Had Walter's Mother been in the car with them when Ken drove everyone to soccer practice last week? Had Eme been in it? Maybe she would buy that color. What about Ken's shudder? The color was far too bright.

Dinner needed to be prepared. Cat got up to cook. Duty needed attention. Everyone returned in good spirits. The evening continued in normal fashion. The children got special goodnights. The parents quietly slept on their own sides of the bed.

CHAPTER FOURTEEN

On Sunday, Suzanne conceded to Michael Ken's resemblance to Michael Crichton. Within five minutes of that admission she fell into tears while a baseball game in the third inning played background. Michael automatically patted her shoulder without taking his eye off the game, but he was relieved Ken hadn't called. He felt sure Ken was history since over a week was a long time in his sex life to avoid the target of his aspirations. Right after the game he was going to Caramello's, and he hoped Suzanne would be all right with going to O'Rileys alone or staying home and going to bed early. It wouldn't hurt her.

It was evident the man had returned to his marital senses and responsibilities. He knew the tears and weepiness Suzanne wasted on Ken were necessary female costs, but now that he had been a good brother and distractedly listened to her emotional ravings with an occasional pat on her shoulder, he was pleased it was over.

Workdays passed without a compelling or transparent reason for either Ken or Suzanne to pretend a call. They both knew what they wanted from each other. The naked hand on the table between them was Ken's next move. It had been almost two weeks since he left her apartment and she missed him. Pride was also hurt that he hadn't wanted to use a graciously offered exit good-bye fuck.

Overton's paper orders from Ken were called in on the main phone line and went directly to the order department where people were planted to chairs. Mary Ellen called Suzanne directly a few times for samples or small orders. Suzanne imagined Ken telling her in an irritated voice to do this or that, just so he wouldn't have to follow up with her. The jerk. Suzanne was surprised she felt lonely and deserted. Worse, her private true hopes in life had been presented to him and rejected. When told what the real Suzanne wanted, she was dumped without further notice. Once again her honest words about what she wanted and would surely deliver to the right man were turned down.

What surprised her was that on top of the sting of being dumped, she remembered a few quirks about the man himself that she had deeply enjoyed. The Damn Prince now had additional standards.

For a man who was a proud workaholic, Ken had a surprising streak of spontaneity. He liked getting in his beloved Expedition and going on unplanned excursions. Ending up ten minutes or two hours away in any direction had been fun and surprising opportunities to hear him talk. On a lunch break they walked along the paved walkways by the Jordan River in the middle of the Salt Lake Valley. They strolled as friends might walk, side by side, without touching, aware they were in public with other walkers and bikers. The distance they kept was compensated by the words they spoke.

"Suzanne, you're young for me. There's fourteen years between us." While he talked Suzanne noticed a woman raking her backyard, that was fenced next to the parkway. Days spent alone as a housewife one after another must be very lonely and sacrificing. "I must seem old to you."

Suzanne noticed the line of silvery hairs above his ears before answering. "If you say that, I must seem too young to you."

He was always surprised how quick she was to play offense, "That's not an answer."

"What do you want to hear, Ken? That I think you're old but dashing in your maturity?" They walked a few steps, waiting for a mom on a bike pulling a baby in a low slung rickshaw to pass.

"I want to know if you really want or need an older man or I'm just an interest before you return to guys your own age."

"I could ask you the same." Neither one of them gave an answer. Neither one was quite ready to show either their heart or a weakness.

The turning point for Suzanne was the Wednesday he called at nine and begged her to make an excuse to be away from the office until three, when he promised to have her back. At ten they were on the road headed to Brigham City, sixty miles north. Only an hour. Suzanne let messages stack on her phone. Ken took four calls. He told Mary Ellen only to send the very important.

They ate lunch at a Utah landmark steakhouse, celebrating

grease, soda pop and blonde waitresses in flowered cotton. Later, Suzanne waited until they were on the freeway, headed south to Salt Lake, to be sure this hadn't all been for sex. "You're headed back to work?"

"Yes."

"No sex?"

"You want sex?"

"I mean, why don't you?"

"I do. But I'm trying to show you that's not all I want. I want someone who will be with me to do this kind of thing."

When she asked the next question she needed to see his face, so she turned in the seat belt and faced him squarely. She picked up his cell phone, turned it off, set it back in the cup holder and said, "What about your wife?"

He shrugged, not wanting to answer but her stare left the next words to him. "She likes to go. She likes to do these things, but on different roads. With a different schedule."

"What does that mean?"

"It means people change. Cat and I are different from each other."

"How?"

"She'd be happier married to a college professor."

"Does she know that?"

"Cat will do what she needs to, to get by."

"So you're deciding for her?"

"Back off, Suzanne," he looked at her, his clouded eyes reflecting the sky were not angry. They dilated hurt.

"I can see, Ken, you are that lonely man you once told me about," she turned back in her seat and watched the freeway ahead. "But I think you like being lonely."

"I haven't liked it since I met you. You need to know I love my wife and I don't want to hurt my kids." He paused and the weight of his words pushed Suzanne back to her seat. "But now I know you," his words were the sound of his soul slipping away from the center of gravity. Add something in that conversation to the list for The Damn Prince.

Suzanne also liked that Ken was a man of his word. If he said he was going to be somewhere he was and he understood when you

149

told him what you expected and wanted in a deal of the heart or printing. If he could produce he did and if he couldn't, well, she supposed that was why she hadn't heard from him.

Then there was the way he looked her in the eyes for meaning beyond sex and listened to her intelligence. Not many did that. There was a respect between them Suzanne appreciated. The energy she received from Ken was a mossy green electrical heat of dedication and perseverance. She was sure he was a man who would always be true to his heart.

Because she was in honest mourning over losing Ken back to his family, she had not called Sugarloaf. He was for pleasure, renewed energy and fun. Not revenge, not ever a second choice.

Monday morning Suzanne was sitting in a meeting at Harkness. Fifteen people sat around an old walnut table with bagels, coffee and orange juice separating them. The meeting would last another forty minutes at least, but the last thing she heard during the dry list of sales quotas, paper promotions and employee regulations was when her boss, Carter Holmes, said he was taking a group to a thank you dinner on Friday. Ron, his wife, Krista, their highest spending customer, and Suzanne and her highest spending customer, Overton would be there. The customers had accepted, Ron and Suzanne were expected. Suzanne could bring a date if she liked.

"What am I going to do, Michael?" Her voice was tight, near desperation. He answered his phone on the job and balanced the phone, nails, and a hammer.

"It will work, Suze. He won't say a thing and I've seen you act."

"I didn't want to do this. I never wanted to get involved with him."

"I know," and he did. She always had a fear of married men. He couldn't tell if it was because they were candy or poison.

His words of belief stilled her. Like their mother, Michael could soothe Suzanne with tones of care. A calming center opened and Suzanne knew she would be able to handle Kenneth Overton, his stupid wife whatever her name was and their stupid company, Overton Printing, and her idiot boss who put her in this situation.

"Then I'll try to be gracious. How's Caramello?"

"She's fine. Wants to know you better."

150

"She's crazy."

"I know. Every other female had self-preservation instincts and wanted to keep you away."

"That's because they knew I loved you more than they did and I was watching."

"Well, good. Maybe this is a good omen."

Thursday afternoon she was sitting at her desk, shuffling a few papers for invoicing when her cell phone rang. She didn't look to see who it was.

"Suzanne, here."

"Hello, Suze." Her heart stalled before kicking louder.

"Yes, Ken." She sounded calm enough.

"Can we meet now?"

"No. No I don't think so."

He paused. His voice was intent, near beseeching. "Please."

"Ken, what do you want?"

"Please meet me at Ginger's. Half an hour?"

Her body weakened to water. There was no more bone; only hot feeling, anticipation, a fluttering of sex between her legs she knew she wanted.

"All right, Ken," she said and hung up. Suzanne didn't leave the office for forty-five minutes. Let him wait. She could be in control if she wanted. And she wanted. When she opened the door to Ginger's it was the last reaches of dusk that lit her from behind. She stood a few feet in the door and looked but all she could see were jostling shadows and she heard the laughter of people who had suffered a workday and were half a drink too far into the night.

In the diffused light she saw Ken stand to let her know where he was. The same table where they met the first time. The cocktail waitress was at the table when she sat down. Ken was ordering a second.

"Beer. On tap."

He smiled, "You like beer."

"I'm used to it."

"A young person's favorite."

"I am a young person."

Silently, they regarded each other. Suzanne was stiff, primly seated. Ken watched and drank her in. When the beer was placed before her, she didn't move.

Ken leaned forward and looked deeper into her eyes, "I told Cat last night."

Alarmed, Suzanne picked up the beer, "Told her what?" She certainly hadn't been notified of this terror.

Ken shifted in his chair, whether from discomfort or pride she wasn't sure. "I told her things were not working between us. That I wasn't sure what I wanted."

Suzanne waited for the man on stage to come to the punch line.

"That, that, it wasn't working."

"You didn't mention me."

"No."

She didn't know if that relieved her or made her angry, "Ken, I don't get your point."

His eyes lowered, "I know." An ice cube in his glass cracked and then the rest of the cubes shuffled order above the fading golden liquid at the bottom.

Ken leaned forward, his hand moved across the table and met her fingers. He touched the tips and moved along their length, softly, tenderly. Their fingers intertwined, his moving, hers still. "Suzanne, please." People she couldn't see were sitting at a table behind her and she withdrew her hand for privacy.

A man of his word, Suzanne remembered. He thought. He decided. He cleared the deck. He acted. He expected.

"You're confusing me, Ken," was this another short-lived affair to prop his ego or was the man standing up?

"It's been confusing to me, too. But it's you I want, Suzanne. For my life. For your life, I hope."

Moments ticked. Suzanne finished her beer. She looked across the table and deep into him, "Prove it."

"All right," he sat straighter and half-smiled as though he had waited for her challenge. A nod to the waitress brought a third and a second. "I'll be away from my marriage by December 1 if you promise to have me."

"You have children."

This time his eyes did not meet hers. "I'll always have children."

"So what is it you are saying?"

"I'm saying, I need until December first. Then I'll be yours if you'll have me."

"And the children?"

"The children are part of the deal," from his hips to his feet he switched sides. "But they have their mother, too."

The flash in Suzanne's memory was of she, Michael and their mother dumbstruck in the kitchen as they stared at the woman with the tight curls in the fuzzy sweater who stood before them, severing their lives with sudden amputation. After his last look into her eyes, her father had not given a backward glance. The air didn't move in the kitchen as the three of them heard the slam of two car doors and the turning of the engine heavily revved, to make sure it would get away. The father she had grown to dislike as he fell into a drunken sleep before TV she discovered disliked her more. Here she was. Suzanne. The other woman without disguise or pretense.

"You need to take care of your children."

"I will. I expect to. I want to take care of you, too."

"I can take care of myself."

"I know, Suzanne. But I would like to assist."

For the first time that day, she smiled.

"Does that mean you would take me?"

"So, I could have what about Overton?"

"As much as you want." Offering his business was offering his heart.

She sat up and looked hard. He was the one who answered, "What do you want?"

"Part ownership. On paper."

"That means your ass is on the line."

"My ass is on the line right now."

"Now I know you would take the business. What about me?"

"And do you promise the man as easily as the company? The fucker, the wanderer over country roads? The man who looks me in the eye?"

They stared at one another until she answered her own question, "Yes, I would take you."

Ken leaned back and smiled, his best Michael Crichton imitation Suzanne had seen. A deal was struck.

"What about tomorrow night?"

"Cat and I are coming. It's business."

Half an hour later they walked out of Ginger's. The October moon was waxing to the full moon of Halloween. Ken put his arm around her and sniffed as he kissed her hair and ear. "Let's go to your place."

"Let's go to your road monster."

Ken opened the back of the Expedition. When Suzanne sat on the carpeted truckbed and lifted her skirt, she consciously challenged female territory.

CHAPTER FIFTEEN

"Look at this dress, Cat, isn't it beautiful?" Eme's eyes glistened along with the red, blue and green rhinestones embedded in the crocheted sheath. Swaying on the hanger, it already moved to the sway of Eme's step.

"It's beautiful, Eme, and will be more so on you."

"I'll try this one on and this one," she took an emerald green silk from Cat's arms. "And one more. It's a waste to go in a change room with less than three things." Eme laid six dresses across Cat's lap in the wallpapered faux French dressing room with two mirrors. The department store was quiet on a late Tuesday afternoon and they had the bride changing room with supporting bridesmaid rooms trailing the hall to the cashier at the end. Eme slipped on a dress, and began wriggling and adjusting sleeves, waistline and hems to best advantage before looking in the mirror.

"What do you think?"

"I think the others will be better."

"I think so, too," Eme unzipped the green silk. "Have I told you who I'm inviting to the wedding?"

"No." Eme repeated thirty names, four of them Cat's family. All thirty were expected to attend the ceremony and dinner at Snowbird in just over three weeks.

"I think I will be able to wear this dress Christmas morning, too," Eme turned to see her backside in the studded, crochet dress, "If you serve caviar and champagne."

"Don't worry about using it twice. A wedding is only itself. Perhaps we should all burn our wedding clothes for purification before becoming disillusioned."

"Great. Tell a bride that."

"I'm sorry, Eme." It just slipped out. "I'll change the subject. Can you get Sheldon to donate something to the Cancer Care House silent auction?"

"You're begging?"

"Yes."

After Eme bought the rhinestone crocheted sheath, they drove separate cars to Eme's house for tea. The maples on the parking strip were dancing with the wind as rain clouds hovered and moved toward the mountains where they would be caught as cornered rabbits and be forced to give rain. New yards do not have this sound of wild skirted trees reaching to the sky, thought Cat.

Eme prepared tea while Cat watched like a lurking shadow. Water was started, china cups were placed on the kitchen counter with the teapot and rough dry tea leaves were dropped in its bottom. Cat stepped beside Eme; they stood inches apart waiting for the water to reach near boiling.

"Why did you make such a fuss over Ryan, Eme? You didn't really like him. Or even know him."

"He was my foil, I think, a cover-up."

"You're afraid of Sheldon," the revelation came as a simple statement.

Eme nodded as she moved the teapot on the burner.

"Why?"

"He loves. More than I do, I think."

"You love. You love a lot."

"I do love, Cat, but I expect with my love and I parade love. Sheldon gives it without parading."

"You deserve his love. It's a wonderful thing for you to receive."

"And a great responsibility. Married people with children know that. What do you think Ken gives?" A deft shift of subject.

Cat hesitated, thinking, "Ken gives protection. His mental and physical strength, I would say. He's a wall against the world."

They walked into the living room with the tea and sat on the couch, "That sounds right. That sounds like Ken. How is he? I haven't seen him lately. How's Overton?"

Cat's tears came as the day's unexpected storm. She told Eme of the lipstick, Ken's unfounded accusations that she did not care and was not up to whatever in the hell challenge he was talking about, his coldness and anger. She hadn't seen that anger for so long she thought he left it behind in years that were gone. Her mother hadn't been told. She was confused, ungrounded, unsure what to do and Ken didn't seem to want to do anything but blame. She felt accused without stated charges. Undermined from behind and within her family. And she didn't know why.

"I'm sorry, Eme. I'm sorry," after a flood of words out of order and reason, passing by only as they could squeeze out of her heart, she cuddled in her friend's arms and ended.

Eme's words to her as she left were, "Remember, Catalina, you were on your way to the Future of Inner Trinity when you met Ken. You still are." Eme referred to their secret pledge to believe in each other's future. The questioning days of college had given private opportunity to laugh at male religious domination and imagine females had personal sanctity and opportunity. They had grown up past the cusp of 60's feminism that pretended right but not provided opportunity. The Future of Inner Trinity believed self-belief, right to change and honor of self-discovery would walk a woman to inner peace and outer success. Cat smiled remembering youthful possibilities. Eme watched her leave through the glass window in her door, afraid for her friend.

The time from the Tuesday afternoon of wedding dress shopping to the morning of the Harkness dinner cut life from Before to After. As she woke on Friday she listened to Ken's breathing, wondering if his waking breath would kill her. She could easily die if Justin and MoMo would live well without her. And perhaps they would, but she just wasn't sure. She needed to attend their needs; their growing up to life. When they were ready to live and be on their own; then surely at that moment she would die. As her father died on her.

First, she had to live through Ken's business dinner with Harkness. Duty. To herself. Her children's secure future. Ken. Overton Printing. Wednesday night Ken waited until the children were in bed. He poured her a glass of wine she did not asked for. He did not have a drink. Ken was always good at keeping his wits about when it was important. They sat before the muted television, its shadows playing on their faces.

"Cat there is something I need to tell you."

Ken's words bubbled like water from a mountain spring.

Emotion was deep and true, full and strong. Ken was sure. Sure of what needed to be done and where he needed to go in his life. His life. Cat did not hear all of it and it was for the protection of a soft inner self that she did not. After all, one person's view is not another person's experience. Even in the same marriage. So, Ken talked on, trying not to be cruel, but certainly being direct and closed to compromise or even aware that Cat would have an opinion or would care to state it. Yet Cat didn't hear it that way on that night. It was too much. Yes, he was distraught, unhappy and thinking this should be the end, but she did not, could not hear the finality in his voice. He didn't say point blank he was leaving, nor did he offer solutions or compromise. Ken's method was to aim the gun, pull the trigger, and let the small caliber bullet cause internal bleeding that would give him time to get away so he would not witness the death of his marriage in Cat's eyes. Coldness held his last words in the air before they fell on Cat.

"I'm sorry it's this way, Cat. This is not how I wanted it but I don't see a way out. We've changed." He stood and went upstairs to bed. Perhaps she was in shock because she never believed Ken would speak this way to her. This was a voice he used with troublesome employees and rude people in stores. Perhaps there could be reconciliation. A miracle. That was why they slept in the same bed. Habit on his part. Hope on hers. It had always been a comfortable bed.

Wednesday night to this Friday morning passed as the hours between death and funeral; except there wasn't a physical body to mourn. There hadn't been a public posting so she could receive condolences. She had not updated Eme or told her mother. The children had only been touched and murmured over. They were confused and quieter, but the past weeks had been confusing and they moved fears aside because they needed to so their lives would proceed. Perhaps if she could just get through this small bit of time it would be a good change. The darkest before the dawn theory. She looked toward the window to pre-dawn darkness.

At 5:41 Ken got up. Uncaring, unnoticing of her beside him he raised himself from a moment of peaceful sleep to fully awake. He walked to the combined closet and bathroom while Cat didn't move. Or cry. Or think. Or appear awake. While shower water ran, she tried to hear the children breathe and could not.

When Ken came out of the bathroom she still had not moved.

There had not really been a full sentence of thought. He leaned and took her hand laying inches outside the sheet. How did he see in the darkness. Midnight darkness and hot noon sun suited him best. He shook her hand as though he were ending an appointment.

"I'll be home at six for you."

"Eme, Eme, call me back," Cat left a voice mail when she got up. I need to talk to you, she thought. I need to breathe. She and the children finished morning routines and Cat was left alone as she often was on Fridays. After pouring another cup of coffee she sat on the couch and stared at the backyard. October light was encompassing as a lover's arms. Not as yellow and young as May, October cast shadows of red desire. Of life's need to finish what it had started. That she understood.

Eme called from her windowless office. "Cat, what's happening?"

She listened to a staccato rambling account of the last few days. In deference for crumbling hope and Cat's feelings she did not interrupt. "I'm sorry, Cat. That's awful. I'll see if I can leave the office early and come over."

Cat nodded yes but answered no, "No, Eme, we have the Harkness dinner tonight and I need to be ready."

Mid afternoon. she prepared a long bath of bubbles, shampoo and oil. While the water ran she walked naked to the kitchen and poured wine. The tub was so warm sweat popped on her forehead. Sun shone through the window, breaking into a prism of light touching the reflecting bubbles. A finished glass of wine, closed eyes, a silent house except for the dying bubbles counted as blessings. Her hands followed each side of her body from her head, breasts, ribs, waist, hips, legs until they could not reach further and she lay there suspended. Glimmering light drops fell from behind her eyes, down the darkness inside her body, out her toes and she felt opened. In that bare passage of time she was life expectant, a woman preparing for love. Reflecting in the mirror when she stood silky wet she saw a frightened woman losing the man of her life.

The dress she chose was a simple black A-line. When she bought it for their anniversary dinner two years ago it had been 'of station.' Now it felt matronly, too married. She put pearls around her neck that hung past the neckline. No. She took them off and picked up a gold filigreed necklace dotted with garnets Eme gave her for Christmas, saying she needed more pizazz and color. The garnets at least drank in moonlight; maybe it would reflect on her. Thick bangs and wavy full hair fell to her shoulders. Plain and direct; as at home and unnoticeable in the grocery store and a PTA meeting as this dinner.

Cat was sitting with the children and the baby-sitter watching TV when Ken ran in the door and headed upstairs.

"I need to clean up. Ten minutes." He was down in nine. Cat stood, walked to each child and kissed them before following Ken to the garage. Silence was crushing. They didn't always talk when they drove in comfortable married peace, but tonight it was underlining fear for Cat and Ken's lack of care.

"Perhaps we should go to a marriage counselor," Her voice was soft, purposefully oatmeal bland. He had changed to a white starched shirt and tie with a blue blazer. Shifting shoulders were his answer. Didn't matter. Okay.

The restaurant was a popular local dark cavern for steak, located in a high-rise city hotel. Ken leaned over, "Well, here we go, Lina. Be pleased. This is a step in the right direction for Overton to be recognized by Harkness."

Inside the restaurant they were led to a back table where five people were sitting at a long table set for nine. Introductions went around. Cat met the top man from Harkness, whose name, Carter, she recognized from mailers, and his wife, Nancy. Another sales person named Ron and his wife, Krista, were on Carter's right. She walked toward Ron, shook his hand, nodded all around and sat beside Ron. Across the table she recognized Overton's salesperson. Suzanne was the blonde droplet of beautiful, assured young woman Ken introduced months ago. Ron's client, Slimmer (easier than Sylvester he said) Deacon and his wife, Misty, who owned a local ad agency followed behind Ken to sit between Nancy and Suzanne.

As pre-dinner drinks finished there was a moment in conversation when everyone at the table but Ken and Cat were involved. She leaned to him and whispered, "Now isn't it this man, Carter, that you went fishing with?" Ken twitched his shoulder away and brushed her hand.

"No, Cat. It was someone else."

"But you said it was the top person at Harkness."

"Another guy. Deacon's the one I did that pewter catalog for this summer. Try talking to his wife." He turned to listen to the conversation between Suzanne and Misty.

Cat sat back, lifted her wineglass, watched the people around her. Heads bobbed and weaved like chickens fighting for space, respect where there was none. Her blood bubbled and ran through her, making her light and aware. Thoughts crushed up and over while she sat with strangers; feeling as if she were in a subtly cruel amusement park funhouse. How many other top guys could there be at Harkness? She was familiar enough with the company to wonder who Ken could be talking about. Voices began to blend and the words of others were slurred, not by their voice but in her mind as the blood bubble led fear and suspicion through her body. She turned to talk to Ron, doing as she was told while behind she heard Ken's bright, easy manner that once was familiar to her but now was only for Suzanne and Misty.

Hors'doevres were on the table but Cat leaned forward to hear conversation; not pick up food. Hunger had fallen away since Wednesday night. Very little food and the hunting adrenaline of unacknowledged hunger sharpened her vision. Carter initiated a toast to thank his top sales people and the good and wonderful clients they had brought to the family of Harkness. Direct focus was on Carter, but raw awareness saw fully and peripherally when Ken looked across the table at Suzanne. Lust shone from his eyes, lifting them wider in a way she had not seen for so long that without witnessing it now she would have thought it lost in a youth no one could recapture. Suzanne answered his look equally and without regard or awareness of Cat. Automatic response was to turn away; she had seen something both private and dangerous to her safety.

Ron, next to Cat, turned and asked polite questions about Overton. She nodded and answered as she could. When he asked about press and equipment, she turned to Ken to speak across her. He and Suzanne were talking everyday words of common conversation but when he turned his eyes glistened.

Surreal floating seconds moved dinner slowly. Ken split time between Suzanne and the advertising agency couple. Cat listened and nodded, pretending to be part of it, saying a bit once in a while and dipping in and out of conversation beside her and across the table. Two, sometimes three conversations surrounded her with a background of clicking silver against china, ice against glass, walking waiters and whispers of people at other tables. A calm ghostly voice whispered clearly through her whole body as she concentrated on cutting steak on the plate, "Do you really want this life?" She didn't answer.

After Bananas Foster and Seven Layers of Decadence was ordered, Suzanne excused herself and lifted a phone out of her purse; saying she needed to step away to call her brother. Cat saw the direction she went, waited a minute and then told Ken she was going to the restroom. It was in the opposite direction that Suzanne walked. The hollow tiled room ricocheted the click of her heels scraping a high note hurting her ears. Alone in the closed stall a rush of vomit and emotion rose from her belly. The sound of a turning paper roll and flush stopped the surging knife blade and she was back to surreal timeless survival. The woman who left the stall made quick primping sounds. When she opened her door, of course, it was Suzanne. She must have circled back a way Cat hadn't seen. They nodded as wary observers in a check-out line and turned forward to the mirror. Suzanne lifted her lipstick. Cheap, gold brightness stung Cat's eyes. Awkwardly, they both moved quickly to finish.

"Great color."

"ShaNa Boogie. Stupid name."

Cat rolled her hair behind her ears. "Did you get in touch with your brother?"

Suzanne's smile was slow, sensuous even by a woman's observation, "Yes. We're meeting in an hour. This will be over by then, don't you think?"

Cat's low slung head wave was a beaten schoolgirl's. Suzanne again looked toward the mirror, ran fingers through short hair for spike effect and turned to leave. The door swung closed behind her.

The turn in Cat's stomach was so severe she doubled over and stumbled to the stall. The gagging was stopped body function, her desire not to breathe and a reaction from her stomach that she must. After three gasps for air she leaned against the wall. Two women entered, laughing and Cat closed the door to be alone.

Months later, Cat marveled that in a public bathroom when

she had been alone for the first time with the woman she knew was her husband's lover the suffocating emotion was not anger, fear or sadness. It was waving drowning desire. She wanted to know the flaming passion of having a man want her, Catalina Margaret Daniels Overton, so much that he disregarded his life, everything he held dear.

It took so long to remember desire because the second thought was what stayed. Realization that Ken did not believe he was jeopardizing anything for Suzanne. The beautiful 'everything' of their marriage that held promise on their wedding night was a never materialized ghostly dream. What the birth of the children had done for Cat had not taken with Ken. Children riveted her to Ken in loyalty and need beyond herself. She felt failed as a mother, as a wife; as a woman.

Dry-eyed, in shock and somber, Cat returned to the table. No one had missed her. Only Suzanne's lidded watchfulness noticed her at all.

"Thank you, Carter, for the dinner. It was very enjoyable." Shaking hands good-bye, Ken then turned to include Carter's wife, Nancy, with Ron and Suzanne at her side. "We appreciate Overton," Carter said in measured good buddy tones. Deftly, Ken walked to the advertising agency couple and began a good-bye conversation.

Cat stepped over to Carter. He was a big man with a friendly Friday night face, "I know Ken appreciates your service for the company." After he nodded and said thank you, she continued. "Isn't your partner a fisherman? I think I heard that."

Carter answered easily as though she had asked the time, "Nobody but me on the lonely top, Miss Cat. No one fishes at Harkness unless its for higher sales."

The turn of the Expedition's wheels up the driving ramp reverberated angry squeals along the close concrete walls as Ken drove from middle earth to city night streets. The man eyes that had glistened in desire; now blazed. "You certainly weren't at the party tonight."

She turned to him, "What do you mean?"

"This was a perfect opportunity to dazzle a little for Overton and what do you do? Nothing. You barely talked."

Cat cringed, unable to talk. She remembered talking to everyone at the table, but now her brain was jelly and there wasn't ability to think. Self-preservation settled in automatic and she shut down to half-awareness to make it home to her children and through this ugliness.

"Well, why not?"

"Why not what?"

"Why couldn't you talk to anyone? Everyone else was having a good time!"

They were coming to the attendant's stall and they were quiet while Ken offered the validated card. On the street they tailed a car in front of them as if it were a magnet requiring they follow through the yellow light turning red. "What's wrong Cat? Can't you do it for Overton?"

"Do what Ken?" By keeping him talking her body would not fall apart from words that would spill out if she talked.

"Care about it. Do your share." His voice was rising. "Do what needs to be done to make it succeed. To get food on the table for you, for the kids?"

Her voice choked, cracked. They were both staring straight ahead. "I work there, Ken."

"Once a week. Maybe twice," he was clearly disgusted with her poor attendance.

As she spoke the words she knew it was disaster, "What do you want, Ken?"

"Want? Want?" his eyes were not blazing now. They were crazed. She wondered if one more breath would make the air in the car explode to fire. "I want someone who cares. Someone who wants what I want. Someone who will be with me."

Unable to gauge a safe answer she didn't answer. Seconds ticked and she heard his breath. "Ken, I, I care."

"Care for what, Cat?"

"Care for you."

"That's not enough." The last five miles home all she heard was Ken's feet playing the gas and brake, the sound of the engine, the traffic noise of other cars. When they walked in the door of the house from the garage to the family room Cat wondered how Ken's voice would sound to the baby-sitter. When it was as clear and friendly as it had been with ad agency people Cat knew she had been suckered. Ken knowingly played her for his ends. He went to bed. She sat on the couch to settle.

Saturday morning Cat's eyes were overburdened and distended from a night of restless napping on the couch in front of TV. Three times she moved from the couch to the bed to try sleeping by the very peaceful Ken. It reminded her of a piece in *Life Among the Savages*, by Shirley Jackson about movement in the house through the night as parents and children traded sleeping spaces and blankets. Only she was alone. Rising fitfully she would go to the kitchen for a drink of water and slowly walk in the dark about the house without pattern, but always stopping in each child's room before settling for yet another restless turning of time in the bed or on the couch. In all the tortured sleeping and mindless walking there was no conclusion of thought because there was no question before her to solve. There was only worry, fear, aloneness and an extreme awareness of potential catastrophe in her life and that of her children.

Hearing the anger and meanness that bellowed up from the dark part of his heart with the fire of hate was not unknown to Cat. The first time she felt its heat and heard his contorted voice was when they were dating. Ken had been splitting rent with two guys in a cinderblock six-plex between the city and the university. One of the guys had taken Ken's share of the rent money and bought beer. Cat was walking up the steps to get Ken for a movie when she heard. The voice was a wild and terrible animal let loose to kill. When she tapped on the door, Dave, the third roommate opened it. She walked in to see Ken in a rage of anger that turned his face to a bloated, bulging mask and filled the room with the smell of spit and hate. The other roommate was ashen.

A week before Ken quit his last job and started Overton Overnight he came home in a rage that lasted two hours. Surprised, Cat listened to his anger touching the cutting knife of hatred in words that didn't seem to describe how she had known the kindly Mr. Presson. Ken's emotion was so persuasive and oversized that Cat could only nod agreement with Ken's need to get out of that place and start his own business.

The last time he had been like this was after being turned down for a loan to buy a secondhand press when it was still Overton Overnight five years ago. He came home from the bank and was so upset she sent the children to the bedroom they shared so they would only hear his roaring, not have to see how it changed his face, elongated his movements and sharpened his body smell. The frothy hatred that glowed from his eyes, the waves of heat that rolled off him were not any more pleasant or understandable, but she knew it existed deep within him and once it was spent he returned to normal. Kathleen had told her it was him; not the world, not her.

Ken's great anger and show of beasty power was always followed by heartfelt desire and soul searching to change the situation. As anger waned pathfinding gained momentum. After confronting the roommate in college, he grabbed her hand and ran with her to the car. Half a mile away they parked at a city park and the movie was forgotten as he poured out his heart over financial worries and hopes for this future. Nodding and listening for over an hour, it was then Cat realized the depth of Ken's heart in the projects he felt important. If he couldn't see his way in the world, he would hammer and chip at any enclosing wall until he made his way.

After the anger with Presson he started Overton. After the disappointment with the loan officer he built a stronger financial presentation, but he also out glowered and verbally manipulated the next polite loan officer who looked across the desk at him. He admitted to Cat the man who refused the first loan had been right. He was not prepared.

The difference this time was that the anger was directed toward her. And he was not making any moves to change the situation. At four, she wondered if dawn would ever break again. Then, for the first time, she was in a solid mindless sleep until Ken woke her while she was on the couch. Grey light shadowed Ken's face without promise of a sunny day.

"You should go to the bed, Cat. It would be more comfortable." It was a statement of fact, not invitation or care. He did not wait to see her up before walking to the kitchen to make coffee. Because she did not know how to be around him she walked upstairs, past the rooms of her still sleeping children.

In bed she listened to Ken making coffee, a car driving by, the newspaper coming and Ken opening the front door. She leaned to the side of Ken's indention in the sheets, ran her fingers over it, into the deep lines he left in the sheets and sniffed fully, through her throat, down to her lungs, trying to understand. Remember.

Justin went downstairs first, greeted by his father whooping, "It's Justin, man of the year, hale and hearty."

"Oh, dad," he answered sleepily and happily as he headed to the cereal and then by his dad's side to watch cartoons. The noise wakened MoMo and she soon followed and was greeted by Ken, "It's Princess MoMo, fairest in the land. May she ever rule the foolish masses as she rules her dad's heart."

Oh, Ken, Cat's heart quaked, how you rule this house. How you rule all of us. Ever the master and man. Ever the head and lord. Giving due only as the reflection applauds you.

Twenty minutes passed while Cat listened for cues. The children and Ken were in comfortable Saturday morning presence of each other, TV and newspaper. She was in oblivion. No wish to think. No wish to know. No wish to do. Cat got up, showered and with a freshened as possible face, wet hair and a clean robe went downstairs.

"Time for waffles. Who wants waffles?" Her voice felt gruff and phony cheerful but the game was playing. Two children raised their hands.

"Okay. It's waffle time. How about you, Ken?"

He waved a no and concentrated on the newspaper. The morning was dotted and finally stalled at a dead-end by Cat trying to draw Ken into conversation and him retreating.

"What do you think the President should have done with the tax bill, Ken?" she tried to sound like an interested voter as she read the paper over coffee.

"Who knows?" he shrugged not looking at her.

"Ken, do you think we should turn the water off this weekend?" Winter was approaching and fragile underground pipes needed protection.

"Ya, sure. I'll do it tomorrow," he said without looking away from the TV he was watching with the children.

"Let's take a drive. We can all see the fall leaves. I'll pack sort of a picnic and we'll drive the Alpine Loop. Okay?" The half day mountain drive was an annual outing to see the fall colors thrown like a casual quilt over the mountains.

"I'm going to the movie with Walt, remember?" Justin settled his unavailability.

"I'm going to the birthday party," MoMo reminded everyone.

"Then I guess the Alpine Loop's out of the question." No one talked. Cat hated herself through her words spit like dry salty dough. She wrestled the moment for its moisture for her children, their future. During breakfast Ken's languor over the newspaper was deliberate and measured but when he put the paper down after seeming to read everything, he didn't stop being busy with tasks. He fluttered about the garage, wrote down the furnace filter size, walked around the yard to check the water sprinklers and fixed a leaky faucet in the down-stairs bathroom. Cat was avoided and yet her life was served. Ken drove the children to their events before going to a store. He would be right back, he said.

Eme's wedding invitation came in the mail. Flourishing type in gold printing on a panel card announced Eme's and Sheldon's wish to share their joy at a ceremony and dinner at Snowbird in three weeks. Standing at the mailbox she opened the invitation and held it a long time, rubbing the gold words before going back in the house.

The morning hours finally ended without seeming movement while Ken was at the store. When he returned Cat was sitting as a self-protective child at the end of the couch. Her arms holding her legs as she hunched forward, hugging herself for comfort.

"We need to talk, Ken." Softly, fear in her voice.

Ken put the sack of filters on the kitchen counter and then turned to her, "We know there's trouble, Cat."

"Is there trouble between us, Ken or just another woman in the way?"

"The trouble between us has nothing to do with anyone else," he was now seated in the chair and looking at her with what Cat saw as simple, focused hardness.

She was afraid. Life was cracking like ice hitting cold water. "Is there another woman?"

"No. There isn't another woman." He stared at her, unblink-ing, as though it was a magic trick needing attention to accomplish.

"What about that Suzanne last night?"

"You've always been a jealous person Cat. She's my salesper-son. We're a big account for her."

"Why are you so angry at me?"

"It's not anger, Cat. It's realization. You and I are just different. Our goals aren't the same."

She lifted her head and her mouth dropped slightly. "What do you mean? We've got the children, this house, a business. We've been married for twelve years with the same goals."

"They've changed. The children, yes, but a house is a house. I'm killing myself working to take care of the children and you and everything in this house. Every day I'm trying to land bids with margins so slim that every month I need more jobs. Jobs in a city that's cheap and dirty. Ready to trade anyone in for a one time better deal. And we can't make it on business cards anymore Cat, in case you hadn't noticed. I need runs of 20 and 50,000 to pay for everything. I'm working against an industry that's changing every month with more and more expensive equipment that some dumb ass sales kid in another company can turn a spin on to make a customer drool. I need help. I need everyone to have the same goals as me."

He didn't wait for a reply. He didn't want to hear one and he also knew he had sprayed her with an invading smell of emotion that she didn't know how to answer. Cat never answered large emotions. She cowered and licked inner wounds like the idiot animal she was named after. Sure of his attack plan and not wanting to hear this woman's mewing, he got up, got the sack of filters and headed to the basement.

Ken was right. She couldn't answer his emotion. Even with the name of Suzanne's lipstick she needed time to sort thoughts. Her sweet, comforting childhood had not prepared her to stand up for herself. The assumption had been respect was always given, love was without question once it was given. It did not need to be earned or re-earned. And the foundation of a lasting marriage was infinite trust. To imagine infidelity was a first act of betrayal.

Motionless, she sat on the couch and listened. His steps back up from the basement went to the heavy beat of her heart. He walked to the phone and while she listened he called his salesman, Dan, and said he'd decided to join them for golf in the morning. Rain or shine, unless it was snowing, he'd be there. Every time Ken moved from one place in the house to the other Cat was sure he was headed to the garage to get in the car and leave. He put the phone down, went to the refrigerator, got a beer and returned to the chair. The TV was clicked on and Ken turned his attention to the screen.

She was a fly on the wall. After fifteen minutes Cat realized the children would at last be home so she went upstairs to comb her hair and make sure her shocked ashen face was as normal as she could make it. She sat on her side of the still unmade bed and waited for them to return; unwilling to wait in the emptiness of Ken's presence.

When Justin and MoMo returned they moved effortlessly to the comfort of watching TV with Ken, creating an illusion of family normality. If family habits were not known, if there was not a memory of the buoyant laughter and teasing that had been lavish and joyous, it could be said the Overtons spent a normal Saturday night. Only those who had seen a previous camaraderie, and been touched by the care for one another would know the depth of the stiffness between this man and woman, this father and mother; that reached the hungry frightened hearts of the children.

Ken finished another beer as he switched between news, late night comedy, wrestling and a movie. They let the children stay up as buffer zones to keep them civil and a comfortable distance from each other's company. Before eleven Ken carried MoMo up to bed and half an hour later he carried Justin. Cat intermittently looked up from a book to watch with him and once to get another glass of wine. They did not talk. Their civil physical presence with each other was a victory to both of them.

It was almost midnight when Ken stood and tossed Cat the remote. "I'm going up now. I've got an early golf game."

When the bedroom door closed and Cat knew Ken was in bed she switched off the TV and sat in the dark. For an hour she stared at blackness through the glass doors and windows. Reflections played with glimpses of shadows and the moving light of clouds. When she went upstairs she slipped as silently as a dying fall leaf between the sheets.

The weekend passed in measured time that hung as weights on Cat. No one else seemed to notice that every second lengthened and slowed. Ken was up and gone in the dark of the fall morning for his golf. The children ambled down hours later to find Cat on the couch holding a coffee mug and staring into space with the Sunday paper on her lap. Her smile was not easy, but it was present as she watched them through the morning.

"Hi, Dad," Justin said, after beating MoMo to answer the

phone. "Okay," he leaned away from the phone and said, "Dad's going to be home in about an hour. If you want to take that drive today we can go and have dinner somewhere." Cat nodded and it was settled between father and son.

Dappling light and urgent autumn colors lightened the day. The children were comfortable and the adults pleasant. The winding canyon road took concentration to drive while Justin and Ken kept a casual conversation going about the subtleties of baseball and the frankness of football. MoMo joined in as well, but Cat knew nothing about the games and was quiet. Ken is making this afternoon a memory, Cat thought as he pulled the Expedition to an overlook and invited everyone to step outside and stretch. He is creating this afternoon as a last memory of togetherness before an end. He wants the children to hold it and he wants to hold it as we step into a place he is taking us.

CHAPTER SIXTEEN

Suzanne and Ken were lost. There is something profanely found in being lost in another person. The warm wet lust, the pure lovely unquestioned sweetness of believing life is yours because you have found it in another is a blissful drunk. A purposely lost and ignored deep-self alternately snickers, mourns and is frightened as the body revels in sex, sweat and a need to believe. The need to mesh with another. Later the lovers might wonder how they gave themselves up, laid themselves bare, and never questioned or wondered that they dissolved to nothing in another. In days, or months or years they may decide they were sweetly innocent and dear or stupidly naive and dependent. But for now, for this too short time of passion, it is a mind-numbing blessing to be lost. Few want to be found.

The meeting of two persons in sexual, frenetic, wonderful clutching is dissolving the boundaries of self, the losing of self, the finding of self. To touch another's body with limitless invitation and equality opens a person from inside out like lush, perfumed, over-hanging early summer roses dropping petals like women drop underwear. Life yearns to be enjoyed; admired.

Ken and Suzanne enjoyed. Wednesday morning he called her. "Can we meet at noon? I've been so good to wait so long." His voice was measured grinding saws in hundred-year-old trees.

"Yes."

Shoes were stepped out of in the living room. On each side of Suzanne's bed their eyes didn't waver from the other. Limp cotton dropped in silent turns until they stood naked, ready and lost in claimed desire. Seven turns for Suzanne counting earrings, seven for Ken. His eyes followed the ladybugs and dragonfly up her leg. Touch was sweet, when they met in the middle, anticipated, felt beyond reason.

Suzanne breathed Ken in as they moved; receiving the energy of man she so needed. He was hers in air, the wetness of body, the fire of desire, the earthy smell of lips, hair, breathe. Workday, family was lost.

The sun moved from behind trees to slant through blinds that striped them in shadows and sun before they parted. Suzanne sat and reached for the phone. Ken reached from behind to touch her nipple as lightly as a butterfly lands on a leaf. She shuddered, opening her legs away from his as she dialed and then talked on the phone, "I'm not feeling well. I won't be back in the office today."

She nodded in conversation. "Oh, it's nothing. I just need to catch it now before it turns into something. Will you call Barons, you know, The Printing Barons, for me? Tell them I'm not coming," She turned to Ken and smiled, "I'll be there in the morning."

She gave the phone to Ken, "Do you need to call someone?"

He shook his head, eyes glazed as he watched her move across the sheets. Her breasts swayed; warm creamy pillows, lush and soft, "You forget. I am the boss."

They fell into each other's arms, chests, hips, legs, hands, hair, fingers.

Ken fell away to half sleep. MoMo was dressed as a princess, her wand writing her name in the air. Justin put in plastic fangs and held his vampire cape out for him to admire. Last night they had tried on their costume for tomorrow, Thursday, Halloween. His light rest was fitful. Suzanne touched his hand and he calmed.

Evening was beginning to lay darkness before he went to the coral bathroom. A mental veil needed to be crossed to another life of wife, children, newly replaced furnace filters and raked leaves in plastic bags so this haunting woman of wonder and fulfillment in a seven-hundred-foot apartment would be his. The coral color was infusing. He liked that it did not fit in Salt Lake City at all. It was a color of great inward happiness, strength and abandon to convention. Only brave people could use it.

Ken leaned on the bathroom door frame, darkness surrounding him like it did Sugarloaf. Suzanne's naked body lay in shadow on the bed. His eyes looked to the ceiling as he described Cat's Wednesday routine with Shiners, how she picked up the children from Justin's soccer where MoMo had followed to watch. They would be home by 6:20. Dinner would be started within minutes.

"The kids will be upstairs and she will be at the stove. She'll turn to say hi, and turn back to what she is doing." He left out that she always walked over to kiss him before returning to peeling potatoes or boiling rice or cutting tomatoes.

His hand could not stay away. Under a spell of her slim, lively body of promise and future he gently ran his palm across her chest, hoping to touch her being and take it with him in his fingers. Then he leaned to kiss her neck.

"Good night, Ken."

"I don't want to leave you."

"Then come back at midnight. I'll be here." She knew he wouldn't.

Suzanne was intoxicated with body and spaceless joy. She met with Michael, Eddie, Sierra and Trent at X-Cess and danced until midnight. So good, so good. The joys of the body when there is promise of deliverance of the heart as well is so good.

The passing days of October 31 to November 30 remained in Ken's contract.

CHAPTER SEVENTEEN

A year ago, Mary Ellen tried to save a marriage then finally and gladly lost it. The twelve sessions had been too little too late, but Mary Ellen was pleased with the insights she learned about herself and what a marriage could and could not deliver. Which was why her dating was so sporadic now. Any man within radar distance had to pass a mental checklist before a first date. Did he look like he'd rather spend a weekend deer hunting with guffawing, belching guy-buddies or take her to a weekend retreat of hiking, spas, long dinners and sex? She also dearly liked that her 'ex' had been chastened by the marriage therapy experience and forced to observe his selfishness from a therapy standpoint. At least in relation to *her* needs. In the end, they both agreed he was entitled to a guilt-free mental checklist that *"his"* woman should like hunting trips and marathon potato chip weekends in front of TV.

Cat remembered the name of the therapist. Dr. Roger Dalton. After making an appointment she called Eme. "How are the wedding plans coming?"

"It's a mess. I love it. Sheldon and I are trying to figure out what to give as favors. He wants brandy, but I reminded him of the children. He thinks the children can give theirs to the parents."

"It wouldn't make us unhappy."

"Maybe not but I don't think it's fair. Maybe we'll have to do two kinds of bags."

"Not married and already compromising," Cat shifted as she stood, "Eme, how about getting together this week or next? Any time in that schedule of yours?"

"Always time for you, Cat. Friday lunch?"

It was arranged. The next call was to Ken. "I've made the appointment."

"What?"

"Ken, you agreed to a marriage counselor and I've made an appointment." Cat heard the presses behind Ken. The steady clack-itedy hum filled the space of her nervousness. "I want you to write it down at the office so you won't forget."

"I'm not at my desk but when is it?"

She intentionally called him at Overton so she wouldn't have to say this in person. Unpleasant business needed to be said in neutral territory, so maybe when he was home life could be superficially pleasant.

"Next Monday. The 4th at two."

"I'll put it down." They hung up. Cat sat at the kitchen table. A marriage counselor. How had they come to needing that from her happiness, her complete peace with life such a short time ago? Sha Na Boogie was on the counter in front of her where she stared at it to reconstruct history. What she really wanted was for it to melt to noth-ingness and not ever have existed.

She sat at the table in the serene quiet of home. Cool light streaked in long V fingers through the French doors. The waning days of fall still held heat and vibrancy in her garden while her body, her house felt chill and silent. There was nothing to hear but the words in her head. There was nothing to see but Sha Na Boogie on the count-er. There was nothing to feel.

Any talk with Ken was a fearful dead wall of hurt; a disap-pointment to herself. Fear that the smallest thing could turn a cool atmosphere to ice. She felt extinguished and overrun. Outmaneuvered by design.

She rubbed her arms for warmth but the chill was rising from her heart and spreading outward. Only when she prepared for the Harkness dinner had she poured a glass of wine in the afternoon while the children were at school and Ken was at Overton. But today she poured the wine, took a full swallow and poured again before going to the backyard. It took only five minutes to finish the glass before putting it down on the patio bricks. Ken put the furniture away on his very busy Saturday. She walked to the middle of the backyard.

Her clothes were heavy and too many; but looser than a few weeks ago, hanging easily. The sun was a sweater. Cat returned to the patio and picked up the empty wineglass, went back in the house, poured another and went upstairs. She took all her clothes off, put on her blue bathrobe and returned to the backyard. Again she emptied her glass, put it down and then walked to the center of the yard before laying down. Now the sun could reach through the bathrobe, could touch her when she lowered herself on the grass that was beginning to hibernate for the long winter. The earthy smell of dirt and decaying green opened her nose. She breathed in and relaxed.

For half an hour she lay in the sun, feeling connection of self and dirt. In a light sun warmed sleep she dreamt a train whistle coming toward her, while she stood in a waiting crowd. She held a light bag of her dearest possessions (what were they?) and when the train stopped in front of her she didn't know whether to jump on or not. Everyone was a stranger. She would be leaving much behind. Where was she going?

When she woke she did not remember the sad fear of talking to Ken or feeling extinguished. Instead there was a faint steady current of life from earth unsettling her cells to move in new directions as it traveled from the back of her body where she touched earth to her head, neck, arms, chest, belly, groin, legs, feet. Relaxed and as ready as she could expect, she went upstairs to dress and be ready for the children and Ken.

The week was as ponderous as summer's ripening of a peach. Slow and slower if one is eager for the fruit to ripen or for days to erase pain. Tuesday she did not call him at the office. On Wednesday when she was at Shiner's she did. El told her the new Michael Crichton book was soon arriving. He knew she watched Crichton for Ken. Did she want to reserve a copy? But when she called he was not there. Mary Ellen said he had not come back from lunch. It was three.

Thursday was Halloween. Justin was a vampire and MoMo a princess. They were packed off to school and she was in the office at nine. The workday was stiff but polite. Every night Ken was home by half-past six. Afraid of answers Cat did not ask reasons for anything. Why he was coming home early. Why he was not in the office on Wednesday. Why suddenly she felt like an employee at her husband's and her business. Why neither of them cared about the children's Halloween costumes.

On Friday during lunch, when she could have told Eme they were seeing a marriage counselor next week, she could not. Eme's glowing eyes, bright lights of happiness around her, melodic voice talking about wedding and Sheldon trivia was simply too tender to smash and ruin with her worries. It felt good to bask in Eme's happiness as she had in the sun on the drying lawn. Instead, to release pressure she called her mother. Even the edited version easily drew murmured throat sounds that were muffled mixtures of hurt for Cat and a questioning, confused anger at the son-in-law she admired for his abilities and until now, loyalty to family.

Ken was home at six, aglow with ideas. Aglow with a happiness she did not recognize. "Let's go to a movie and dinner," he looked at his wife and two children. "We haven't done that in a while. Justin and MoMo will choose the movie and Cat will choose the restaurant and I will drive. It's settled. Everyone meet at the car in half an hour."

Justin and MoMo ran for the paper laying on the table. Ken went for a tall glass of water and settled in front of TV and the news. Standing alone, Cat felt her face, smoothed her thick unruly hair and went upstairs to prepare. In front of the mirror, she leaned forward and touched her thinner cheek and then stood back. She looked better in the thinness of sadness.

The assembled family headed to a teenage angst movie of one line jokes about bathrooms, school, teen sex, parents and adult life. Cat found little humor in it but Ken guffawed with the kids. It wasn't until they were sitting in the family Chinese restaurant and the waitress appeared for orders that Cat realized Ken had not directed one word or glance to her all evening. Nor had he touched her as he once did as they maneuvered in public with the children. "What will you have, Cat," he deferred to the waitress.

Cat was baffled and haunted. The surrounding noise of background music, clanging dishes, her children's voices and Ken's happy laughter were knives landing on her heart. She was removed, isolated from the secure warmth of routine and life she so needed; the only kind of domestic life she had ever witnessed or known. Her parents' home was always a peaceful sanctuary of murmured approvals and gentle compliments. The scraping noises of metal chairs on wooden floors at school, the competitions of the playground and learning, all fell away when she walked in the door to hear her mother's rhythmic movements. It seemed her mother's body radiated power to the rafters, basement and out to the garden to keep it safe and infused with life for her father and her.

The weekend continued. Ken was home every minute. When the children were settled in bed on Saturday night it was almost eleven. Ken returned to TV but Cat sat at the end of the couch and sat facing him.

"Ken, are you having an affair? Are you leaving me?"

"I've agreed to meet the marriage person."

"That's not what I asked. Are you leaving me? What is the matter. You aren't talking to me. You aren't saying anything. You aren't the same. What's happening? We haven't made love. All you do is go to work, drink and talk to the kids."

He turned from the TV halfway through her words and watched her as a frog under a microscope; distanced and unconvinced.

"Cat. I said there were problems. Our lives are different. You like some things, I like others."

"What do you mean? We've always had different interests at some point. We've been doing the same for years."

"And I don't like it."

"What don't you like?" her eyes blazed.

"You are much happier sorting laundry, making grocery lists, going shopping with the kids, working at Shiner's with books. Overton is a bother to you. A burden. Maybe I'm a burden to you."

"That's ridiculous. You know it's not true and I work at Overton."

"You work one day a week. Six hours. Maybe seven."

"That's all you've asked for." She sat back, surprised.

"No it isn't and why do I need to ask for it? Don't you know how I work? What the business world is like? I need support. This isn't like the little sweet world of your parents. It changes every day. Women are doing it, too."

"Would it help if I worked at Overton's more? Is that all this is about?" A secret dark chamber in her heart quaked. She felt cornered, as though she was backing through the door of her own jail.

His smile curled into thin lips, "You don't really want to do that."

He was right.

The importance of Justin and MoMo fade to the background

at this point because two adults embroiled in an emotional game of whether the marriage is worthwhile or not do not have time for needs of children. The parents will do what they can, when they remember, but their own survival is on the forefront and will be treated that way. It is a temporary situation that children immediately understand, but being the self-centered little half-grown people they are, without great reasoning ability, and an undeveloped capacity to care about anyone more than themselves, they are alternately incensed and heartbroken to their core that their security is threatened and they are being ignored.

They instinctively understand, perhaps better than the adults, that this is a time of hibernation of their souls as they protect themselves from their parents and the poisonous wrath that surrounds them. At least Justin and MoMo saw it that way. For several weeks they silently absorbed the coldness, anger and sadness in the house. By the morning of Ken and Cat's marriage therapy appointment they began to slink to the kitchen silently, pour their own cereal and stay as unnoticeable as possible whenever either parent was around.

"I may not be here when you get home from school today," Cat said as she poured coffee with her back to them. "I'm sure you can make yourselves busy with homework. I'll check it when I get home." She hadn't checked homework for two weeks.

Cat pulled into the parking lot ten minutes early to wait for Ken. She wanted to walk into Dr. Roger Dalton's office together, as a Goddamn salvageable twosome. At a few minutes after two, Ken pulled in the lot and she got out of her car. He looked at her with a stranger's face. She did not recognize the man who stared through her. His dark features were taut and focused. Ready for battle. The mouth was straight, silent, and did not give recognition. Cat's shoulders fell though she kept her head up. Already she was losing. Ken did not want to be here.

"Hello, Cat," he was deferential.

They took the elevator to the third floor. Both feared a waiting room filled with miserable people. They were alone in the small, softly lit space. Five comfortable wing back chairs were placed around the rectangle room in five points. Two racks filled with drooping magazines were easy distractions. A smiling woman about Cat's age welcomed them from behind a window, and of course, gave them a form to fill out on a clipboard. A demanding buzz preceded the invitation to walk through the door to see Dr. Dalton. Leading them down the hall, she gave a quick glance. "A second appointment is automatically set as a courtesy, but if you do not want it, please call by Friday." She politely smiled through her practiced act.

Immediately, Cat was relieved by Dr. Dalton's presence. He filled the hallway like an oversized, unkempt angel and favorite uncle. His broad smile underscored relaxed eyes that were certainly scanning them for clues, but not with judgment. Arms were stretched out to meet them. Ken went first and Cat followed. She could see sunlight through his wavy hair and she knew he must not be settled with its thinness as he swept his hand through it after shaking her hand. He followed them into his office where two more wing back chairs faced a four-legged wooden table and a single swivel chair with a high back. On top of the table was a notepad, several pens and pencils, a tall desk lamp and a box of tissue. Along one wall was a bookcase filled with thick leather-bound books. The drapes were a sun filtered dull gold leaving Dr. Dalton's face in shadows and theirs lighted for scrutiny.

"We do not decide who is right or wrong in this room," he said as he took his seat. "That's a task only God or his associate should handle. Not us. We look at two sides of a coin and discover what can be worked together." He smiled and looked to both of them for agreement. Cat tried a wan smile but Ken only surveyed him.

"Ken, tell me a bit about yourself. Did you grow up in Salt Lake? Brothers? Sisters?"

"I grew up in Salt Lake with both parents. Two older brothers and a younger sister. I started at the U. of U. but I was never a student and dropped out before the first year was up. I went to work for a printing company as a delivery person and have been in printing ever since." The short biography. Dalton nodded, believing that would urge more but Ken stopped.

"Did the two of you meet in college?" he glanced between them, seeing who would pick up.

"No," Cat said, "we met through friends. He was working. I was just out of college, working as a second grade teacher." After several minutes Cat came to the end, "When our first born was a baby and before our daughter arrived Ken started Overton Overnight."

"I remember hearing that name. Is that you?" Dalton seemed

genuinely pleased to meet the people who started the enterprise. Ken picked up on the interest and soon ran through the years of business cards, flyers, small stationery sets done overnight and cheap.

"What a lot of work. I must admire you for all the work it took." Dalton glanced admirably at both of them.

"But times change, computers changed everything and I had to move on. To survive I had to get into offset printing and now it's direct to plate." Cat was silent, adding nothing.

"What about you, Cat? What did you do during this time?"

She told about raising the children, running babies back and forth between home and Overton, working at Shiner's, how the three days a week at Overton's, changed to two days and now one day. She knew Ken worked long hard hours and was under a lot of pressure and she tried to help where she could and keep a warm and comfortable home for him to find comfort.

"You never did say, Cat. Where did you grow up? What about your family? Are they here?"

"I grew up in Logan. My father was a manager in a small bank. My mother stayed home. I was an only child who came to Salt Lake to college and started teaching."

"But love interrupted?"

She laughed, "Yes."

Twenty minutes later Dr. Dalton indicated the hour was almost finished. "I have one small task for you both. He handed them each a pencil and a small notebook size piece of paper. All my new couples are asked at the end of the first visit to write in one sentence or less what they believe is the major problem they are facing."

Both reacted with the same startled look. After they finished, folded the paper and handed it to him, he stood.

"You are a charming man and woman. Certainly your years of marriage speaks to maturity for both of you. I hope we can meet again and dig a bit deeper. Life can seem so complicated during certain stages of our lives. Don't you agree?"

Yes. Their shoulders rose and fell. Cat's mouth pursed. He was leading them out a back doorway that did not pass through the waiting room. They shook hands, he smiled and wished them well.

"That was a wasted hour." Ken's voice had a bite that hadn't been there during the visit. Cat was stung. She thought it wonderful to remember the first days together. The innocence and hope had lit a sparked light in her eyes.

"Why do you think so?"

"What advice was that? Life can seem difficult in certain stages? It is difficult in all stages. Just different ways. Are you sure you want to continue?"

"I don't want to continue this. I just want us to be happy again and this seems a way. I don't understand what's going on and I'm trying to find out. You're not helping."

Ken shrugged his shoulders and got in his truck, leaving Cat to get in her car.

Dr. Dalton watched through the side of the drawn curtain. He was always grateful when clients parked in viewing distance. Then turned to the two papers.

Ken's broad heavy scrawl wrote, "Cat is no longer a partner with the same goals in life."

Cat's lighter, evenly spaced and easy to read script read, "I'm not sure. Ken's work is demanding."

Chapter Eighteen

"He wants to take you to dinner." Michael leaned on the table at O'Riley's to be sure Suzanne heard over background music and people talking louder than they were an hour ago.

She didn't look at him and shrugged, "I don't know."

"Look, the ugly Mr. Crichton hasn't left his wife and kids. Wife and kids," he emphasized, "and when's the last time you went to an expensive restaurant where you didn't have to buy?"

She thought of the dinner Harkness paid. "I know." It truly was unfortunate Ken was married when this all started.

Arnie, Arnold Greenhall, who had been hanging out with the group on a scattered schedule since August, placed a call to Michael that morning stating male interest. A call Michael kept to himself. Last week he overheard Arnie ask her out and she said she was a little committed. It must be a little commitment, he quipped, because of the time she spent at O'Riley's and X-Cess. He laughed when she turned without a word and walked away. The two of them had played pool a few times. A few weeks ago he beat her in the best of five games. He pushed a stiff arm up in victory with a loud, "Yes!" after putting the last ball in the pocket.

"You can't be committed to a man with a wife and kids. That would be too stupid for you," Michael looked as if leveling her. His blue eyes seemed flecked with golden sawdust as he looked past her 28-year-old façade into the depth of knowing her forever. Her own words were being used against her. It was part of the 'always keep an upper hand' talk they vowed to one another. During Suzanne's last year in high school she persuaded her younger brother it was best to keep the upper hand in a love relationship if one was to get what was really wanted in the long run. If only Mom had been that smart. Strategy was not sneaky; it was good groundwork. She was irritated he was losing ground with Caramello who was scheduled to walk in the door any minute. His eyes would go glassy and thinkless as soon as she appeared. If Suzanne were lucky, Caramello would come soon, so Michael would stop talking about Ken.

"Okay, I'll go," she said. She still had three weeks and two days. She liked nice restaurants. Arnie was good-looking.

"I miss you," Ken whispered the next day when he called on the cell phone. "I don't like not seeing you."

"You can see me. You haven't asked." It was true.

"I can't see you often. I need things to go right."

She was silent. She had been told the game plan. Be a good boy so he wasn't caught doing anything wrong and then just get out December 1. She suspected it was a financial consideration; not an issue of love. Oh, hell, maybe he was also trying to let the kids down without splatting their insides from a sudden drop. He had to be given a little credit for that.

"What are you doing tonight, Suze?" he whispered. "Are you mine?"

"Ken, I'm yours when you're mine." He was satisfied with the answer.

"I want to be with you Suze. I do. We'll go off together as soon as this happens. Away to be alone together."

"I would like that Ken, very much," she felt flushed and ready to touch him. Licorice, sweat, ink filled her nose as she inhaled to imagine smelling him.

Three hours later Arnie appeared at her door. Five minutes late, but an acceptable leeway. "Would you like to come in for a drink, Arnie?" she moved aside for him to enter.

"No, I'll wait for the drink. But I will come in to wait for you," his eyebrow lifted. She took another few minutes before they left, leaving him to glance at the starkness of what a paper rep earned who made a weekly point of saving ten percent. In the bathroom mirror she saw her blonde hair standing at attention, a black sleeveless dress and the coral necklace. Her lips shone.

"I like that dress," he nodded toward her while they sat at the restaurant table. A short candle and two full wine glasses were between them. Hors d'oeuvres were coming.

"Thanks."

Arnie talked with the charm of Virginia underlining Utah's

185

desert history of starkness, utility and unfinished syllables. When he bent his head to cut steak a light shone on him and she decided rather than summer moon shimmer, his hair had the color of dying aspen leaves, yellow, fringed with black. A very wonderful, earthy look. Ken's looked like the result of two women conspiring against a man at a hair care counter. Arnie was entertaining, easy to talk to, attentive, good-looking. Too bad she had already given her heart and didn't think she had a reason to change. When they sat in the car in front of her apartment it was almost eleven. The junipers along the building were bent and broken of spirit.

Arnie leaned to kiss her and she kissed back, he leaned further to hold her closely and instinctively she moved toward him. Her hips almost raised. Suzanne fell into him and then, startled, she sat up to break away.

"Thank you, Arnie, thank you, but I need to go now," and she gathered her purse, opened the door and went upstairs to her apartment without turning around. All she thought was, "What am I going to tell Sugarloaf?"

Raylene's call woke Suzanne the next morning. "Want to go shopping? I need to spend money I don't have today. Let's go drink at lunch and look at slutty clothes." At least her Saturday would be filled.

"Why do you want to spend money and buy slutty clothes?" Suzanne eyed her over a pastrami sandwich.

"Carson."

"Carson?"

"He's a Taurus. A true land loving territorial bull without humor."

"What did he do?"

"He scatters the crowds. He makes it impossible to talk when he's so intense."

"I don't get it."

"I like how he's always around for me, but he also is a choke hold. We were at a party last night. His friends. You'd think he'd be relaxed. Instead when a few of them gathered around me to talk he sat like a vulture watching blood drip."

"So why the slutty clothes?"

"To convince myself I'm mine. Maybe I need a new man."

Suzanne told Raylene about the afternoon she called in sick. "Sounds like he called again after being turned down for dinner."

"It took a while but he did."

"Good, I'm glad it took a while."

"Why?" Suzanne didn't get that.

"Because it shows he had much to consider with a family at home and he still chose to call you. If it had just been sex, he could have found someone else."

"I hadn't looked at it that way."

"So what's the real situation now?"

"We agreed to the first of December."

"He's supposed to be free by the first of December?" her eyes narrowed, assessing possibilities. Raylene's hair glowed in an autumn ring of golden red around the sun.

"Yes."

"That's quick to end a marriage. Assuming it wasn't over anyway."

Suzanne nodded, "I don't know, Ray, who can know?"

"Well, today's the 9th. What happens either way?"

"If he's free then he's mine. If he's not, well, I guess I'm free again."

Raylene's voice lowered, "So you want him that much?" Suzanne didn't move. "Why, Suzanne?" They both knew she wanted the deeper, not flippant answer.

"I'm tired of being alone. I want to go somewhere further than Harkness. I want someone who knows where he's going." They were both quiet. The sound of the restaurant was a drum circle keeping their awareness to each other. "I want someone with a little age and weariness I know how to lighten. Who won't leave me."

Raylene sat back, "Then I think you may have found your man."

It turned out they didn't look at slutty clothes. Instead they looked at dishes. Raylene admired a few pieces that would match the colors she wanted Carson to paint the living room. Suzanne touched a few designs that would bring coral into the kitchen.

"What do you think of Caramello?" They were walking down the mall hall with people passing. Suzanne signaled they were moving in front of three slow teenagers with a hip that kicked her purse to the left.

"I can tell by that little nose movement you're jealous."

"Okay, enough about me. What do you think of Caramello?"

"She's an underground river. Refreshing and secret."

"What the hell does that mean for Michael?"

"I'm not sure yet. Either his best and secret find or a cold and mysterious drowning pool."

When they parted, Raylene leaned and hugged Suzanne. "Be careful, Suzanne. Claiming a man is claiming a life."

Suzanne's phone rang in the dark on Monday morning. The sound tore her dream away and left her unsure which world was hers. When it rang the second time she turned in bed to see a fluorescent 6:09. Her arm outside the cover met cold air.

"Hey." Her voice scratched.

"I woke you." She nodded instead of answering, then growled a yes.

"Can I come over, Suzanne?" Ken's voice seemed unsure.

"Yes."

"I'll be there in ten minutes."

Her head lifted to start for the shower but she lay back, content and warm. No soap, water, shampoo, conditioner, hair gel, lotion or lip gloss. Let him smell yesterday.

The key in the lock hurtled Mr. Crichton from the blanket in the corner of her room to the front door. Suzanne turned on her back to watch Ken remove his clothes; dropping each piece carelessly except his shirt; laid carefully on the dresser. Sniffing her neck, running his fingers through soft hair, he leaned deeply onto her after lifting the blanket and letting his full weight take her. "I need this time. I need this time. It will keep me going."

Half an hour later she stepped from bed to wash for a day at Harkness.

Ken heard the noises of her morning as music, a sweet promising melody of remembrance that would be his charm as he faced the rest of the month. How she moved in the bathroom with running water, an opening drawer, a hair dryer's whine were substance of proof she existed beyond imagination.

It wasn't enough. He needed reassurance, a talisman to keep with him when he looked at Justin and MoMo. In grey light with yellowing edges he surveyed her room and was surprised how bare it was. Desire had not noticed. A small TV was on a laminate table in front of the bed. Above it was a cheap framed print of a woodland scene and a small brook. To the right was the window with white curtains that looked to be made of wide strips of medical gauze. On the left was the dresser where he laid his shirt. Six drawers were stacked. The top small drawers leaned down, not meeting squarely, like drooping eyelids above the face of other drawers. He got up to look through a tray of scattered cheap jewelry her fingers ran through without care for order. The coral necklace was to the side. He opened a top drawer while listening to Suzanne's sounds, predicting when she would come out. Panties were exploding bubbles of color: red, yellow, blue, green, black, white, orange, purple. In the corner was her folded business card. He opened it and read, "Fuck me easily Ken and die."

Suzanne had passed the card at the dinner with Harkness when they said hello. When Cat had gone to the bathroom he'd answered and given it back. In his heavy, hard script was, "I won't." This would be his talisman. Tucked in his pocket, it would be with him. He wanted to rush in the bathroom and look at her. Look at this woman who could take anything from him he had to give and return it hard and heavy. And take more. He knew it would feel good in his pocket and remind him of her. Her.

Gently, he tapped on the door. "I'm leaving now, Suze. Can I see you?"

"Come in."

Inside the steamy sanctum of a coral bathroom he may have been overcome. "I love you, Suzanne Flint. I love you." They stood three feet apart. Her dripping and dressed only in the silk of her own skin. Him dressed and buttoned the second time for a day's work.

Suzanne lifted her leg and put it on his arm; leaving a wet spot on his shirt. "Good. Life is waiting for you here."

CHAPTER NINETEEN

When Ken left the house Monday morning, Cat heard his Expedition roar like a warlock from his foot on the accelerator. Quietly, she lay without moving, listening to her house; the furnace turning on and off, the mysterious cracking of the house as it settled, another car leaving Sunshadow Estates, the wind moving a screen in the bathroom window. Though she tried to hear, she could not make out her children's breathing; or the sound of earth turning on its axis preparing for winter. She did not know if the paper was in the driveway.

Life was looking around a corner. There was denouement. A swooping arc of undefined time was finishing a rainbow. Innocence. Habits with Ken. The children's early years. Her thirties. Or simply the dying of one year working toward another. Cat rose from bed to prepare for the day as Suzanne felt Ken lift the sheet and lay his weight on her.

Showered and lotioned, Cat returned to the comfort of sheets and pillows and turned on the bedside lamp. She picked up the book on the table. *Dr. Jung once replied, "How can you find a lion who has just swallowed you?" The chief characteristic of the inferior function is that it is out of control."* The book was *Ecstasy,* by Robert A. Johnson. Her life did feel out of control in areas she was unaccustomed to observing. Her way of knowing was through skin, feeling waves of information or noticing movement within bodies. She was unaccustomed to interpreting direct action easily seen by others. There wasn't enough time or ability to see the lion she was living in. And it was fearful. When Cat put the book down because it was time to wake her children to begin their day, Ken was holding the note, "Fuck me easily Ken and die." "I won't."

Later, Cat arrived at Dalton's parking lot before Ken. As they walked silently to his office she wanted to ask about Mary Ellen,

Rhonda, Miguel and Dan. People she thought would be friendly neutral conversation. Just to hear his voice through the forbidding silence.

"Glad to see you, glad to see you," Roger Dalton expressed as they came through the door to his office. They both nodded. Ken curtly, Cat apologetic. He observed Ken's strident directed walk apart from Cat and her silent, hidden walk that held her behind, inside her clothes and herself. A variation of several themes he saw every day.

"Lovely November weather, don't you think?" he watched where their eyes went. Ken's went to the side and out the window to the parking lot, Cat's to the floor.

"Well, Ken, I want to hear what you think is a comforting, wonderful, perfect home life for you," imagining had been a good tool to use and letting the man talk first was usually better received and relaxed both people.

Ken shifted but he was intrigued by the question. A thinking pause filled the room. Cat smelled ink drifting toward her and felt a welling of tears that made her turn away. Ken was not going to talk about the home she had provided.

"A place away from work. No worry. Sex. The children happy. A happy wife." Roger Dalton nodded, "And you, Cat?"

"Peace. Tranquility. Ken. The children playing. Books." She stopped talking so again Roger Dalton nodded. This time he looked to both of them and waited to see who would answer.

"So, how do you see your home?"

Ken's voice felt so strong Cat lifted her left hand and rubbed her ear. "Cat's not happy. And therefore I'm not happy. She keeps a fine house, always has. She could run a bed and breakfast. But she's disinterested. Distant. I don't think she really wants to be part of my life. My business takes all I have to run it well and she's not there. Not supportive. Not part of the team."

Cat shrank to the far side of her chair and color drained from her face. Her voice was raspy and she felt her hot face starting to contort. "I do, too. Yes, I do. I work at the business. I support you on everything."

"I blame her parents," Ken was looking straight at Dr. Dalton as though he were a teacher and Cat a recalcitrant child who shouted an immature outburst. "They overprotected her. She didn't have a chance to be strong."

The fifty minutes were miserable and long. Dr. Dalton's quiet words guided the tangled, convoluted, angry barking and defensive talk to a neutral place, he wanted opinions, nuances, and to watch reactions. Ten minutes before the time was to end he began nodding more and interjecting words to defuse and settle. Ken's eyes were a focused dog's, aware he had cornered his prey and with a witness in the room, a witness who would know he deserved to win. Cat's eyes were wounded. Dalton was sure that during this hour an innocence in her had been smashed like a smiling pumpkin in the hands of ranting teenagers.

Dalton watched through the curtains as they walked to their cars. Ken took strides that made Cat skip fast. At his car he stopped and turned to her. They exchanged a few words and then he abruptly opened his door, sat inside and closed it. She stepped away as his car drove off. She slowly walked to her car and disappeared inside. When his next patients arrived she still had not driven away.

Her eyes were red and make-up was wiped away with a tissue when she walked in the house. She looked down and did not let the children see her fully. They were busy and did not notice her beaten walk, pasty cheeks, red eyes, broken voice. In the bathroom she washed her face and reapplied makeup. *Ecstasy* was a strange title for her to be reading now, she thought as the picked it up from where it sat. She walked to each child's room, patted them on the head, glanced at homework and then went downstairs to sit on the couch with her book.

Within an hour Ken was home. He went to the fridge for a beer, nodded at her and went upstairs to Justin's room to play video games. MoMo joined them and Cat could hear three tones of laughter.

That morning she snipped a dozen marigolds that were still blooming. Any night the frost could kill them, but tonight they were jubilant with their straight stems looking boldly to the sky. With laughter in the background, she leaned over and plucked one stem from the small glass vase on the coffee table in front of her. That one hardy marigold was used as a bookmark in a slim book, *Ecstacy*, with the tagline, Understanding the Psychology of Joy. Suddenly, the numbing contradiction of being the target of Ken's anger a few hours earlier, and the laughing joyous voices of her husband and two children playing a game upstairs brought her to realize what was really happening. In the darkening November twilight the flower, book, laughter and knowing she was the target of her husband's deepest anger stirred a new awareness. It was the simple and unadorned truth laid before her: Ken had staged this afternoon's rampage in Roger Dalton's office and he was now fully enjoying his children without her or any thought about her. He was urging the marriage to end.

The thought was so clear it ended the tears rising from her belly. Why he wanted to leave she still would not understand, but it did not matter. She was absorbing the information, the knowledge that flowed through the house in the air. Ken was finished. Until the three of them walked downstairs to watch TV Cat sat on the couch, motionless. Her hand was wrapped around the marigold and she stared toward the stairs where their laughter reverberated from wall to wall surrounding her.

Wrapped in shock and unavoidable truths, Cat was silent and self-protected. She made dinner, was pleasant, directed the children to baths and tucked them in. When she came back down to read a little longer, Ken had turned the lights off and gone to their bedroom to watch TV alone. She no longer existed in the house.

Cat went upstairs, walked through Ken's TV view and went in the bathroom to prepare for bed. Shadows caught her eye as she undressed and she turned to the bathroom mirror. Her body had the languid fullness and sloping lines of bearing two children, but she had never been ashamed of it. Her skin was smooth, tight enough and clear. And now it was only eight pounds too heavy. This body served her purposes, was healthy enough and gave her ability to move about.

Deeper thought never seemed necessary or worth the inevitable disappointment of comparison to the young bodies strutting on TV and on magazines lining grocery store check-outs. When she came out of the bathroom the TV was off and Ken was quiet in the dark.

For the first time in twelve years of marriage there was fear of him. Her whisper was unsure and broke cracked and loud. "Ken, what's going on?"

The dark made his voice everywhere. "Cat, I've wanted to tell you for a long time. Since summer. But I haven't known how and this is just the way it is. We've outgrown each other."

"Outgrown each other," so polite. Her voice was a twelve-year-olds, "What about the children and the life we've built?" Her arm swept wide, "this house?"

"The children are ours. We'll work it out. We bought this house. We can sell it. It's a house."

"You've got to let us try. We have a marriage with children. You dump this on me and just say it's over? Without a chance? Without fighting for it? All your fighting is for Overton Printing is that it? Is that more important than the children, than me, than our history together?" Flourishing her arms she stepped away from the bed and turned on the light. Her nightgown fell from her shoulder, her face without make-up was sterner, "You've been thinking this since summer and you keep it a secret? Nothing said? To the very people who love you?"

He kept his head on the pillow but his body tensed, his chin tightened, causing the side of his forehead to jut out. He was forcing quiet.

"All this and now you have nothing to say?"

"Cat, it's too late. Maybe I should have said something sooner, but you are who you are."

"Is that supposed to make me feel ashamed?"

"No. It's supposed to tell you what you already know. We're mismatched and have been for a long time."

Cat spent the night on the couch in the family room. The light of the moon touched her face as it could not in the bedroom with Ken. Alternately, she talked to God and herself. Yes, she knew they were different. In fact, they always had been. Him more aggressive, her the book person, him interested in sports, her happy just to be around him and the children. Didn't he tell her a hundred times he liked that? He told her that a hundred times and it must have made an impression that didn't need reassuring because he had not said it again for several years. At five-thirty she heard Ken come down the stairs, open the garage door and quietly leave.

She was so bent and worn while the children prepared for school that they asked her several times if she was okay or if they should call the doctor or Dad. "No," she said, she was fine but, of course, they knew she was not. After they left it was eerie quiet; the faux French mansion was a prison. She didn't want to be there, but had no where to go. While the tub filled she poured a glass of wine. In deference to morning she added a strawberry.

Naked, she watched herself in the mirror and waited for the tub to fill. What would she do without Ken? When she sank in the bath water it was to the warmth and security of an unremembered womb. Since the day she met Ken she felt protected and safe in his presence. Without realizing it she always felt the cover of his invisible umbrella of masculine power and she had been secure under it as she had never been anywhere else. The warmth of Ken's strength, the caring of his protection was a current of security she believed would always be hers and she returned it with... There she stopped. What had she really returned to him? That he wanted?

Tears landed on her arm as she dried. A clean robe was at the end of the closet and she walked to get it. On the carpet was a folded piece of paper under a pair of Ken's folded pants, hanging upside down from a chair kept in the closet.

Suzanne's blue raised ink business card was folded tightly but she recognized whose it was as soon as she saw it. Cat's body felt drained, near bloodless. She opened the card. A water droplet from her hair fell on it before she turned it around to read the two handwritings. "Fuck me easily Ken and die. . . I won't."

The last of Cat's imaginary marriage and the hope of renewing its gossamer walls crumbled. First she called Eme, told her of the note that "showed it was over." The written words wouldn't spit out. She was sorry to deliver the news the week before her wedding, but she would be in Jackson Hole for a few days and needed her to know. She would see her on Saturday at the wedding. Cat's words were half sobs that clicked against each other like knitting needles changing the direction of Cat's life. Eme listened, nodding and murmured soft ohs and dear Cat. "Call me, Cat, please call me."

She called Ken. In staccato, she told him she found the business card, she was leaving for a few days to think and the children needed him to care for them. They would all be going to Eme's wedding on Saturday so be ready. He mumbled little response. The clack of the press behind him covered his last words. The next call was to Shiner's. She would not be able to go in tomorrow. She could not call her mother. Before leaving the house she made reservations at The Bear Trail Lodge a few blocks from town and requested a room overlooking the valley.

With the suitcase packed she left the bedroom, but stopped at the top of the stairs. Bending from the knees she put the suitcase down, turned back to the bedroom and straightened. Out of her top drawer she slid her fingers to the back and found Sha Na Boogie. She walked in the bathroom and carefully wrote on the mirror so she wouldn't ruin the lipstick. Perhaps she would need court evidence. "No fucking, Ken.' On a sticky note she penciled, "Stay with the children," and stuck it underneath.

The suitcase held too many clothes, but she hadn't wanted to think about efficiency. Books, paper, wine, a camera and colored pencils were added. On the seat beside her she put a handful of CDs to play on the way. But first she stopped at the children's school, pulled them from class, made sure they understood she was fine but needed to be away a few days. Daddy would take care of them.

From a chair by the window she watched the small town's night lights mirror the sky. Staring into the peaceful forever, she could let thought surface. Things had been changing since spring, perhaps May. It was background noise too low to hear clearly and her belief in the strength of love and marriage discounted it; believed it was a temporary blip not worth making a big deal over. Marriage was like that. Each person needed to give and receive occasional quirky space. She remembered how affectionately Ken would look at her in the first years of their marriage as she cuddled to sit by him and read while he watched TV. When she fell on the bed it was with a worn ragged peace that let her sleep deeply until the day's light crept in the room.

Her eyes opened, she did not move. Ken did not make movements in the bathroom. She couldn't hear the children breathe. There was nothing she needed to do. For herself or anyone else. She surveyed the room. Pine dresser and TV amoire with black ornamental iron pulls. Very western. Two swivel chairs upholstered in snowflakes had a round pine table between them. The wine bottle, almost empty, stood on it with the bathroom glass she used. Beside them were two notebooks she brought, the leather hotel book, and the wine opener. Forest green drapes hung heavy but not closed letting in light through sheers. She rolled in bed to view the room entirely with the outdoor prints on the walls, her clothes on the floor, the suitcase to the side on the aluminum legged holder. Her private kingdom in a little bubble of time.

She didn't want to think beyond this room and was vaguely irritated she told Ken and Eme she was leaving town to 'think about things' when her real mission was to leave everything behind, run and not think about anything. Pretend nothing unusual was happening. Out of sight, out of mind is what came to her and an unreality laid on her that at this moment she didn't have a husband and two children had never been born. Her mind wanted blankness.

Lying in this bed, devoid of her familiar room, children, husband, house she felt freed and at peace. Everything she left three-hundred miles away was too painful. In this lovely place of holiday fun, where her parents brought her for Forth of July celebrations, she wanted to enjoy life. She lay naked and rested while her hand touched her hair, cheek, shoulder, breast, hip, belly, hair. Today would be hers.

Room service was luxury. Good. She ordered what she wanted and showered before it came.

The day was meandering, without purpose, thoughtless, unplanned. Exactly what Cat wanted. There was a walk around the grounds of the hotel reminding her of years ago walking between her parents. Then a drive to town, a bit of time at an antique store that caught her eye on a side street, a bookstore, a stop at a deli for snacks, a drive to Lake Louise, a stop by the road to sketch a grove of trees. At Lake Louise she sat at a worn wooden picnic table anchored in cement, listened to water while holding a pencil above blank paper, forced herself to draw and then threw it in a Forest Service garbage can. There was a stop for gas, another walk around the hotel, and a drive-by assessment of stores she might visit tomorrow to find presents for Justin and MoMo.

Evening. What to do. Surely not call home. When she arrived she left a voice message on the home recorder so they would know where to find her, but it was certain she did not want to call them and be weepy. No, this was time to be - what? Remote? Independent? Sassy? At least unavailable? Then she was irritated it sounded like she was playing a game when she was only, only trying to live, to survive learning she was not wanted by the man who was her body's only woman history.

She listened to news on TV little interested in the middle east, economy, a murder trial in Florida, the smiles and tousled hair of British royalty. All of this was going on so clearly and independently without her. At six, she opened a bottle of wine. Tonight she wanted to go from her room but she didn't know how or where. It was important to be around people.

Cat flipped through the leather-bound guide on the table to Restaurants. She had seen the bar downstairs to the right when she walked in the front door, Spurs. There hadn't been a tagline, definition or apology. They did serve dinner and it sounded, if not approachable, at least a place where she could run back to her room. The other choice had been Six Horses, "A team for steam," where there would be a band and 'fun to remember'. Well, she wasn't ready for remembering.

Protected in black; she wore the indefinable. It hid her. Dissolving her like children's candies that turned to fizz in water.

"Window or bar?" the maitre de asked.

"Window."

She ordered a gin and tonic. She would sip and be forced to stay longer. Time passed, dinner was ordered and Cat held ground. Alone in a place of enjoyment. Pride would survive this evening. The television played, the bartender talked to three people who were insistent that all talk revolve around whether snowmobiles should be allowed in Yellowstone Park. She shifted in her chair, waiting, wondering, hoping she could go to her room within an hour and pretend she had been sophisticated. Sign the charge card with flair and go back to the room. Charge it to Ken. Charge it to the company.

Black can be sultry. The man walked by and their eyes met but Cat looked away. Cat was halfway through her salad, baked potato, almond crusted trout and wine. Every bite was being felt and tasted in a slow dinner pace that didn't look like she was racing to leave.

"May I sit with you?" the man returned from behind her. He looked expectant and was so polite it seemed he was asking for the small courtesy of sitting at her table in a busy cafeteria. She nodded yes.

"Thanks, I've been alone all day gathering soil samples and haven't talked to anyone. Thought I'd come downstairs just to be around a few people." He was a burly man with an easy cowboy western walk that needed more room than city people gave. His hands were dry tree stumps that made the drink he held child-size. Easy twinkling light came from his eyes and Cat was not afraid of this friendly stranger.

"Why were you gathering soil?"

"Follow up on a study. Trying to figure what this earth may be good for around here besides skiing and driving over. I'm a geologist for a company in Boise."

"Oh." Cat wasn't too conversant. Talking skills had abandoned her.

"What are you doing in Jackson?" His eyebrows were lifted and listening.

"Not much. Just visiting for a day or so." She knew that sounded evasive, "I did some sightseeing today." That sounded more directed.

An hour went by as they exchanged full real names, because both of them were too honest not to do so, said appreciative phrases on Jackson scenery, commented on national news and talked about whether they liked snow or rain better. Half way through Cat laughed at a small thing he said with the first real voice she had returned. His eyes deepened and looked with appreciation. The warmth of his eyes, the acceptance of this man covered her slowly like a warm blanket in a cold night.

"Where are you from, Lina?"

His eyes were too interested and kind to lie, "Salt Lake City." That was the critical information he didn't even know he needed to piece together why she was there. Cat felt flawed and suddenly sitting in a bar with a strange man in a resort town was cheating. "I came to have a day or so away," she whispered.

"Sometimes a person needs that." He looked straight in her eyes, seeing corners and pathways in her woman's body that had never been touched. Cat changed during dinner. She wouldn't be able to tell you how. It was a subterranean subconscious shift because she wished it so. They talked without feeling time. Deep life invites without demand or advertising. It is tender and shrinking. If you are lucky it will show a flash of blinding sword light, hoping to catch your attention, but it returns as quickly to a shadowed background whisper difficult to hear. You must claim your invitation and come on your own. That night Cat was invited. In the end, they looked deeply, well into one another. As persons, not cheating or deceptive but in care and appreciation.

When they walked the huge lobby of lodge pole furniture and Indian rugs toward the elevator their conversation stopped for the first time. During their lost time as they lifted hands to talk and drink, they had noticed each other's wedding rings. The man pushed floor three. Cat pushed four.

"Nice to meet you, Lina," he nodded and started out before suddenly turning and taking her hand. He held the door with the other. The focused look in his eye startled her, compelled her to look in his eyes.

"You're a beautiful woman, Catalina. It's been good to talk to you. Take care of yourself," he let go of her hand, turned away and stepped out, letting the door close.

"Mom! Mom!" MoMo rushed for hugs. Lina leaned and sniffed the oily sweat of her daughter. Justin followed equally happy to see his mother, but not as loud. She kneeled on the floor to receive and give in a flow of chests, arms, shoulders, heads.

"Hello, Cat," Ken turned from his chair, watching.

"I prefer Lina," and she turned away from him. It was a quiet sentence that hung like yesterday's laundry above the childrens' notice.

"Justin, there's a sack on the front seat. Will you get it without opening it?" she smiled as large as he did and both children ran to the car. Lina walked to the refrigerator. A glass of wine would be good after a long drive, but she also needed cheese, an apple, crackers, grapes. The children were back before the plate was arranged.

"Let me finish," she smiled again and they lit under the happiest smile they had received from her in weeks. It could be imagined her skin glowed.

There was a slower walk to her presence and she breathed evenly, fully as she walked to the family room balancing wine and a plate of snacks that would be dinner. The long skirt hung a little from the last weeks of eating less and she walked lighter. Ken turned to watch her, TV remote still in hand.

"For my first born, comes the first present," Lina presented a smaller sack inside the sack. Justin tore open the paper to find a box of flashing orange, red, yellow fishing lures dancing around the box already seeming alive.

"Fishing lures!"

"Yes, Justin. Your father will teach you how to use them. The two of you will be great fishing buddies."

"Good, Cat. We'll go in the spring, Justin," Ken's look was killing.

"What's mine, Mom?" MoMo jumped up and down, leaning on her, trying to drink her presence in from three lost days.

"Here you are," she presented a small ribboned box. The dainty turquoise necklace soon dangled on Momo's neck. "I love it, Mommy," she stroked it. "Real jewelry."

"And of course I have something for you, Ken," she walked to an oversize purse she brought in and opened it.

"Thanks, Cat," he was happy with a bottle of twenty-year-old bourbon. Maybe eight dollars was avoided in Utah taxes.

"I take it everyone is ready for Eme's wedding?" They nodded. "Good, I talked to her on the phone today and she's expecting the rest of you at five. I'm going up early at two."

"I've got to work Saturday. I've had to take time off with the kids and I need to be there," Ken said in tones she didn't interpret.

"What does that mean, Ken?"

"It means I'm going in at six and I need to work all day."

"I don't understand."

They looked squarely at each other. "You've been away, I've taken time off, I need to be in the office."

"Are you coming to Eme's wedding?"

Lina could see him think. The measure of the man sat before her in the high back oversized chair with wide arms she had chosen especially to take the rough wear of his hands, head and back as he watched TV. She looked though a dozen designer fabric books to find something as masculine as Ken that would take absent-minded abuse and still look decorator approved. He did not want to go to the wedding, but she had believed and now saw it was true, that he was torn between his friendship and admiration for Eme and Sheldon and spending time as a failing, falling apart family. Which meant time with his wife.

"Are you coming to Eme's wedding, Ken?" she whispered,

hoping to be compelling and not begging. She did want him there for Eme. A last show.

"I'll be there, but you need to take the kids. I need to work until I have to come."

"Settled. The kids will come with me." She straightened.

Ken and Lina slept in the same bed without touching. Neither acknowledged the other's presence. When Lina woke at 3:40, Ken was softly asleep behind her. When she woke again he was gone.

Grey light opened the day, filling the room with an artist's brush depth of purpose. As though the day would have meaning. Because it arrived on slow ponderous feet of gloom it should carry weight of meaning. Lina doubted. It was a Hollywood trick, a writer's tool, a poet's pretension, but she knew this slow grey day that held sure doom of one marriage ending while another started was the same day young couples would welcome a first baby, reunions of long lost loves would meld, fortunes would be found, puzzles solved, questions answered. Just not hers.

"This requires some explanation, particularly at airports. I always make a point of telling the airline ticket agent just how many skulls I have with me in my baggage - not to shock her, but to make sure that, in case the plane crashes, investigators will know why there were more skulls than passengers aboard. This is mere professional courtesy to my colleagues, who will have to pick through my remains in the event of an accident." That was the first paragraph she read from *Dead Men Do Tell Tales,* by William R. Maples and Michael Browning before the children woke. Her life was skulls in old baggage that needed to be worked through unless she died before it was possible.

The children ate toaster waffles while she sipped coffee and looked out the back window. While she was away a deep frost covered the night wilting the marigolds to over-steamed, tortured spinach. Autumn was falling into winter. Death of this year would end in birth of next year. Lina stared at her back yard. There was intrigue below the cold and now barren dirt. Hot earth, roiling, over a 1000 degrees was only a few miles below her artificially warmed floor. The cold she felt standing above a molten uneasy plate of earth was the vanity of believing in human importance. It could all rush up, drowned her, ruin her at any moment.

"Eme, Eme!" MoMo screamed as she rushed to the warm, engulfing embrace of her pretend aunt. Eme was radiant, flushed with excitement.

"You look beautiful, Eme, we're so happy for you." Lina said wrapping her arms around her friend. Eme was dressed in the flowing crochet dress, bias cut gown with a generous neckline and inset rhinestones. This wondrous, bursting woman filled the air with electricity and love.

"I'm happy, too. I didn't really expect to be, Cat, but I am," Eme stepped back into the room with the three of them so they could help her finish preparing for the ceremony. Sheldon and his father, who had flown in from Florida, were in another room.

The two friends sat in the chairs by the table, locked hands and looked at one another. "I've decided to be Lina from now on." Eme's face opened with a flushed over reaching smile from her heart, "Oh, Lina, you are on the way to The Future of Inner Trinity."

For the first time in two days Lina thought she was going to cry. Her forehead scrunched up. Empathy is so seductive. But she caught herself.

"We'll talk another day, Eme. This is your day," she paused, "Ken will be here by the ceremony. He needed to go into the office." Eme nodded. "And I have something for you. I got it in Jackson."

Eme took the package Lina held. Inside was a twist top silver box with a pinecone handle that fit in her palm. Before opening it she turned to the card with it. The front showed a standing woman in windswept thin nightwear holding a lamp to darkness. "May you ever be lighting the dark."

"That's how I think of you, Eme, lighting the dark for me to follow." Inside the silver box was a scoop of dirt she had gathered on the soft shores of Lake Louise.

"From a lake shore to you, Eme. To remember what we're made of."

Ken was five minutes early and looked rushed but pleased enough to kiss Eme well, shake Sheldon's hand and sit with his family. It was part show-time with expected roles and part sentimental journey. Eme knew. Lina and Ken knew. Sheldon had been told. This was a last time together. They enjoyed the time as borrowed and paid with interest. More valuable because it was owed. Owed to time that would scoop it away by their next meeting. Owed to eternity to record and reckon.

Ken drove home with Justin talking about the basketball season and pointing out all the cities of the NBA in the Atlas Eme and Sheldon had given him. Lina had MoMo, who slept most the way from Snowbird, her head resting against the window and her gift of a plush toy rabbit. The adult brandy was secured on the floor. "You are the Sunshine of My Life" played on the radio. She turned it off. Lina followed Ken down the canyon watching his taillights, reflecting his brake lights, turning as he did, staying a distance behind as an observer and participant. "This man," she thought, "this man of my life. How softly you have slipped away with good intention, hard work, sweet pleasure. And still you are gone. To another already. The dear touch of your face in the morning filled with softness of sand under your eyes and prickle of cactus on your cheek will not be mine. The sound of your sleep. The light of your eyes when you disagree with a referee's call, the smell of your sweat after yard work, the stance of your hips when you are angry. Will not be mine any longer. I will miss it. You jerk. You asshole.

Then she smelled the trailing memory of the man who looked at her over dinner in a bar. The man who drank in charm she didn't think was there, who tilted his head when she tilted hers, who smiled with a wild acceptance when she lifted her wineglass, who was awkward in his chair to leave it so he could walk her to the elevator, who had ears too small for his head, who didn't touch her as they walked, who took her hand and said she was beautiful. And said she should take care of herself. She smelled books, life, mountain air, lingerie, lipstick, herself busy and alive; not afraid, cautious or worrying.

The lengths of the Expedition and the Audi reacted to the garage opening at the same time. The children were carried to bed. The man and woman, husband and wife of twelve years, lovers for fifteen, silently had a drink of wine, a glass of twenty-year-old brandy and wordlessly fell into bed to make very satisfying love. A love of end. A love of thank you. A love of revenge to what now would be lost to both. A good-bye to what could have been. A closing of the far book of possibilities that now would write a final chapter through space.

The fight was over. When sex was finished Lina recoiled to

her side of the bed, but this night, for this moment, her body needed the peace of a surging recognition before good-bye. Good-bye.

CHAPTER TWENTY

Suzanne had unfinished business.

Stroking Mr. Crichton while she sat on the couch watching a sitcom rerun was not helping her sort it out. The low sound of the TV and the cat's steady purr were irritating, just plain irritating. Purrs and TV noise weren't blocking out the thoughts of other people filling her head. Their mind shadows made a circle around her. There was her mother's sweet, timid smile under glistening eyes and arms always outstretched to hold her. Ken. A lumbering bear man who threw things out of his way to make his own path and delivered what he promised which she expected to be security and future. The swivel-hipped polite Arnold Greenhall. She hadn't slept with him and he still had crawled into her comparison chart. He would be a legal playing ground and a lot of fun. Eventually, he would make her be educated and then leave if she messed up bar exams. Sugarloaf. Thinking of him, she shifted on the couch. Sugarloaf was freedom, expression without due. A man who gave her male strength by touch, took what she gave, came back when called and never asked for more. And there was Michael. A born conscience, too well-loved to discard when he was irritating. If he would only get out of the way and be quiet. A conscience was very inefficient to goal reaching.

An hour ago she left O'Riley's. Fled O'Riley's. Michael once again started on why she was being so stupid with a married man when she could have Arnold, a man with clean fingernails, or even the real Mr. Crichton. He had been on the internet and it looked like he was free. Send him an e-mail with a picture, Michael suggested, or give him a call. Michael would write a letter of endorsement. Coming from a brother it might make her look vulnerable. The true story could come out later.

The hollow cave voice of her mother's words rang in the back of her head, "Suzanne, you like too much excitement. Focus on what you truly want and pay attention." Was that advice when she was twelve and her mother was luminescent and clear-eyed or when she was sixteen and her skin was writing paper and her voice chimney whistles?

"Did Mom ever give you advice on how to live?" she asked Michael two hours ago over the half-tuned voice of a Monday night folksinger at O'Riley's.

"What?"

"Did Mom ever tell you stuff about what you should and should not do to live? Cause she did me and I wonder if you ever got her stuff cause sometimes it rings in my head." She sounded indignant.

He laughed, "She probably told me more about how you should live than how I should."

"Really? What did she say?"

"Not that much," suddenly he was evasive. He remembered more than he wanted to say and she knew it.

"What did she say, Michael? It could be important. All she told me was pay attention or be a good girl or stupid stuff like that." She paused, "I can't believe I miss her stupid words."

"I know she was worried about you. She thought you were very strong."

Suzanne looked at him hopefully. To get him started she offered something, "She thought you were very stable and needed a woman who would appreciate steadiness."

"Do you think Caramello appreciates me?"

Suzanne nodded yes, "She'd even be fun at the Thanksgiving dinner table. Now, what did Mom say about me?"

"She thought," he paused and took a long swallow of beer while he thought about the words, "that you were strong and alive. I think she was a little jealous. She wished she had your style when she was younger. But she said she also thought, and maybe this has something to do with dad leaving, that you would only be strong as long as you owned men. Once a man owned you, it would be over."

Suzanne stopped, her eyes glassy and she stared at him. Michael faltered, seeing her surprise, "It's a compliment you know that you're so strong and alive and sexy. Ask any guy here."

"You've just reminded me of something I need to go do. I'm

leaving now." And she put her beer down, unfinished.

So here she was. An hour later. Suzanne leaned her nose into Mr. Crichton's fur, nuzzled him once more and shooed him off her lap.

Sugarloaf was who she wanted. It had been six weeks. Long enough. She called him and he promised Wednesday. When indecision and fears erupt, it's always better to take some kind of direct action, she thought. It got movement started.

"I miss you," Ken said Wednesday morning when she answered the phone at work.

"I miss you, too," and she meant it. A week had passed since having sex with him and she needed substantiation. Monday, before she met Michael, fled O'Riley's and before she called Sugarloaf, she made a delivery to the back of Overton. Ken had come out to receive it and walked to her car at the end of the parking lot, perhaps forty feet back from the dock. When he leaned down to say hello to her through the driver's window in full view of anyone who might be watching, she took his hand and slipped it up her skirt, urging his fingers to touch. The two men standing back in the shop were shadows to her, so she figured they couldn't see. He caught his breath or lost his breath, closed his eyes and stifled a moan. Glassy-eyed, he went to the trunk for the paper before walking away without saying good-bye.

"Suzanne," he now said on the phone.

She was silent.

"I'm almost there. It's the kids. They mean a lot."

"I know."

"You will like them?" It was a question.

"Yes, I will like them."

"They will live with Cat. But we will have them, too."

Guilt. She could smell it through the phone. When he did not continue she talked, "When will I see you, Ken? It's been a while. It's hard to believe you're missing me."

"You know I've had the kids. I need things to be right when I leave. Then there's work here. We're busy," he was rambling, "A wedding. Can I see you tonight?"

She felt victorious. "Not tonight, Ken. I'm busy."

He was silent again and she could feel his brain working. "Busy?"

"Well, Ken, you've got a wife, children, a big house, a company. I've got a busy night."

"I miss your body."

"I miss fucking you."

As they hung up another line buzzed from the front desk. "A customer to see you up front, Suzanne." She wasn't expecting anyone and seldom had anyone drop by. They expected her to go see them. The click of her low heel and movement of slung hips caused at least three male co-workers to look from their computers and phones to follow her steps.

"Outside, she said she'd be at her car," Joanne rushed to say before answering another call. Suzanne hadn't brought her jacket for the dark day, but she had on a warm black turtleneck and long pants. As the glass door closed behind her, she recognized Cat. Oh, god. She was at work and hoped nothing would happen. But there was also no turning back. The woman was leaning by the trunk of her parked car, her arms moving restlessly with nowhere comfortable to rest. Suzanne walked over and stood five feet away. The woman looked haggard, old, but then she was older. That dark wild hair needed better management, she thought to distract herself. She also noticed the cut and material of the woman's navy blue pantsuit with thick gold buttons was more expensive than anything she owned. The lines on her face, the color under her eyes, the lack of life in her eyes, pale cheeks with a few prominent freckles, was the shadow of her mother. Suzanne could see the sadness, jealousy, desperation in those staring eyes. Let the woman talk, she told herself. The woman, what was her name, had come to see her. She put her feet a few inches further apart to give balance against the stare and waited. She heard the door close when her father and the woman with the bouncing breasts stepped like dancers taking their leave from the stage, out of the kitchen, out of her life.

"Are you taking Ken?" it was half whisper; half croak.

Suzanne did not answer.

"The children are mine. I'm the only mother."

If Suzanne thought of the children at all it was only when Ken mentioned them and then they felt like what Raylene described as nephew and niece. "Yes, you are."

A car passed behind them and Suzanne couldn't see if it was anyone she knew. Hurry up, woman, she thought, I don't need this.

209

"Ken's not always so easy." Both women had seen the same lusting fire in Ken's eyes that offered warmth and future. A deep radiating heat they both believed would be theirs forever.

"Men aren't." Lina heard Suzanne roll the word men on her tongue like warm chocolate.

"Are you taking Ken or playing with him?" The woman's nose started to run and she moved a finger under it. There was saliva in the crease of her mouth. Suzanne wanted to walk away from this pathetic person who was begging to keep love she freely squandered, but she saw her own mother through memory's eye.

Catalina straightened her back and looked into Suzanne's eyes. She was numb with the younger woman's perfect face, flirty hair that could never look bad, slim curvy body that Ken had enjoyed; unruined by childbirth. A moment from a social issues college class flashed before her, "Help your younger sisters climb behind you," the instructor admonished. "Women need to reach a hand down and make room for each other."

"You'll be giving up things with him." Lina's words surprised Suzanne. Was it a motherly warning? More likely, a bitch with her best years behind her.

Words stirred from a deep unrealized well and were spoken before thought. "You'll be gaining things without him."

"Are you taking Ken?" Again the question was asked. She was insisting on seeing the knife that stabbed her.

A fall wind whispered up Suzanne's body before she answered. "I'm not taking him. He's coming."

Neither of them understood the warnings they gave and received. They did understand the directives. Lina stepped back to the car door still facing Suzanne. Staying any longer would compromise her ability to speak without screaming. In the rearview mirror she saw Suzanne open the glass front doors and was inside. Huge shaking sobs rocked Lina and her face contorted. Nostrils flared, leaking snot to meet with tears to fall on the wool of her most expensive pantsuit.

The earliest Sugarloaf could come was half past ten. Time enough for a bath, wine she had been trying to learn to enjoy, a little fruit to fill the body. She dressed in red silk.

His door tap was easy and quiet. She answered in the dark and felt his hello by his hands. Suzanne made love, had sex, fucked and all during the deaf movement of time she had a second screen of her mother's words. Owning men. Owning her. She did not think of Catalina. The waving movement of sex, the soothing of body, the energy of life was hers tonight and she met Sugarloaf with an evenness and purity that she had never truly given or received with anyone else. She did feel free with him as she hadn't with anyone else. They all expected something when sex was over, even if it was only cheap admiration or a beer. With him she could only give and receive from a man she didn't know. Did not know his birthday, his age, where he lived, his home phone, whether he had children, if he was married. She did know he liked being with her and she was his well-kept secret. He knew she lived alone, was not married and didn't have children. It felt pure. Without mercies, angers, hurts, keeping of accounts. Good. She wanted to feel free.

CHAPTER TWENTY ONE

This story shouldn't be told. It encourages similar stories by adding to existing consciousness. Perhaps it gives permission and excuses. Or it could be as others believe; face the savage truths and hurts of life and deal with them. Both are meant to erase or reduce pain. Truth stands mute. How is it possible to know when to look and when to quietly look away?

Lina's Aunt Betty stretched to the mashed potatoes at a family dinner when Lina was eight and stared into her, "If you don't want something in your life that is bothering you; if someone is mistreating you and you don't know what to do, rise above it. Forgive and live," she lifted and turned her shoulders, as if posing for a business public relations photograph. "That's Buddha like, Christ like, God like. Your mind is the strongest part of your body." Her parents sighed, allowing Aunt Betty her strangeness and believing she was entertaining instead of instructive. Unfortunately, they never counterbalanced with their daughter the idea that being aware of surroundings and taking action when necessary was not nosy or weak, it was self-protection.

Lina, who is now suffering from wondering if being called Lina is a pretension or a genuine step into a personally defined womanhood, is also wondering what happened to what she believed was her life. Where was the marriage like Mom and Dad's? Her unexamined life expectation was of a polite and enduring friendship with reassuring sex. It might be wondered how a woman in today's world can think like that when headlines at the news stand blare "20 ways to make a man a sexual slave," or "10 new ways to use your tongue to drive him wild," or a plaintive, "Chances are your husband cheats." Instead, she was blind her husband had a fumbling affair and dropped hints she should have pieced together in time to save her naïve marriage. She was a treasured, protected child and no one believed she needed self-defense or to have a questioning mind; including Ken, and all of Utah.

Ken deserves sympathy, too. The guy works like a Mack truck every day of his life and no one does anything but expect more. Lina wants serenity, peace and to imagine she is a comfort. The beloved children expect attendance at school functions and sports events. MoMo wants his lap and adoration. Justin wants his hair tousled and to be wrapped in an encouraging large male voice shadowing his way to manhood. Ken only wants help to support their world. Help that freely gives very good sex maybe, but he is not happy his business plan marriage has not produced long term bottom line results. He has never threatened to withdraw from the children. He likes being a father and a husband. Children are endearing to him as they exist. It is a bonus they are a point of proud fruitful male expression to other men. Reasonable compensation will be offered for twelve years of marriage to a woman he loved as he could and found a slippery sandstone wall he was never able to scale. Now he wants. No, now he needs a woman who anticipates his fears and buffers them away in dark feminine power. He needs to feel encircled and feel her in his blood as he works without question to provide.

And Suzanne. Poor little half-orphan girl and half-deserted child who is needy and knows how to hide it with a strut butt. Only Michael applauds her great show. She's offering to be with a man who has another woman's children he is devoted to; and work a job description he outlines. She would admit she wants comfort and security, but she doesn't yet understand they will not dissolve her loneliness and grief. The five dreams of her mother's lost and beaten face looking into the victorious lipsticked face of her father's lover on a Sunday morning are too ephemeral to openly touch her days. Unacknowledged fear won't let her think of having children. A very promising and maturing womanhood is being interrupted to hold a man whose natural action will be to take many decisions away from her while she clings to his reasonable breadth and comforting arms during the night.

All three of them may be crazy and blind, but they pay bills on time so they are seldom noticeable.

"Hello, Mr. Shiner," Lina spoke as he brushed by. She was

shelving books and did not look up, but he stopped.

"You've got a cold, Cat?" Care was in his grating old voice. She shook her head, again not looking up.

"Then something is bothering you. Now I see it in your shoulders."

She turned to him, submissive as a beaten puppy and pulled hair behind her ear. A dark hair caught in a sleeve's gold button. Flushed cheeks, red-rimmed eyes looked at the old speckled hardwood floor. After all these years he still disliked evidence of personal life in the store but now it was for a different reason. As a young man struggling to be successful he believed the store was as much him as his toenails, and it was important to show the buying public a façade of perfection. He didn't want employees to disrupt the flow of perfect lives doing perfect business for perfect profit. Now, after all the years of his own life he recognized the effort of separating the literature, art and science invading him from books that exuded thought waves. He became a conduit within his store, and at last a skeptic of business as a human goal. His only objection to unhappy employees was simply that they were unhappy.

"Let's go to my office, Cat. You need to relax a few minutes." She put down a book and followed his bony quickly striding back for face cover. Sitting in his tiny windowless office, in the safety of this man she had known since she was eighteen, she wanted to bellow in pain. She wanted man's recognition that another man had done her wrong. Tears fell like steaming tea water in her lap.

"Ken?" It was usually the important other person in life.

Her head bobbed, the thick curls far happier than the woman underneath.

"Work or home?" He knew her ties to Overton.

"Home." The worst choice. Time ticked on the desk clock. Silence held them in place. The quiet patience of Mr. Shiner enveloped Lina, slowing her emotions enough to speak.

"He's leaving me."

There was nothing Mr. Shiner wanted to say.

"He's having an affair." The words circled the room unchallenged.

"We've gone to a marriage counselor, but it's not working." The story was out, the worst spoken. Two minutes ticked.

"I'm sorry, Cat." She nodded to the softness in his voice and the tears started once more. Mr. Shiner remembered a box of tissue in a bottom drawer and leaned down. He put the box out on the desk. Lina reached for one and broadly wiped her face, pulling off make-up, tears and sweat from the heat of feelings.

"Well, that's it. That's all, Mr. Shiner. I don't know what else to say. I don't know what's going on. I don't know what I did wrong."

Why did women always blame themselves, he wondered. Literature to encyclopedias to magazine articles on grocery store shelves held stories of men's fucking against women they expected to be faithful to them. His answer was to run his hand silently along his mouth to keep from coldly commenting on all human failings and the way small things wreck terrible havoc. Ashley, his twenty-year-old granddaughter gave him hope. She told her boyfriend of a year to go to hell when he didn't approve of her weekend with friends. Maybe the watershed of the last century women's movement was finally hitting ground dirt where real male female relations evolve.

"Cat, I've known you a long time. You're a good and beautiful young woman. Sometimes life just doesn't go as planned."

Her shoulders trembled. She liked hearing good but beautiful and young were an obvious ploy to stop tears. Unable to meet Mr. Shiner's gaze, she stared at her lap. The chair creaked as he straightened to stand and leave.

"You're a beautiful woman, Catalina. I've seen you grow from girl to woman and I know it. Take care of yourself." The quiet close of the door left her alone in the office to hear his words through her. As he gave other employees before her, he allowed privacy in his male room to collect.

You're a beautiful woman, Catalina. Take care of yourself. The words spoken as a kindly afterthought by a stranger when the elevator had closed. Two men had spoken quietly the mantra she needed to open her own heart to herself.

"You're a beautiful woman, Catalina. Take care of yourself," she said aloud in Mr. Shiner's office where voice bounced off old plaster and returned to be heard again. The words circled with the ghost of Suzanne's clear young face she had seen this morning when she stopped at Harkness before coming to Shiner's. "I'm not taking him. He's coming," were the words that followed her out of the room.

When her shift was over she picked up MoMo at Trista's and Justin at Walt's. With each she turned in the seat to welcome them in the car with a wan but warm smile. They both beamed in its small cover from November's night darkness.

"You two go do homework now. I'll start dinner," Lina said as they walked into the dark house. Their feet clamored up the stairs and Lina headed for the kitchen, turning on every light she passed. From the refrigerator she tossed bread, lunch meat, cheeses, lettuce, mustard and whatever else she thought could be put into the sandwich each would make themselves. Light flooded the kitchen and family room, reflecting off walls. From the pantry on the other side of the refrigerator she gathered cans of soup to display for personal choice.

The shadows of night met the starkness of her lighted house at the French doors. A few feet beyond the window her ghostly reflection floated. A transparent double staring back at her. She put the cans down and walked toward herself. Near the door she stopped, staring at the specter through glassy dried raindrops and dust. She moved to the side and watched her face roll in waves through glass and across the cold dark backyard. Noise from the children's rooms was a soothing buzz of music with computer hum and clicks. For several minutes she stared, occasionally moving to see the angles of her face change like an interpretive painting. Drawn to look deeper into her image her eyes glazed until she lost the face and looked beyond to her wintering yard.

Caught in her thoughts, she didn't close the door behind her as she stepped to the patio. Lina looked at the dying, stiff stems in the pots. Shriveled petunia blossoms hung from the tops, discolored and old. Perhaps they tried harder than I imagined, Lina thought, to be hearty in a world that wanted only a lovely uncomplaining summer garden. She discounted effort in a landscape that didn't fit its nature. Maybe this lonesome, unprepared plant, so far from its native home in Argentina was doing its best. Life always thrives where it feels at home, nurtured in whatever secret passion it desires and suffers from effort where it is not comfortable.

Marigolds had a more varied history. A book she opened during a hot summer's day when not many people wandered through Shiner's traced its homelands to Africa, India, France, Mexico. She walked to the stiff marigold corpses. Yes, here was strength, dashing flamboyant alive colors to the end, until its night of death. She broke a stem.

"Mom, Mom, where are you?" MoMo called from the bright kitchen. Lina held the marigold and returned to the house.

"Right here. Are you ready for a sandwich?"

"Lunch for dinner, Justin" she yelled. "Lunch for dinner!"

After sandwiches and soup the three of them were in Justin's room when Ken arrived home. The sound of the garage door and the engine idling in the driveway as Ken waited for it to lift caused Justin's and MoMo's eyes to meet. Lina noticed the quick look and was sad for them. Their parents were not at ease with each other and they felt the discomfort.

"Anybody here?" Ken yelled.

"Up here, Dad!" Justin answered. Ken walked into the room where they were gathered around the computer, giving a last check to his spelling list for a test the next day. "Maybe Dad can give me a sentence for lambent," he hoped.

"First, tell me what it means."

Lina and Ken acknowledged each other. MoMo ran to her father's arms and he lifted her. Stay there, little girl, and learn, Lina thought; learn more than I did.

"Say goodnight to her Ken, and I'll take her to bed. You can say goodnight to Justin." She leaned and kissed her son's head as he stared at the screen. Her hands patted his thick oily smelling boy hair. Tears held in her eyes and did not drop.

"Come on, MoMo." They went to her bedroom where MoMo curled in her covers as a ball; her hair spread like a butterfly and she looked openly at her mother.

"Is Daddy mad at me?"

Surprised, Lina stopped patting the bedcovers and sat by her daughter. "Mad at you?"

Her eyes opened as bright crystals under water, "He's always mad."

"He's not mad at you MoMo. He has other problems. It is not you. I can guarantee it."

MoMo looked away, pursing her lips knowing more words would unloose a flood. "Daddy loves you MoMo. It's work and maybe other things. It's not you." She kissed her daughter. "I'll ask

Daddy to come say goodnight to you so you will know it."

She said goodnight again to Justin through the door and went downstairs. As she got a wineglass from the cupboard she spoke to Ken, already seated in front of TV.

"MoMo thinks you're angry with her. You need to say goodnight." He stood immediately. Lina's throat caught. He loved his children. It was only her. Only love for her was negotiable; replaceable. And dead.

Overfilled wineglass in hand, she sat at the end of the couch and waited. Background TV noise was welcome to muffle words in the air and keep them from the children. Words she didn't want to remember and didn't want to say. Lina listened as MoMo's door opened and closed before Ken knocked softly on Justin's door and went in to assure his son. Ken returned and sat facing the TV.

"Ken."

He didn't move.

"Ken."

Still, he didn't move and she realized she only whispered, only mouthed his name afraid she would not say it easily or with affection. Perhaps he would not hear her plea, the desperation rising from her belly. She took a long swallow of wine and waited, hoping the kindly alcohol would enter her bloodstream and numb life.

"Ken." She spoke more clearly and he looked at her. "Ken, what's happened?"

He clicked the TV off. They were left in lamplight facing each other. Lina's ears perked for movement from the children's bedroom. She didn't want them to hear.

"What do you want, Cat?"

"I want things the way they used to be." She looked away, ceding losses. "I want to know why you are still sitting here watching television and saying goodnight to the children." Ken was silent, assessing, trying to read beneath the skin for his next move.

It could be said Ken was kind. He had not brought Suzanne home while he got a few clothes and a shaving kit. Over the past weeks he had taken Lina in quick steps so a brutal, more sudden departure would not leave her dumb. Kindness, in the eyes of the giver has many faces. The next assault was a blow with Lina against the ropes, but conscious enough to hear.

"I want Thanksgiving with you and the children. Then I'm leaving. You can stay in the house for now." He stood and walked up the stairs to bed. Lina was rooted to the couch, listening to night sounds of the house, unable to feel.

At four she was still sitting on the couch. A flood of light fell on the floor from a full moon. Long shadows laid sharp fingers of iridescent light in angles and lines. Perhaps they were lambent. Finally, emptied of thought, she drifted asleep.

"Cat." Ken's voice was warm water, soothing, sad as it fell to meet rising headwater. Lightly, he took her pale thin fingers, every other one in his every other one. His gentle connection when he faced fragile female. "Cat, I'm sorry." Her eyes opened to see him dressed, ready for the day, and a wave of soap and aftershave helped her sit straighter. "You'll be happier." She peered at him through a fading dream. "You used to look at me for something you needed. Not anymore."

Her head cocked, "All about a look?"

"No. What the look says. You don't need me."

"I've always needed you."

"No," he kissed her fingers, "you're with me by habit. Fear. I don't want that."

Neither of them spoke. He tightened his hold on her fingers, not looking at her face, "You'll always be the woman I wanted for everything. But it didn't work. Now I need a woman who needs me. A woman who will let me inside of all of her. Her head. Her body. Her heart."

Catalina looked wildly, cravenly at his moussed, slick hair, bending before her as a child asking grace.

"You haven't let me for a long time, Lina. You want yourself now."

An hour later the children lurched out the front door, escaping the dense air of their mother's heaviness and her ghostly face to join Walt and his smiling mother for a ride to school. Lina watched their flight from the living room window, knowing it was from her. The only words she had spoken that morning were a soulless soft, "It's time to get up." She stood by each of their beds, mouthing the words as a machine instantly waking them to fear.

Eme was unpacking from Utah's second choice of a holiday after Disneyland, a three day Las Vegas honeymoon. She was sorting quickly with most of it going in the dirty clothes or in a pile to the dry cleaners. Sheldon was at the office, but she had taken time to get a few things done and 'just because.' Just because she had a husband now and their team effort would mean more freedom for each of them. They had planned their dream future.

Lina called minutes earlier to say she was on her way over. Her voice was hollow, a listless mewing kitten. Eme didn't understand what had happened. It was frightening an outwardly good marriage could collapse so completely. But at her wedding Eme knew. Ken's eyes were lax, unfocused, and never settled on his wife. He was polite and affectionate to Eme, congratulatory to Sheldon, and his usual interactive father style with his children was normal. He was otherwise alone, without Lina.

Ken's presence had always been strong and self-possessed. Through the years she admired the single-minded career path Ken forged ahead of his wife and children to make them comfortable and use his strengths well. Not since Lina's and Ken's wedding day had she allowed herself to question her best friend's choice of man. It seemed disloyal to interpret the shard of light in Ken's eyes as he looked at his bride on their wedding day. Had she worded it rather than felt it, she would have called it claiming unquestioning trust for private use. Eme was afraid of a ruthlessness directed at her friend, the woman Ken had promised to love as a girl.

Eme's eyes widened when she saw Lina at the door, but she bit her lip and held her friend close while she sobbed. Lina's pale skin was streaked in red blotches and leftover makeup. They rocked for a minute until Eme began to baby step both of them to the couch.

"I'm sorry, Cat." She murmured when she thought the time was right.

"Don't call me Cat anymore. I'm Lina."

The sound was so muffled and angry that Eme lifted Lina away and looked at her. "That's right. You told me. I'm sorry. I won't let that happen again. Well, I'm glad there's a little spirit here. You're not all goopy tears."

"And I want a glass of wine."

Eme got up smiling. "It is a little early, but rules are meant to be broken." Eme put a plate of pumpkin spice bars on the table that would stay untouched.

Lina did more crying than drinking, but holding the glass with two hands balanced her thinking. She told her about Suzanne and that Ken was staying home only through Thanksgiving.

"What are you going to do," she paused, "Lina?"

"We went to the marriage counselor. Last Monday, the third trip, Ken left halfway through. Just stood up and said he needed to get back to Overton." She took a swallow of wine. "I stayed and talked to the man. Dr. Roger Dalton. He really is very good. Certainly very kindly. When Ken darted out he looked at me with such compassion I started to sob. I've lost weight, Eme, and half of it is tears."

"What did Dalton say?"

"Nothing. Nothing about Ken leaving. He asked me what I wanted to do. I said I wasn't sure. It just felt like my days were getting darker. We won't be going back to Roger Dalton." They were silent while Lina strummed on the glass. " I did something I never thought I'd do. I went to where she works. I asked her if she was taking Ken. I was such a slobby mess crying through it, Eme, but I had to do it. I had to look at the horror of it and know what she was doing."

When Lina was stilled without words Eme asked, "How are Justin and MoMo doing?"

"Poorly. Well, okay as can be expected, but they don't like it."

A glass of wine later Eme had a suggestion, "There's a pile of sycamore and maple leaves in the backyard. Want to roll?"

Half a dozen maples and sycamores looming above arbored the yard. The generous green leaf umbrellas of summer that were home to migrating birds were now bare grasping branches naked against winter. Eme and Lina fell like children, rolling in the crinkly, paper stiff, woodsy smell of dead leaves.

"Let's race!" Lina yelled jumping up and running to Eme at the end of the yard. "Here we are!" They were lined up like two bags of leaves. "First one to the other side of the yard wins!" They rolled and screeched as they sighted each other halfway across. Gasping, choking laughter played like piano notes. The laughing surprised Lina. She hadn't felt it in her throat since sitting with a kind gentle man over dinner.

"I met that Suzanne before."

"*That* Suzanne?"

"Yes, *that* Suzanne."

"When?"

Lina looked to the sky; her eyes reflecting the soft glisten of sun hidden behind clouds. "She's Overton's sales person for Harkness. Ken introduced her at the office and she was at that business dinner. I guess instead of a cash discount, Ken took a fuck."

Eme didn't know whether Lina was being funny or serious. She choked on a laugh.

"And another thing, since she's being a fuck and probably getting the best fuck Ken's ever given, I'm thinking it might be good to be a fuck." Lina's shoulders straightened.

"You are?" Eme was surprised; her cave brown eyes were merry, entertained.

"Yes," she held a handful of dry leaves to her face. "I want to be the thinking man's fuck since Ken never did much thinking beyond efficient press runs. It would be new." Eme quietly considered the turnabout the two friends had in the last week.

"Eme," her voice was a beseeching far-off foghorn to the lost.

"Yes, Lina, my Catalina."

"I'm going to miss him. His smells, his body, his arms. I do love him." On their backs they looked up at the looming stark branches. Lying on the ground they were wrapped in all the maples and sycamores could offer during a winter's rest.

"It's gone too far. I know it. I have to let him go," she breathed in endurance. "Not because I want to. But maybe a bit of me does. He's going anyway." Cat returned to Suzanne. "She didn't try and make it easy for me to see my life die. At the end she said, 'I'm not taking him. He's coming.'"

Eme motioned to be still and wait while she went into the house. Her arms were held behind her when she returned and sank on the ground. She brought her left hand around and opened it to a whelk seashell; Eme's definition of her frail heart when she knew it was time to leave. Lina watched; numb. Slowly Eme brought the other hand from behind her and there was a rock; hard earth to be hit and absorb sadness at being left behind.

"Which is it?"

Lina looked at the fork to her future, picked the seashell and rubbed its bony surface hard against her thumb. She wrote her husband's name on it with the marker Eme held before slowly lifting her head to look to her friend. "Before I hit it, I need your help."

Eme made the call to Harkness. Suzanne had politely left her cell phone number on the company's voice mail. When Eme introduced herself over the phone and explained what she wanted, she was sure Suzanne's surprise release of air was youth's prideful insolence that there were rules she hadn't learned. The meeting was arranged for three that afternoon at Ginger's. Eme noted to Suzanne that Lina had decided on a place she knew Suzanne would be familiar with and it would be best if she brought a friend with her. A witness. But not to worry. All of this was to give Suzanne what she wanted.

"I think I'll have Thanksgiving Sunday." Lina set the seashell down on leaves smelling of death. Eme lifted a meat tenderizer from a pocket and handed it to her.

"Is this business or a funeral?" An hour later Lina methodically moved through her rack of clothes before settling on a black suit with a pink blouse she had worn to two funerals and one bank loan signing. She laid her clothes on the unmade bed from Ken's night alone. In the shower she turned the water as hot as she could bear and stood until her shoulders and arms were red. At half past two she was meeting Eme at Ginger's; early enough to be prepared and go over all of it one more time. Drying her thick hair took time, too much time today, when she needed to hurry, but she also wanted to look as good as possible. Twice she put on make-up, still unhappy about how little it helped a sleepless night and an approaching birthday. Clean, dressed, perfumed, and looking drained and carved from candle wax, she got in the Audi and drove to Ginger's.

"Let's sit over there," Eme nodded to a round table on the far right side by the wall. It was the first time either had been in Ginger's. Except for one man at the bar and three men finishing a late lunch in the back they were the only customers.

"No, Eme, I think up here would be better," Lina headed to the table on the second tier where Ken and Suzanne had closed their deal. "Round tables are too friendly and I want you where we can send each other eye signals."

When Suzanne and Raylene arrived a few minutes after three, they were as nervously relaxed as possible with a glass of wine in front of each of them.

"Raylene." Suzanne's voice was clear. Accustomed to speaking up.

"Eme, Emeraude," The pervading gentleness and inward sight of Raylene unnerved Lina. Was everyone under thirty suddenly beautiful and smarter than her, too? She grasped Eme's full name to clutch a crown of greater power.

The two younger women sat down. Suzanne by Eme and Raylene by Lina. Lina stared at the coral necklace. Had Ken given her that? Blood raged across her temples.

"We know what is happening here." Seconds were minutes, but Eme waited for all jostling due to sitting to end. Still her voice was frozen. "We know what is happening here," she repeated, "and it is best settled now. Children are involved."

"Mountain Dew," Suzanne said to the waitress. Raylene also nodded.

"What Eme is saying is what I need to say," Lina's heart swelled. For herself. For the first time, only for herself. Raylene shifted in her seat to look at Lina. Lina smelled strawberry and honey and imagined clacking train wheels rolling through France.

"I know. I know," she couldn't say anyone's name without crying. "But I have to, need to make it as right as possible." Intimidated by the young women's drinks, she felt her need stronger and took a long drink while the three watched. If apparent confusion made Suzanne feel less guarded perhaps it was good. "It just is. So, here we are and here is what I need.

"What Ken and I work out, I suppose will come. There will be a reasonable split of household goods, fifty percent of the house's equity, and standard child support. I will not ask for alimony. What I need from you Suzanne is a witnessed guarantee of 2% income after vendor costs of Overton every year until MoMo is eighteen in a trust fund for the children. Ten years. If the company dissolves or is sold before then, the total amount would be due as a company debt." Lina and Eme looked at Suzanne. Her eyes opened and she looked at Raylene, down at her drink, tapped it and looked at Lina.

224

"That's stupid. Why would I agree to that? No."

Lina sat straighter. "Because you want Overton as much as you want Ken."

Suzanne looked for the bluff in Lina's eyes. There was none and for the first time Suzanne was engaged.

"Ten years is a long time."

"I've been married twelve."

"Still too long," Suzanne brushed the inconsequential marriage aside and tousled hair. Ken has kissed that, Lina thought as Suzanne continued. "And unnecessary. The children will be fine. I know Ken, he will take care of them. And what makes you think I can agree to this? Isn't it Ken's decision?"

Lina's eyes narrowed as she gained emotional ground. If anyone at this table knew Ken it was her. And she was beginning to understand Suzanne. A naïve baby bird needing an outstretched wing to hide from rain.

"I can ruin Overton," she looked evenly and for the first time calmly. "I can dismantle it piece by piece."

The three women looked at Lina with respect, alarm, curiosity.

"And I will if necessary."

"What is this, some kind of blackmail? Ken would know. It's his fight. There's nothing I can agree to that would have any meaning."

Eme saw the clutch in Lina's throat, "No Suzanne, you are right. What Lina is saying, is this will be in the divorce settlement. You need to agree and get Ken to agree. If not, Lina will drag it out and she knows how to ruin what is right now a very successful company. She is an officer of the company. Part of the original incorporation."

Silence waited with the four women while Suzanne absorbed implications. "Who are Overton officers?" Her voice was caution hiding anger.

Ken hadn't told her everything. Lina was slow to answer. "Ken is 51%, I'm 49% and his father is a silent third partner without a vote."

When Suzanne looked down Eme continued. "It's only $20,000 per million per year, after vendor costs and before company costs. Do you know what Overton did last year? What they can do in the future? Especially with your help?" Eme aimed to compliment Suzanne's pride.

Raylene knew of Suzanne's research. Printers only took home 6 to 8% gross profit.

"A small sum compared to losing all of it."

Raylene's satin notes were warm, "What would Suzanne gain by this?"

"Besides an intact company?" whispered Lina.

"Besides Ken?" said Eme.

"Yes, besides that," Suzanne spiked her hair. This was sales. Always go for more. "If I'm to agree to this and have to work to make your kids rich there are things I want."

No one spoke. A waitress circled; drinks were not empty.

Her voice softened, wording an unspoken secret wish, "I want him left alone outside of regular visits. The kids can see him the day before his birthday. His birthday is mine. All holidays are mine unless I agree with you to something different. You may have to make up reasons why they can't come. You will take it. It will never be me."

It was close to four and people were wandering in to finish a day early and start an evening. The three women watched Lina as she regarded Suzanne. She didn't want to be the one to say no to the children and their father. So far everything Suzanne wanted Ken had provided. She hadn't seen Ken when he wanted his own. She was speaking as a lover, as a possessive horny young thing. Not a lifetime job description. Suzanne believed her bed power would win every decision like Lina believed her goodness would protect her.

"I can do that. You and I will make our arrangements." That would not be in the divorce settlement.

Suzanne saw the rise of color in Lina's cheeks. Was it a flash of returning life or was the woman covering a lie and relieved this was nearing an end?

"Here is what we all need to sign," Eme was kind and definite.

"Suze, I want to speak with you," Raylene turned in her seat and rose, leading Suzanne out of hearing distance.

"Will this work, Lina? What about taking the heat for holidays and Ken's birthday?" Eme's eyes looked directly into Lina.

"Do you think she or I can keep Ken from the kids if he wants to see them? Do you think I can keep Ken from a printing press or another woman?" Lina's wan smile was a resignation to loss as Suzanne and Raylene returned.

After outlining the agreements, Eme made a note about birthdays and holidays in careful teacher handwriting before presenting originals to both parties. The four women signed two originals.

Formally, stiffly Catalina stood while Suzanne rose impatiently. Eme and Raylene lifted slowly as emotionally encumbered sisters, acknowledging each other as worthy helpmates to two confused women. Lina held out her hand to Suzanne, "In ten years you will have paid for Ken free and clear. Perhaps I should have been smart enough to know the cost."

Lina did not feel pleased as she drove from the parking lot where her husband and Suzanne first had sex in the Expedition. She felt naked in a dream of a thousand people watching as she tried to find a blanket.

"Thanksgiving is tomorrow, Ken and children, Justin and MoMo." All three stopped eating cereal and reading the newspaper to look at her over the kitchen counter.

"Today is Saturday. Thanksgiving is tomorrow. There may be another one Thursday, but tomorrow we will have our family party. Any objection?"

Three heads with dropped jaws indicated no.

"Good. I'm leaving for the grocery store soon. If there's anything you need let me know. Otherwise, I'm only shopping for Thanksgiving. Except, Ken, will you stop at the liquor store and get some wine and marsala? I need it for the sweet potatoes."

Catalina Marie Daniels Overton tried not to do a lot of thinking or feeling. She turned her efforts to doing. MoMo went with her to the grocery store, prompting her in almost every aisle for necessary Thanksgiving items. Aluminum foil, flour, nutmeg, cranberries, celery, onions, and on it went. As MoMo skipped ahead to find the nutmeg Lina choked in tears watching her.

At home there was more planning, washing a tablecloth, polishing silverware, vacuuming and ironing napkins. Mid afternoon she turned to food. The children were with friends and Ken, well, Ken said he was golfing and when Lina checked, the golf clubs were not in the garage. The three-year-old house, imprinted only with their short history was silent, a bit dumb she thought, as she threw the tablecloth out. Not very comforting at all with its wide spaces, high ceilings, and hard angles. The silence and largeness of it scratched her ears and after filling salt and pepper shakers she turned on the TV, switching from golf to a cooking show.

Her only rest was to call her mother. "Hi, Mom, I'll see you Wednesday. Yes, we'll be there. I know it's a change of plans but I'll explain more then." For weeks her mother had asked her to come for Thanksgiving. Aunt Betty looked three days older for every one she now breathed and it was important to see her one more time. A few cousins from Cheyenne would be in town and everyone wanted to see the sophisticated Salt Lake City folks with their own business. From the beginning Lina had politely said no. Too many obligations here, Mom. Ken just can't get away. The children are busy. She suspected her mother saw through the rambling excuses, but she had not pressed and Lina appreciated it. The full truth of her failing marriage had been too hard to say until she was sure. "It will be without Ken," she finished and her mother asked nothing.

Cranberries simmered, sweet potato casserole with pecans was layered. Marsala would be added if Ken brought it home. A pumpkin pie was put in the oven, stuffing for a twelve pound turkey was hidden deep in the refrigerator with salad plates and wineglasses. When the children and then Ken came home after dark, she washed lettuce and green beans, set the table and had tea. She sent them to buy that night's dinner and they returned with hamburgers, fries, onion rings and ice cream.

Civil. That was the word Lina put to the conversation at the dinner table and through the evening of television. At least civil between Ken and Lina. The children were quiet but happy, sensing their behavior would anticipate and anchor this Saturday night. MoMo settled in Ken's open oversized lap. Justin moved from one end of the couch to the other; torn between being an independent pre-teen to needing the arm of his mother when he felt anxious and unsure. Ken had a number of beers and Lina had wine before the children went to bed.

The parents stared at the TV screen, unwilling to talk. After twenty minutes Lina stood to head for wine. "I'm sleeping in the bed, Ken. You can have the downstairs bedroom. It would be more comfortable than the couch. I've put a few of your things there." In a small vase she had arranged dead marigolds for the bedside table. His linear thinking wouldn't get the joke or the hurt.

"You're suddenly prepared," granite words hurt but she knew that's all they would do. She would not, could not break.

"We'll tell the children Monday night. We're leaving for my mother's on Wednesday and you'll be free." She started to the stairs, stopped before the first one and turned around. He could not see her shadowed face. "We'll be back on Saturday, so I hope by then your clothes will be out."

Lina had not changed the sheets over the last days Ken slept in the bed. Tonight she leaned into his pillow and where his chest rested to smell deeply. Was it man, Ken, simply male sweat, cologne, ink, paper, and now another woman, a beautiful young woman with more life and blind undirected energy than she possessed. The smells of her marriage bed. Did the sheets of three nights, worn and indented, to fit a man all smell the same? She doubted it, but she didn't know. When she turned and tried to drift to sleep she pulled far to her side and did not move to his again.

Silver sparkled, linens were stiff, crystal prismed. Marsala was splashed on the sweet potatoes. An hour before it was ready Lina's lilting voice let everyone know it was time to change clothes to the dress she insisted on seeing.

"It's ready! Everyone come!" she stood at the end of the table. Kenneth and Justin were in white shirts and slacks. Catalina and MoMo were in velvet.

"Ken, please say the Thanksgiving blessing," Lina looked down and lifted her hands to hold Justin's in her left and MoMo's in her right. It was a photo perfect meal with iced glassware, starched napkins and glistening silver. The winter twilight hour was shared with great generosity of spirit and memory and served with as much presence of mind as Kenneth and Catalina could provide their children.

CHAPTER TWENTY TWO

Yesterday's meeting was exhilarating. Suzanne left Ginger's with Raylene feeling like she was watching skids of paper leave the dock on a major sale. When the woman called she was wary. Deserted women can be nuclear waste and she didn't want trouble at Ginger's where she was known to be on business duty. But it turned out okay. The twice-told tales of raging indulged kids wouldn't be her problem. From the beginning they would be controllable. She didn't want to think about the money she would be paying for those kids. They would be getting more a year just because they existed as Ken's children as she now made for going to work every day. She would just learn how to step up again and think in larger, more global terms. Hearing her mother fret over the cost of ground beef was replaced by realizing the cost of apartments and cars. Then she learned about $10,000 and $20,000 printing jobs and companies that made millions. She was now stepping up again in life. The subject in her head needed changing.

Suzanne silently amused herself by listing all the reasons Arnie was wrong for her while she waited for the Cherokee to be cleaned and vacuumed. It was Saturday with time to waste. Two rings came from her purse before she answered the cell phone. Ken talked through her hello.

"Suze, Suze, Cat's letting me go. She's having Thanksgiving tomorrow and then it's over. I told you." Suzanne heard as much delight as shock in his voice.

"Oh?" His information or lack of it would tell her what kind of a games player Cat was. She hoped the people sitting with her waiting for cars could only hear her voice. She got up and sauntered away. A man shook his newspaper.

"It means I'm free Monday." Good. That's all he had to say.

"Ken, that's good."

"Yes, it's very good."

"But you have to understand."

"Yes?" His voice questioned. Perhaps it was confidence she heard roll down his throat.

"I was counting on December 1." She could afford to play.

"What does that mean, Suzanne?"

"It means I have a few things to clear up. A few details. I promised Thanksgiving to my brother and a few friends. I have to make things ready for you," she paused, "you understand." A young dark-haired guy whirled a dirty rag over his head to let her know the car was ready.

"What does that mean, Suzanne?" An edge of anger and fear was rising.

"It means you had a life to live without me and I have a few details to clear up, also. I will expect you at my place at midnight Friday morning. And that's three days early." They hung up, neither too happy with the other, and both feeling the rising need for sex they weren't sure how to quell.

Arnie didn't come in X-Cess until eleven that night. He spotted Michael, Suzanne, Raylene, her odd boyfriend, Eddie, Diane, Trent and Caramello at the back table immediately. He slid in the booth by Caramello, saying hello to everyone. One more drink and he'd be ready to dance. Suzanne looked ready - so ready he wasn't sure there could be anything under that dress.

"Let's dance."

She got up, smiled and they headed out. Arnie hovered like a hawk over a dove as he led her to the dance floor. The whirl of body, heat, emotion, not enough time and too much desire swirled in heavy waves over and through the bodies dancing to Lip Manure. Three dances later they headed back for another drink and to sit. The music was slower and neither were sure they trusted Arnie to its heated closeness. They were the only ones at the table.

"You're beautiful, Suzanne."

Cocking her head, she closed her eyes, opened them and lifted her lips to be kissed.

"Why won't you go out with me again," he whispered after the kiss.

"I've got a deal already cinched. It works this week or it doesn't. But in my own terrible way, I'm faithful."

"Another man."

Her head lifted and lowered with her chest. Arnie watched for real or simply stated faithfulness.

"I'm Mr. Back-up."

"I didn't meet you first."

"I'm better."

"Maybe, but one look at you says you're beautiful but not a sure thing, and certainly not a sure thing in the long haul."

"Then let's see what happens with the deal. Want to dance?"

At two, they left with Michael's blessing. He wanted it to work, or play, or be or whatever in the hell it was Suzanne wanted, and waved a big good-bye with one arm while the other held Caramello.

"Goodnight, Arnie," she lifted her arm to unlock the jeep. The noise of X-Cess still rang and her words sounded through cotton.

"Goodnight Ms. Suzanne. I'll see you home safely," and he walked to his car without touching her.

She started her Cherokee. He watched from the Lexus. As she edged out of the parking lot there was no mistaking his car following. At this time of night the streets are not commuter traffic heavy but Suzanne drove carefully allowing for late night Saturday drivers.

There was a lot to consider. The reflection of streetlight, moonlight, headlight; all refractions of her thinking fuzzed with beer. A married man. She breathed in; her spine straightened and her knees parted. Was Ken what she wanted? What she needed? Would he give and take. Already he had given; drives to coral sand dunes, lunches an hour's drive away. His eyes, electrical sparkling lust meant for her. And she had signed yesterday to keep it. Her chest was tight, a breathable claustrophobia. Arnie. Magical. A light handhold leading to places she didn't understand. Maybe he would be gone in a wisp to someone more beautiful. He smelled like frosting. He felt like chance.

Stopped in front of her apartment she was still wondering what to say.

"I need to go upstairs now. Thank you for seeing me home," Suzanne spoke as she walked by the tall languorous, very wonderful Arnold Greenhall.

"You're welcome," he stepped over a fescus the landlord

planted a month ago in a useless attempt to beautify the building. Like putting make-up on an old woman Suzanne thought. There wasn't much room between car bumpers and apartments.

"Arnold."

He stopped. His eyebrows lifted to soak in meaning behind words.

"Arnold, all this can be is tonight. I have other plans and I intend to keep them."

His hipline moved to one side and she wanted to touch it. He understood.

"You're a lawyer. Put it in writing." Maybe she was realizing the value of the legal world. Arnold took out a business card and a pen, both so available. He scrawled out in Saturday night after a few drinks handwriting, "It's only tonight."

She took the card, barely readable in a neighbor's door light and led him up the concrete stairs. Carefully she tucked the card under a yogurt container in a corner of the refrigerator so he would not take it with him. She brought out two beers.

Sunday morning he was still there and she was glad to see him. "Mr. Back-up hopes he gets moved to pitcher's mound," he winked when he left.

Michael called late in the afternoon. "Arnie there?"

"No. He left a few hours ago."

"Oh, well, he was there. Mean anything?"

"What is this? Police headquarters? How is it with Caramello? Are we still on for Thanksgiving?"

"What a lot of questions. Yes, this is police headquarters of your heart since yours is a crime scene. She's fine and yes. A few others might come with us. Maybe Arnie."

Sunday night was spent at home. It had been some time since Suzanne bothered with anything beyond surface wipe-up and pick-up. If the tasks hadn't been defined as housework she would have said she enjoyed the workout of washing windows, vacuuming (a vacuum Michael and she traded as necessary), washing clothes and cleaning the floors and toilet. By the end it occurred to her she didn't know if it had been done for her benefit, health department standards or because she wanted to greet Ken in traditional clean female fashion that indicated worthiness. That idea she didn't like so she didn't dust and the place could have used it.

Before she turned the light out to sleep Suzanne held her sheets of paper with four original signatures to her chest. "This is what you needed Mom." Arnie's card stayed under the yogurt until the first Saturday in December. Insurance.

Rolling boiling clouds with black bellies, streaks of grey and curves to white torsos chased about the valley on Tuesday; the day Suzanne decided to see Sugarloaf. While gathering paper samples, driving to appointments, waiting for clients who greeted her with crazed overworked eyes, or beaten lowered shoulders, she tried to assemble words of good-bye. It would have been so much easier if she wanted to say good-bye. Sugarloaf was the one souvenir of being uncommitted she did not want to give up. Did she need to? She sighed in resignation to her heart. Yes, she did.

As she fiddled at her desk after five, waiting for bravery and a little more night cover Ron walked by her cubicle.

"Hey, Ron," he paused his steps. "I've got a question."

Ron expected something like, how in good conscience do you sell inferior paper for a better commission when you know another is better, but was surprised by something unexpected.

"What do I say to a man when it's over, but I still like him and it's just that I have to?"

Ron considered the question, very pleased to participate in Suzanne's love life. "Tell him to fuck off."

"I said I like him."

"If you're too female he won't understand. He'll think you just want attention. If you really want him gone tell him to fuck off."

"Ya, well, I also like the way he fucks off and it wouldn't be very convincing." No longer questioning, her voice was deeper. Ron stood straighter, closed his arms on his chest and gave a leering smile. "Then I don't know what to tell you. I always understood fuck off."

"Well, it doesn't always mean what you think."

Darkness was reflecting a double Harkness outside from fluorescent light. It was late enough to leave for Terry's. She had not called ahead. Maybe she hoped he wouldn't be there and she could stall the good-bye and keep him emotionally hers a little longer. After her customary attention drawing steps away from the door and an easy scan of the close to a dozen people, she saw him at a table in back of the lights of the pool players. He was rising and coming to her. Suzanne smiled and quickly looked to see if he was sitting with a woman. No, it was two men.

Before reaching her he motioned to the waitress for a pitcher of beer and then led her to a booth in the far corner.

"Suzanne, what brings you here?" Earth rich underground water breaking over rocks spoke to her.

"Good and bad news."

Immediately Sugarloaf knew what was coming. "Then let's not talk about it just yet. Beer's coming and we can enjoy a little time."

He asked if she had gotten any more tickets since he knew she deserved them. She asked him if he would bottle his voice and lips so she could carry them in her underwear. They talked about how long they had known each other and counted the times they met. He teased about her shocking coral bathroom in the otherwise bland raw potato white apartment.

The beer was running out and they stopped talking.

"I guess you know why I'm here." For the first time she noticed age looking through his eyes. "I really don't want to be here. I've enjoyed every time." He lifted his head and put his hand over hers nervously twitching on her lap.

"It's been good, Suzanne."

"I've been having this thing, on-and-off for six months with this guy and it's going to the next step." She straightened and looked at the shoulders that had swayed to her body need when she first saw him through the rear view mirror.

"So, I have to say good-bye, now."

In the angled light and dark of the bar, in the booth in the corner of Terry's, Sugarloaf kept his hand on hers, moved his other hand from the outside curve of her breast, up her shoulder and held her ear to his lips.

"Suzanne, I'm a cop. Good-bye is just see you later." He kissed her ear and patted her hand. "You go now and congratulations."

CHAPTER TWENTY THREE

Monday Lina woke to the small morning sounds of Ken's routines echoing through the walls. Every step from his guest room bed creaked through the skeleton of the house. The toilet, shower water, shaver, hair dryer, then steps across the kitchen floor, and the abrupt running of kitchen water for a long morning drink. Gently, his steps fell on the stairs and stopped in front of Justin's room. The door whispered open and Lina imagined Ken watching his sleeping son in morning darkness. After a minute he walked to MoMo's door. More quietly than he walked up, he returned down the stairs, opened the door to the garage and Lina heard the roaring accelerating engine leaving Sunshadow Estates, *a return to elegance with the casual pleasures of today.*

After the children were driven to school Lina fell to the jumbled thoughts in her head. What was next? How could any life be next? What to pack for Thanksgiving with her mother. A torn wedding photo with Ken's head scissored off? Habit, unfocused energy and the need for time to pass, please, pass, kept Lina going with housework, a little exercise and an emergency call to her hairdresser, Joel.

"I need something sexy and I need it now." As she seated herself she threw words like darts to a target.

"Well, Ms. Sexy, I see the genesis of wanton woman rising from the sea of man's muddy muck in that lackluster overgrown curl on your forehead. Not to mention the bitch who has kidnapped your usually dulcet tones."

Lina tried to smile. "If you have booze hidden away I'll have some. Otherwise, I brought gin."

Joel's eyebrows raised in interest and humor. He blew her a kiss and left to return with wine. He squeezed her in where there wasn't time because of the lost soulness in her voice, but telling sorrows would have to wait for next time. She was pleased, grateful, he would quietly let her drink two glasses of wine, hug him and accept the biggest tip she had ever given.

The hairstyle fell across her face when she walked out the door and required a gentle teasing movement to keep her eyes revealed. Oh, god, if she could only do this hairstyle herself. Her children would be surprised and deserving of explanation, Ken would be surprised and not worth toilet paper.

"I needed a new look. Remember when Walt's mom went blonde? Well, those things happen to mothers every once in a while," she said to each of her children when she picked them up from school.

"Looks good, Mom," Justin said and meant it. MoMo nodded, quietly assessing the foundation of her life which had stayed on very shifting emotional ground. After they each gathered an apple and an ice cream bar and gone upstairs for homework, Lina dug deep in her lingerie drawer for Sha Na Boogie and two white pieces of paper with four signatures. The starkness of evidence was proof she lost her life's bet. She hid them away in a deeper corner of the house and called Ken.

Mary Ellen answered, "Overton Printing. Hello, this is Mary Ellen."

"Hello, Mary Ellen, this is Lina."

"Oh, Cat! We've missed you. Where have you been?" her voice lowered as though she wasn't supposed to be talking to her. Perhaps it was against the rules.

"Mostly, I've just been here, Mary Ellen. It's been awful."

"All Ken said was that you probably wouldn't be in working. Everyone knew something was very wrong."

"Well," her voice caught in a choke, but she knew Mary Ellen would sympathize, "that about says it all. I won't be."

"Oh." Words evaporated.

"I need to talk to Ken."

"I'll get him."

When he came on she could tell he wasn't expecting her. Magpie cries screeched out of her throat and then fell to cave depth as she realized her children could hear, "Get home and let's get this over with. Who the hell do you think you are? I'll bring them to Overton if you aren't here in half an hour." She banged the phone down.

He was there in twenty-two minutes.

Ken looked at her lifeless face under new swingy hair sitting at the end of the couch. Her arms around her folded legs didn't move. She could have been carved wood. He went upstairs and brought the children down.

Perhaps if you are a child, hearing your parents are divorcing when there is still hope in your heart for a return to better days is something like hearing your child is dying when there had been hope in your heart of returned health. The disruption of the generation closest to your own is a breaking of spirit, a dying of innocence that is necessary or at least inevitable but always, always destroying in its first moments. Perhaps, too, it is at best burning embers from which the fabled phoenix of a new self can rise. It is hoped Justin Kenneth Overton and Margaret (MoMo) Overton recover well from this full body blow they received on the day after the pretend Thanksgiving. It is certain their lives will continue from this juncture, as surely as Ken's, Catalina's and Suzanne's. When the dreadful words were spoken by both parents who gave hollow sounding reassurance of their love, they were kissed and held by each parent and told to return to their rooms. Ken stared in hate at Lina.

It could have been hate for his visible uncontrollable weakness and need for woman. The woman who had been given his deepest strongest love and care over fifteen years had not dissolved without him; had not begged, had not once said, "Stay, I'll do what you want to keep you." She refused to honor his biggest prize, Overton Printing, and she forced him to be present at his children's loss of hope. The woman he now wanted, the woman he believed would be the heat of fire, the energy of his life, the woman he destroyed his family to hold, was keeping him away with private days to herself.

Silently Lina withstood his stare, her swollen eyes muddied in smeared make-up and glowing from the ache she felt seeing the fear, horror, sadness on her children's faces. When she spoke it was soft and sure.

"Did you think you were not going to see their hearts bleed?"

Anger was weeping so fully from Ken's skin there was a smell of spit and sweat.

Again she whispered, "Don't you ever hurt my children like that again."

"You can be a bitch, Cat," he threw her name thick and hard.

"It was you who left."

"Don't try and make me feel guilty for what you did."

"If you had wanted to be more of an equal woman, instead of just dawdling around here," he swept one arm around as wide as it would reach to include the whole house. She saw her deep desire to provide home and hearth made valueless. Her womanhood undesirable.

"And if you had loved instead of demanded," Lina felt a sea of water about to pour from her eyes and nose and she rubbed her eyes hard away from the nose, streaking make-up to hair. "Don't use me to cry your tears," she whispered trying to keep phlegm from running out her nose, "I've done my share. Cry your own."

They stared at each other; the air between them stiff as their hearts.

"Get out, Ken. It's Monday. Leave."

He turned on his heel so sharply Lina thought he was going to fall. For half an hour she listened to pounding footsteps across their bedroom floor, the opening of drawers and throwing of clothes. Quietly, the children also listened, both of them sitting on Justin's bed. And then he was gone.

It was ten minutes before Lina got up and went to the downstairs bathroom to wash her face. The vase of dead marigolds was smashed against the floor. He had understood the meanness. When she came out she turned a light on, searched through her purse, found a business card and went to the phone.

"Hey."

"Hello, Suzanne."

Suzanne was quiet. She recognized the voice.

"I just want you to know. Ken is yours now."

"Ken is not mine, until I say he is." She felt exuberant. Like the first time she was salesperson of the month. A winner.

"The papers are signed." Lina stopped talking. Her brain was empty.

"I'll take good care of him."

"I don't care if you kill him."

Now tearless and emotionless, Lina put the phone down. She went upstairs to change the bed sheets. They had not been changed since Ken slept there three nights ago. Encouraged from Justin's room by her meek, normal sounds of movement, the children came in as she was lifting the mattress to fit the bottom sheet. That night they all slept in the marriage bed, brushing arms, elbows, legs, knowing they were the remaining pieces of a broken family.

Lina let the children stay home from school on Tuesday. They were eating cereal in front of TV when she called her mother.

"Hi, Mom, we're coming up a day early. I hope that's okay," she nodded listening. She went on to briefly describe last night without supporting emotion. Next she called Eme, but she moved to the phone upstairs where Justin and Momo couldn't hear.

"It's over, Eme. He left last night after we told the children. It was hell."

"Are you going to be all right?"

"Not right now. But we're going to mother's for Thanksgiving and we'll be okay. We'll live."

The morning was quiet, peaceful, the silence of life recovering after a storm as Lina and the children packed clothes and toys to visit grandma. Her routine check of their bags was cursory and distracted. "I guess if we forget something, we can buy it, or grandma will have it." On the ten minute drive from the house to head north on I-15 they didn't speak at all, but when Lina hit a smooth 75 miles an hour, her shoulders lifted and unthinking, she flipped her new hairstyle with an appreciative stroke.

"The first time I drove alone from Logan to Salt Lake I was eighteen and starting at the U." Her voice had a note of reminiscent cheer. Neither of the children answered.

"It was very frightening, really, but also very exciting. You will find life has its double-edged swords. Happiness and fear too often go together." Neither Justin or MoMo understood what she was talking about but they listened and before ten miles they were talking and looking forward to seeing their mother's family.

Their grandma greeted them with arms opened, kisses, and hugs with slight back rubs. Lina understood the sunlight and shadows within her touch as she understood a sunrise of light and dark in canyons. It had been there forever and was hers.

There was enough family to love and work to do that Lina and the children were in the calm of a meal after a funeral. Everyone had been told before they arrived that Ken would not be there and no one asked why. Everyone gave extra hugs to the three of them and they soaked them in like dry cattails in wetlands.

Justin and MoMo were a room away watching TV when Lina said, "Thank you, thank you mother," They had just said good-bye to Aunt Betty who looked like a frail petal, holding her daughter, Gennie's arm. The house had been full with fifteen people and they were the last to leave. "You deserve an explanation." Lina looked down, afraid. Not of her family, but of life.

Her mother put her arm around her, "There is no explanation, my dear Catalina. There is only life," she paused and kissed her daughter on the forehead. "And it goes on."

Lina was sitting on the bed she slept in as a child when the clock struck midnight, ending Thanksgiving, beginning Friday. The yellow incandescent light that had put her to sleep as a child still marked time in this room. Before leaving home Lina grabbed a book she had already read, remembering it was a sensual story about a lost woman. In *Good Morning, Midnight* by Jean Rhys, she read once more. *"The streets, blazing hot and eating peaches. The long lovely, blue days that lasted forever, that still are..."*

As she drifted, wafted, went to sleep Ken knocked quietly at Suzanne's door.

"I want you, Suzanne," he whispered his words of love through the screen door.

Catalina slept, her forehead creased in a dream. She stood alone atop a mountain of unplanted fertile black earth that stretched every way to a horizon meeting blue sky. Hot raging rivers ran down the sides, wearing it away. "And so I give the man of my children." Her heart ached in words across the landscape and outside herself.

"Catalina," Suzanne's panoramic voice answered from the sky, "and so I give myself."